The Eleventh Doctor

A critical ramble through Matt Smith's tenure in Doctor Who

by **Mike Taylor**

mike@miketaylor.org.uk

http://reprog.wordpress.com/

@MikeTaylor

First Edition.

Published 3 January 2014.

Copyright and licence

Copyright © 2010–2014 Mike Taylor. CC By 4.0.

ISBN 978-1-291-69570-0

The text is made available under the Creative Commons Attribution 4.0 International licence (CC By 4.0), which means you are free to read, share, copy, modify, remix and redistribute it provided only that you credit me as the original author and do not misrepresent me as endorsing any changes you may make.

If you downloaded this book for free, and enjoyed reading it, I ask but do not demand that you buy either an official copy of the e-book or a hardcopy. Actual sales reward me for the work that went into this, and encourage me to write more. But if you can't or won't pay, I'd still rather you read the book than not.

Artwork is provided under a variety of licences and involves a variety of copyright holders, as detailed in the Image and Font Credits section. All but the cover can at least be freely redistributed in unmodified form for non-commercial purposes.

Table of Contents

About this book.. 7
Introduction: warming up to Matt Smith.. 9
    Ages of Doctor Who actors on their debuts.................................15
Series 5.. 19
    Episode 5.1. The Eleventh Hour... 21
    Episode 5.2. The Beast Below.. 27
    Episode 5.3. Victory of the Daleks... 33
    Oh, and by the way 37
    Episode 5.4. The Time of Angels..39
    Episode 5.5. Flesh and Stone...45
    Episode 5.6. The Vampires of Venice...49
    Episode 5.7. Amy's Choice... 53
    Episode 5.8. The Hungry Earth... 57
    Episode 5.9. Cold Blood... 63
    Episode 5.10. Vincent and the Doctor..69
    Episode 5.11. The Lodger.. 75
    What's in the box?... 79
    Episode 5.12. The Pandorica Opens... 85
    Episode 5.13. The Big Bang.. 91
    Series 5 summary and retrospective...95
Christmas 2010: A Christmas Carol.. 97
Series 6.. 101
    Episode 6.1. The Impossible Astronaut...................................... 103
    Who killed the Doctor?...107
    Episode 6.2. Day of the Moon.. 111
    Episode 6.3. The Curse of the Black Spot..................................115
    Episode 6.4. The Doctor's Wife.. 119
    Episode 6.5. The Rebel Flesh... 123
    Episode 6.6. The Almost People.. 127
    The Almost People, redux: let's see if we can sort this out............ 131
    Episode 6.7. A Good Man Goes to War...................................... 135
    Episode 6.8. Let's Kill Hitler... 139

- Episode 6.9. Night Terrors.. 145
- Episode 6.10. The Girl Who Waited... 149
- Episode 6.11. The God Complex... 153
- Episode 6.12. Closing Time.. 159
- What do we know about the Lake Silencio incident?................... 161
- Episode 6.13. The Wedding of River Song................................... 167
- More thoughts on The Wedding of River Song............................173
- Series 6 summary and retrospective..177
- Christmas 2011: The Doctor, the Widow and the Wardrobe.............181
- Series 6.. 185
- Episode 7.1. Asylum of the Daleks... 187
- In praise of Rory (consisting mostly of a digression about how terrible Torchwood is).. 191
- Episode 7.2. Dinosaurs on a Spaceship...195
- Episode 7.3. A Town Called Mercy.. 199
- Episode 7.4. The Power of Three..203
- Episode 7.5. The Angels Take Manhattan.....................................207
- Christmas 2012: The Snowmen.. 211
- Episode 7.6. The Bells of Saint John... 215
- Episode 7.7. The Rings of Akhaten..221
- The reason Doctor Who is the best thing on TV – a discussion....225
- Episode 7.8. Cold War..231
- Episode 7.9. Hide.. 235
- Episode 7.10. Journey to the Centre of the TARDIS...................239
- Episode 7.11. The Crimson Horror...243
- Episode 7.12. Nightmare in Silver... 247
- Episode 7.13. The Name of the Doctor... 251
- A quick thought on The Name of the Doctor............................... 259
- Series 7 summary and retrospective..261
- 50th Anniversary.. 265
- Mini episode: The Night of the Doctor..267
- Mini episode: The Last Day... 269
- The Day of the Doctor...273
- Christmas 2013: The Time of the Doctor.. 281
- The Eleventh Doctor's place in the pantheon..285

Looking forward	289
Appendix A: most memorable episodes	293
Appendix B: Magic moments	297
Acknowledgements	303
Image and font credits	305
A reminder: Copyright and licence	307
About the author	309
Where next?	311

About this book

The bulk of this book is made up of reviews of Matt Smith's episodes, most of them written shortly after they were first broadcast. Although the chapters are reviews at heart, I use them as a platform to discuss lots of other things: writing, casting, acting, the moral issues that Doctor Who throws up, and more.

This book is in no way an episode guide. It's aimed squarely at people who have already seen the episodes and want to read thoughts and opinions about them. If you've not seen the episodes, you won't enjoy reading this. Better return it, and get hold of the episodes themselves. You'll enjoy those.

I've edited the reviews to help them flow better in the context of a broader story, to eliminate some repetition, to free them from the context of the blog where they originally appeared, and to fix some mistakes. But on the whole I've tried to leave them much as I wrote them at the time so that the evolution of my thoughts on Smith and his companions is apparent. That means that along the way I'll be saying some stupid things, sometimes contradicting what I've said earlier, and making some very wrong guesses about how various plot threads were going to work out.

Most of these reviews previously appeared in less polished form on my blog, The Reinvigorated Programmer, which you can find at http://reprog.wordpress.com/. But almost all of the Series 7 material here is new. I reviewed the first five episodes only in the most desultory way on the blog, but here they get the proper treatment. Episodes 8–13 and the 50th anniversary material (*Cold War* to *The Day of the Doctor*) I didn't write about at all at the time, so everything I say about them here is new.

Also new is the introductory material, the summaries and discussion at the end, and a few present-day updates to the reviews. I'll be keen to talk about these on the blog, where the comments are gratifyingly plentiful and insightful. So I'll be posting *about* the new reviews and essays – but not posting the material itself – as placeholders for readers to leave comments. Those posts, when they appear, will be linked from the Doctor Who index of the site, http://reprog.wordpress.com/doctor-who-series-5/

As a matter of style, I italicise the names of episodes (along with those of books and films), but not those of shows. So it's *The Time of Angels* but Doctor Who; and *The End of Days* but Torchwood.

Introduction: warming up to Matt Smith

It's actually been three and a half years, but it's felt like six months. It seemed to me that no sooner was Matt Smith on our screens than his time as the Doctor was up. And I'm really going to miss him. I was sceptical at first: when he was announced as David Tennant's successor, my first thought was just that he was too young – that he couldn't possibly have the gravity that I wanted to see from the Doctor. But it didn't take him long – two episodes in fact – to win me over. Before the end of his first series, he'd become my favourite doctor, unseating the previous incumbent Christopher Eccleston.

Christopher Eccleston

Yes, Eccleston. I was born in 1968, so I was first aware of Doctor Who in the back end of the Jon Pertwee era, around the time of *The Monster of Peladon* and *Planet of the Spiders*. I was more familiar with him from the cut-out figures on the back of Weetabix packets than from the actual TV show, but he was well-established enough in my mind that I remember resenting that upstart Tom Baker who took his place. He seemed completely wrong – for one thing, seeming much younger than his predecessors (though see below). I watched avidly through the early Tom Baker series before losing interest in his later years, and replacing him with the vet's sidekick didn't reignite my interest. I admit to my shame that Peter Davison, Colin Baker and Sylvester McCoy all passed me by. I wasn't particularly upset, or even necessarily aware, when the series was cancelled at the end of 1989.

So when the series was restarted in 2005, Christopher Eccleston's very different take was like a bolt from the blue. Andrew Rilstone said it best (as he so often does) in his review of the very first New Who episode, *Rose*: "Paul McGann was a character who was definitely the Doctor in something which definitely wasn't Doctor Who. Chris Eccleston is a character who is *probably* the Doctor in something which is definitely Doctor Who". He redefined what the Doctor could be, kept the clown, the sage and something else altogether simmering together just under the surface. I felt he might do *anything*. And he often did.

If you'll forgive my taking an early tangent in a book that's meant to be about Matt Smith's Doctor, I'm just going to take a little more time over why I love Eccleston's Doctor so much. It was the combination of the frivolous with the deadly serious – a combination that you might say is the essence of who the Doctor is. Think, for example, of the scene at the end of *The End of the World* when Doctor Chris and Rose, having been with aliens billions of years in the future, arrive back on present-day Earth, into the anonymous bustle of a crowd of people in central London – and Rose sees all those people as though for the first time. And then the dialogue as the crowd passes, oblivious, past them:

Doctor: You think it'll last forever: people, and cars and concrete. But it won't. One day, it's all gone. Even the sky. [Long pause.] My planet's gone. It's dead. It burned, like the Earth. It's just rocks and dust. Before its time.

Rose: What happened?

Doctor: There was a war, and we lost.

Rose: A war with who? [No response.] What about your people?

Doctor: I'm a Time Lord. I'm the last of the Time Lords. They're all gone. I'm the only survivor. I'm left travelling on my own, because there's no-one else.

A beat.

Rose: There's me.

As always, simply transcribing the script doesn't begin to do this justice. The writing is good (notice how simple Rose's lines are kept), but it's brought to life by simply superb acting on the part of both principals – Billie Piper visibly processing everything around her and all that the Doctor's saying, and Chris Eccleston stating the facts as baldly as he can, not allowing an excess of emotion, keeping a tight lid on it all (because the Doctor, alien or not, is definitely English).

And in giving the actors due credit, I'm not taking away from Russell T. Davies' writing here: it was his vision that they brought to life. The "last of the Time Lords" trope has done so much work now (much of it not very good work) that it's easy to forget how startling that was back in the day – a complete change in the Doctor Who universe, and one that cast him in a new and much starker light. It was transformational. And it was Eccleston's Doctor who sold it.

For those who prefer shorter moments, how about the bit in *The Parting of the Ways* when Emergency Programme One is activated, the TARDIS starts to take Rose home, and the hologram of the Doctor explains to her what's happening – and then turns sideways to look directly at her as he says "Have a good life". That is electric. I felt a tingle down my spine when I first saw it, and I feel it again now just thinking about it.

[Five minutes later: I just broke off writing to watch that bit again; and yet again it literally brought tears to my eyes. It is, and I don't say this lightly, perfect.]

David Tennant

So I was very disappointed when it became apparent, very early in Eccleston's first series, that it would also be his last. He'd been the first Doctor who felt like he was playing for real stakes. The first one to take what he was doing seriously. In a sense, the first grown-up (while not neglecting Doctor Tom's dictum that there's no point in being grown up if you can't be childish sometimes).

I was in Priory Park with my wife and a friend of hers who – like so many people in Crouch End – worked in TV. We don't work in TV or even watch it much, so we had no idea who David Tennant was when the name was announced. My wife's friend told us that if we'd liked Eccleston, we were going to *love* the new guy – who, she said, was a proper actor.

And she was right, at least at first. Tennant's debut in *The Christmas Invasion* was all we could have hoped it would be. Having been confined to his bed for the first half of the episode, he came roaring out of the blocks (revived by tea – a nice touch for such a quintessentially English character) to deliver the barnstorming, crazy, inspiring speech to the Sycorax. "Look at these people: these human beings. Consider their potential. From the day they arrive on the planet, and blinking step into the sun, there is more to see than can ever be seen. More to do than – no, hold on ... Sorry, that's *The Lion King*. But the point still stands."

The best of Tennant was superb, no doubt about it. The trouble is, his best became less and less frequent as his time on the show dragged on. With two extraordinary exceptions – *Human Nature* and *Midnight* – his best work was all done in his first series. And the longer he stayed in the role, the more he became a parody of himself. It didn't help that in his second series he was lumbered with a boring companion (Martha) portrayed by someone who always gave the impression of doing her best in a school play. (It's notable that when Martha returned for three Series 4 episodes alongside Donna, Catherine Tate's acting was embarrassingly much better than what Freema Agyeman was serving up. Though to do her justice, when she turned up on The Dreadful Torchwood a bit later, she was much less bad than the rest of the cast.)

By the time of *The Doctor's Daughter*, which admittedly had plenty of other problems, Tennant had become hard to watch. It was all big, shouty declarations, all delivered with volume as a substitute for conviction. No doubt he had some difficulty making himself believe in the material, but you have to do the best you can with what you have, and in that episode and others Tennant was predictable.

So it's a shame that the Doctor who gave us the series' most heartbreaking images (the wall between worlds that separated the Doctor and Rose in their parallel universes) should end up outstaying his welcome so thoroughly. By the time his departure was announced, I was *very* ready to see a new face.

Matt Smith ... finally

But not one so darned *young*. Not one with the same kind of gangly body as Tennant, who looked like him and would act the role in the same way. I didn't want a retread. I wanted a new take on the Doctor, someone older and heftier, who could bring back the sense of actual high stakes that Eccleston had given us. (That's as opposed to Tennant's playground high stakes of every possible universe being wiped out and never having existed. That's not high stakes. That just sciencey words.)

Well, Smith proved me delightedly wrong. I won't say too much about that now, since that's what this book is all about.

Ages of Doctor Who actors on their debuts

I mentioned before that my initial negative reaction to Smith was just about his being so young. I felt that there seems to be a definite downward trend in the ages of the actors playing the role of the Doctor, with the new incumbent illustrating the trend particularly well. Does that intuition stand up to analysis? Let's see.

First, the raw data: the eleven doctors up to Smith with their birth dates, debut dates in the role, and age at that time:

#	Actor	Birth date	Debut date	Age
1	William Hartnell	08 January 1908	23 November 1963	55
2	Patrick Troughton	25 March 1920	29 October 1966	46
3	Jon Pertwee	07 July 1919	03 January 1970	50
4	Tom Baker	20 January 1934	08 June 1974	40
5	Peter Davison	13 April 1951	21 March 1981	29
6	Colin Baker	08 June 1943	16 March 1984	40
7	Sylvester McCoy	20 August 1943	07 September 1987	44
8	Paul McGann	14 November 1959	27 May 1996	36
9	Chris Eccleston	16 February 1964	26 March 2005	41
10	David Tennant	18 April 1971	18 June 2005	34
11	Matt Smith	28 October 1982	01 January 2010	27

Then I plotted those debut ages against Doctor Number and fitted a linear regression line:

Ages of Doctor Who actors on debut

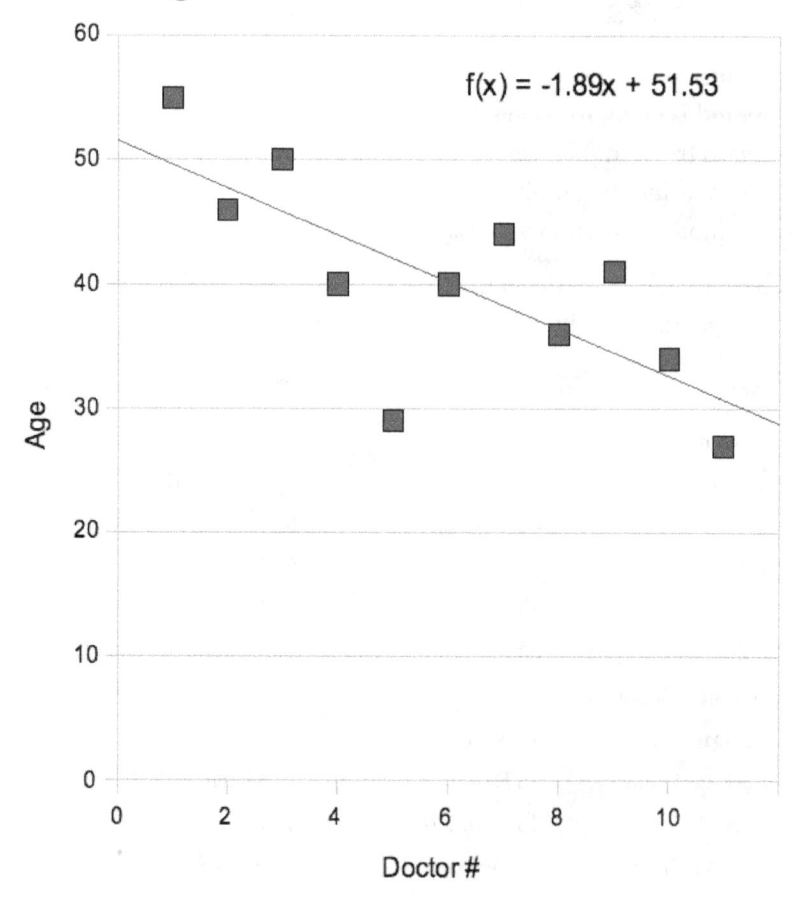

$f(x) = -1.89x + 51.53$

The best-fit is that y = −1.89x + 51.53. In other words, the age of each new Doctor on his debut is approximated as 51.53 years minus 1.89 times the Doctor Number. The banner finding is that each new Doctor is, on average, 1.89 years younger than his predecessor was.

On one level I was surprised by how shallow that gradient is; then I realised that across the sequence of ten Doctors to that succeeded William Hartnell, the best-fit gradient of −1.89 means that the age has fallen by 18.9 years, which is fairly hefty – but still not so hefty as I'd imagined.

Probably my perception was skewed by the first three Doctors all seeming so old, and the last two seeming so young – and the first three were indeed the oldest, though nowhere near as old as I'd thought, or as you would guess watching them now. And the two most recent Doctors are indeed the youngest and third youngest. But in the middle part of the sequence (Doctors 4–9) there is no real pattern, and indeed the overall trend is probably upwards.

But some of those ages take a bit of believing. Can Patrick Troughton (#2) really have been only two years older than Sylvester McCoy (#7)? And could William Hartnell (#1) possibly be only fourteen years older than Christopher Eccleston? Well, that's what it says in Wikipedia, so I guess it must be true.

What does it all mean?

Maybe the trend in *actual* ages of the actors is less interesting than the much stronger trend in their *apparent* ages. Early in the run of Doctor Who, the actors portrayed the character at the upper end of the ranges that worked for them – William Hartnell played him as a man in his seventies and Patrick Troughton as a man in his sixties. (I am talking about human years, of course: Time Lord years are seven times as long, just like the opposite of dogs, or something.) By contrast, the last three Doctors, and especially the last two, have emphasised their youthfulness. Here I am getting into deeper waters than I can comfortably navigate, but it's tempting to think that this reflects a more general change in society – that there was a certain amount of reverence for age and experience in the early 1960s, but that youth is idolised now.

Speaking as one who is older than eight of the eleven Doctors were on their debuts (and closing in fast on Patrick Troughton), I find this disheartening.

That there is still a role for older actors in Doctor Who was rather brilliantly demonstrated by Derek Jacobi, in his compelling role as the amnesiac Master in *Utopia*; but the weight and substance of his portrayal left me hungry for more, and the series has steadfastly refused to oblige me. When Smith was first announced, I found myself thinking that the idea of, say, Ian McKellen as the Doctor did something for me. I thought that it would, paradoxically, be rejuvenating for the series.

Thoughts in 2013

I don't want to say too much about Peter Capaldi at this point, since I know almost nothing about him. The only things I've ever seen him in is a single episode of Doctor Who, where his role was minor (he was the head of the Pompeii family in *The Fires of Pompeii*), and the actually very good Torchwood mini-series *Children of Earth* (where he played Home Office Permanent Secretary John Frobisher). I've never seen The Thick Of It, which is what he's apparently best known for.

All I know about him is the headline fact that he's 55 years old, which means that, depending on when he makes his debut, he'll be either the same age as William Hartnell was or a year older – either the oldest or the joint-oldest Doctor. So it seems I've got my wish. I'm optimistic about this, because it seems to indicate Moffat's desire to shake up the whole Doctor Who pot and go off in different emotional directions. And that's encouraging because the one thing Doctor Who must never become is predictable.

Series 5

Rumours were that Steven Moffat, on assuming control of Doctor Who from Russell T. Davies, wanted to call his first season Series 1, reflecting the broad, sweeping changes in showrunner, lead actor and main supporting actor. Happily, wiser counsel prevailed, and the successor to Series 4 was Series 5. Like its predecessors, it consisted of 13 episodes, broadcast a week apart in a single block.

Episode 5.1. *The Eleventh Hour*

[Posted on April 3, 2010]

I've just finished watching *The Eleventh Hour*, the first Doctor Who episode to feature the new eleventh Doctor played by Matt Smith. My wife Fiona, the three boys and I squashed in together on the sofa and watched the broadcast – with some trepidation on my part. Now I want to get my first impressions down before they fade.

This was a very important episode because so much has changed: most obviously it was the debut of the new Doctor; but it also marked the first appearance of a new companion, Amy Pond (played by Karen Gillan), which means that cast continuity was zero. By contrast, when David Tennant first appeared as the Tenth Doctor, he inherited the Ninth Doctor companion Rose Tyler, so we had a fixed point of reference. As though a new Doctor and new companion were not enough, *The Eleventh Hour* was also the first episode to be helmed by the new showrunner Steven Moffat, who takes over from Russell T. Davies.

So let's look at those three aspects separately ... oh, and the actual episode.

The new Doctor

I have to admit that my heart sank when Matt Smith was announced as the Eleventh Doctor to be, and I first saw pictures of him – he looked like an even younger David Tennant, and I prefer an older, weightier Doctor.

And in some ways, his debut performance bore out those fears: his portrayal of the Doctor resembles that of his predecessor much more closely than any of the other Doctors have – think of the difference between Christopher Eccleston and David Tennant, for example. Smith's voice is very similar to Tennant's, and he portrays the character very similarly too – zany to an almost self-conscious degree, with a hard core and, as became apparent in the episode's final confrontation, the same edge of arrogance. At times, if I'd closed my eyes, it could have been a Tennant episode.

I'm conflicted about this: Tennant was an excellent Doctor, and I can see why the producers might have wanted more of the same; but the essence of the Doctor is surely that everything except his core docs change. I hope that Matt Smith can transcend this initial impersonation and create his own Doctor, as both Eccleston and Tennant so successfully did.

Because his version of the Doctor is so Tennantish, it's hard to make any meaningful assessment of Smith at this stage. I find myself struggling to find much to say about his Doctor that is specific to him. I hope I have more to say next week.

Anyway, he's not rubbish.

The new companion

I have to admit that my heart sank when I first saw pictures of Karen Gillan, when she was announced as the Eleventh Doctor's companion to be. She had Generic Glamorous Young Thing stamped all over her.

Happily, the reality is very different, and it turns out that she can really act. She has a curiously unformed face (rather like Bonnie Wright, who plays Ginny Weasley in the Harry Potter movies), but I was pleasantly surprised to find that this works in her favour. She is like a blank canvas that can readily be painted with whatever emotion the situation demands; and she does this with subtlety.

Now that writing this is making me think more carefully about her performance, I realise that she brought much more in the way of distinctive characterisation to her role than Matt Smith (so far) has to his. Whereas Smith gives the impression of being conscious that he is someone's successor, Gillan seems to be making something fresh.

Of course, this isn't the first time that I've been wrong about a Doctor Who companion actress: like most people I was horrified by the idea of Billie Piper in 2005; but she made Rose believable, memorable and sympathetic. Also like most people, I was sufficiently unhappy about Catherine Tate's over-the-top special-guest spot in *The Runaway Bride* that I all but flatly disbelieved it when I heard that she was going to be the regular Series 4 companion; but once I'd managed to shed my preconceptions and forget about the *Runaway Bride* train-wreck, I realised that she was doing a superb job; in fact I think that she is my favourite of all the Doctor Who companions I've seen, going right back to the days of Liz Shaw.

So the early signs are good that Karen Gillan will continue that much-better-than-I-expected streak.

The new showrunner

During the last four years of Doctor Who, Steven Moffat's scripts have uniformly been among the best of their series: *The Empty Child/The Doctor Dances* in Series 1, *The Girl in the Fireplace* in Series 2, *Blink* in Series 3 and *Silence in the Library/Forest of the Dead* in Series 4. In fact I'd say that with the exception of *Blink*, each of these has been the best story in its series, and *Blink* loses out only narrowly to Paul Cornell's superlative *Human Nature/Family of Blood*.

Not only that, but Moffat's episodes have been good for good reasons: they've been sharp, intelligent, thought-provoking, and apart from whimsical *Girl in the Fireplace* they've been very scary. Not only that, but they've shown us new sides of the Doctor that have felt believably in keeping with what we already know about the character while still stretching the boundaries.

So I was delighted when I heard that he was going to be taking over as head honcho from Russell T. Davies, whose episodes have in comparison seemed rather mundane, with the big end-of-series specials too often going over the top in ways that seem silly in retrospect. (Actually, I may be overstating that last bit: my hatred of *Last of the Time Lords* may be unbalancing my view.)

The question for Moffat is, now that he's going to be writing six episodes per series instead of one or two, will be he able to keep the quality up? (Conversely, I've wondered whether, if Russell T. Davies were given just a single episode to write, would that single episode be sensational? Because his best moments are undeniably brilliant. So it's a shame that he doesn't have an episode in this series, but maybe he wanted to avoid Matt Busby Syndrome – perhaps he'll have one in 2011.) For Moffat, I think it's a good sign that he's had the humility to keep his writing duties down to six of the thirteen episodes rather than the eight that Davies wrote for his first series. Six may still be too many, but let's hope not – maybe he has a decade's worth of great stories cached and ready to deploy.

With all that said, I'd have to say that this initial episode had nothing about it that struck me as characteristically Moffatian, and it could very easily have been a Davies episode in a Davies series. I hope to see Moffat stamp his personality on the show as the series progresses, just as I hope to see Smith stamp his on the title role.

And finally …

The actual episode

Let's see, now – a quick recap.

The damaged TARDIS (see the end of the last David Tennant episode) careens across London, with the Doctor hanging out of the doorway in an ill-conceived action sequence that is played for laughs. I really could have lived without this. The TARDIS crash-lands in the garden of a house where the young Amelia Pond lives with her aunt. The aunt is out, so the girl is the only one to witness another comedy sequence as the new Doctor tries and rejects various foods before settling on fish fingers and custard. My sons laughed like drains so I guess I shouldn't whine too much about this bit. This done, we get on with the story. A mysterious crack in Amelia's bedroom wall turns out to be a gateway to an alien prison from which Prisoner Zero has escaped. The Doctor realises the TARDIS needs attention, tells Amelia he's going to jump five minutes forward in time, but inadvertently disappears for twelve years, only to meet grown-up Amelia who now goes by the name Amy (shades of *Girl in the Fireplace* if we're playing Hunt The Self-Plagiarism).

The Doctor realises that Prisoner Zero has been hiding in Amy's house all this time, using its illusion powers to conceal its presence and later its nature. The alien jailers, played by gigantic eyeballs, come to Earth hoping to recapture the prisoner and warn that they will destroy the Earth if he can't be found in twenty minutes. The Doctor realises that the alien can appear in the form of people who it has formed mental bonds with, and is using the likenesses of coma patients in a local hospital. Enlisting the help of Amy and her boyfriend, he writes a virus that will reset every clock on earth to zero, hacks into an Internet meeting of NASA, Jodrell Bank and other alien specialists, and persuades them to upload the virus everywhere. This they now do. The alien jailers realise that all those zeroes are a hint that someone knows where Prisoner Zero is, and trace the virus's origin as the cellphone that the Doctor carries. After some shape-shifting shenanigans, they recapture the prisoner. The Doctor rebukes them for their high-handedness and warns them away from further interference in Earth's affairs.

Crisis averted, the Doctor returns to his TARDIS, takes a quick trip to the moon and back to check that all is well with its redesign (didn't I mention that it was redesigning itself earlier? It was), and returns to invite Amy to travel with him. Only trouble is, he set the time controls wrong again (again!) and two years have passed since the adventure with Prisoner Zero. Amy agrees to travel with the Doctor provided he can get her home by the next morning, which he promises to do; we realise that that's because her wedding is planned for the very next day. Exeunt, pursued by a bear.

I don't want to be too harsh on this episode, because series openers are rarely outstanding – in fact, come to think of it, *Rose*, *New Earth*, *Smith and Jones* and *Partners in Crime* have all been fairly poor by the standards of their series – but I didn't find much in *The Eleventh Hour* that I think is going to lodge in my hindbrain the way the empty child, the clockwork robots from *GitF*, the Weeping Angels and the Vashta Nerada have done. Maybe that would be asking too much from an episode that also has to introduce a whole new cast, though. Still, although it was enjoyable, it did feel a bit By Numbers.

Next week's episode might be more indicative of where things are going.

A little bit of actual insight to round things off

If I was disappointed that Matt Smith's Doctor was too David Tennant-like, and that Steven Moffat's script was too Russell T. Davies-like, it occurs to me that this might have been deliberate. Given the all-new cast, the production team might have felt that the audience needed something familiar to cling to, hence the recognisable Doctor in the recognisable situation.

If that's so, I suppose it's understandable – for a first episode. But Matt Smith had better start being his own man pretty darned quick, and I want to see more of the depth and insight of Moffat's previous scripts in his subsequent ones.

Episode 5.2. *The Beast Below*

[Posted on April 10, 2010]

2:16pm – zero minus four hours

I realise that I am scared about this evening's Doctor Who episode. I have too much invested in it. I so, so want to love the new series; I so want it to live up to the best of Steven Moffat's episodes in previous series (which, to be fair, is all of Moffat's episodes); I so want his being in overall charge of the series to mean that the plots are going to make more sense, actions have more consequences, and monsters are more motivated. But I don't know if I trust that what Moffat could do for one and a half episodes in each of the previous series, he can do for all thirteen in this one.

Last week's inaugural episode, *The Eleventh Hour*, was Good But Not That Good. I can forgive it, because of the difficulty of introducing a new Doctor and a new companion and a new TARDIS and trying to tell a story. But the gloves are off, now. That hurdle has been negotiated, and *The Beast Below* has no other responsibilities but to be an outstanding episode in its own right.

Can it do it? I will find out in four hours.

3:42pm – zero minus two and a half hours

I find myself wondering why I care so much about this. Why all the emotional investment? Two reasons, I think. One is nationalistic: I've realised that pretty much all the TV shows that I've loved recently (Veronica Mars, Firefly, Buffy/Angel, Frasier, Friends, The Simpsons) have been American, and Doctor Who is the only British entry on the list. So I want the champion of British TV to be a worthy champion. (Yes, Monty Python, Fawlty Towers, Yes Minister/Yes Prime Minister and Blackadder were all British; they are also all between 20 and 40 years old.)

The other reason is broader: when Doctor Who is done well, it's a literally unique blend of the mundane and exotic. The best stories are scary and exciting, yes, but also thought-provoking. The Doctor himself is both very alien and very reassuring – unpredictable yet reliable. In short, the show walks a tightrope. Doing that makes it both fascinating and also in constant danger of falling off on one side or the other. So long as all those aspects are held in tension, Doctor Who has the potential to be brilliant (where script and acting allow); but as soon as the Doctor loses his alienness, say, or the plot emphasises excitement and danger to the point where it's no longer thoughtful, it loses what makes it so special. And I want something on TV to be special in that literate yet accessible way, and I don't know of any other candidates.

Come on, Moffat, you can do it ... No pressure ...

8:03pm – first impressions

I watched *The Beast Below* with Fiona and the eldest and youngest boys as we ate tea in front of the TV. (The middle son is away camping with the Cub Scouts). Then we watched the documentary on BBC 3. As soon as I'd finished cleaning up the meal, I sat down to write this review, and ...

Yes, yes, yes!

This second episode is very much what I'd hoped for on all counts. Last time, I concluded that "Matt Smith had better start being his own man pretty darned quick, and I want to see more of the depth and insight of Moffat's previous scripts in his subsequent ones"; I also wanted to see more characteristically Doctorish qualities about the Doctor. I am delighted to say that we got all that and more.

The 11th Doctor reminds me of the Doctor

First of all, the Doctor was quick of mind, perceptive, thoughtful and observant. I just love that. When he did eccentric things (like taking the drink off the table and putting it on the floor), it was never an unmotivated character tic, but turned out to mean something specific. The Doctor's way into the mystery came from his insight into a normal-looking situation, and his compassion; and straight away he was trying to get Amy to figure it out for herself. As has been said before, it's the job of the Doctor to make people better, and that investment paid off superbly at the climax, when it was Amy's clear thinking that saved the Doctor from making a terrible mistake.

The 11th Doctor doesn't remind me of the 10th Doctor

Second, I didn't feel that Matt Smith was channelling David Tennant this time around. Maybe because from the outset he had something to actually do rather than just having to be the Doctor, he seemed much more his own man, characterised not by arbitrary mannerisms (one thinks of the stick of celery and the umbrella, ugh) but by, well, all the good stuff I mentioned in the last paragraph. Where David Tennant's Doctor too often felt like he was pulling an arbitrary solution out of a big Deus Ex Machina-shaped hat, Matt Smith (in this episode at least) gave much more of an impression that he was slowly putting the pieces together, arriving at an understanding through the same sorts of mental processes that we, if we were Time Lords, might be capable of. I like that: he's a Doctor that I can admire rather than just being dazzled by.

On reflection, Christopher Eccleston's Doctor also had some of this quality of putting solutions together rather than yanking them fully-formed out of mid air; with hindsight, the latter seems to be a bad habit unique to David Tennant's portrayal. But of course this is at least as much a consequence of the writing as of the acting, so please don't think this is criticism of Tennant per se.

Steven Moffat's script reminds me of a Steven Moffat script

Last week I said of *The Eleventh Hour* that "this initial episode had nothing about it that struck me as characteristically Moffatian, and it could very easily have been a Davies episode in a Davies series". This week, no: without either repeating or pastiching himself, Moffat gave us a story that hit several of his trademark qualities, and it was much the better for it: things that would normally seem mundane were made to seem very alien and mysterious; something more complex and interesting was going on than a mere goodies-vs.-baddies confrontation (as with the resolution of *The Empty Child*); and the story taken as a whole made sense. The conclusion pretty much followed from, or at least was consistent with, the set-up, rather than feeling like it was teleported in from some completely different story.

Steven Moffat's script reminds me of a Russell T. Davies script

At the same time, the script had moments that reminded me of the better aspects of RTD's writing, which is an impressive feat to pull off in the context of a Moffat story. Here, I am thinking mostly of two things: that the story made concrete an issue that all of us face in the abstract from day to day (you know, the two buttons that Amy had to choose between); and the interaction between the Doctor and Amy at the end – the sense that, despite their short association, Amy has real insight into his character.

Sadly, that character moment was slightly spoiled for me by its lack of trust in the viewer: the understanding between the Doctor and Amy was conveyed clearly by oblique words and silent eye contact; that was enough. But instead, Amy then had more lines that rather bluntly laid out in black and white what had already been implied, and that broke the moment in the same kind of way that a bad American sit-com spoils a joke by spelling out the punchline that ought to be left hanging in the air unsaid. (Frasier was particularly good at not doing this, at getting it right; but it's in a minority.)

To be clear, I am not alluding to some kind of romantic tie between the two lead characters: no, absolutely not. It's something very different from that. I most certainly don't want to see the series go down that path, and I hope from the bottom of my heart that Moffat has more taste than that. I mean; she's 21, he's 906. It'd never last.

Not that it was perfect or anything

I said earlier that "the story taken as a whole made sense. The conclusion pretty much followed from [...] the set-up". If that seemed like damning with, if not faint then equivocal, praise, then I guess it is. The big reveal, when it comes, is not really quite enough to justify the horror aspects of the set-up, and the pre-credit sequence in particular doesn't really fit the rest of the story when you look back on it from a position of knowledge.

Beyond that … I am sort of casting around for something else negative to say, and nothing is coming to mind. There was so much to like. Karen Gillan's portrayal of Amy was again excellent, Matt Smith was a much better Doctor than previously, there were several laugh-out-loud funny moments, and lots of delicious little details, such as the use of London Underground-style lifts (elevators for you Americans). In fact, the episode was a visual feast, and I will certainly watch it again just to catch all the details of the sets. And again to catch all the dialogue: as is often the case with Doctor Who, some of the dialogue went too fast, and against a backdrop of too much action, to be easily heard (at least while explaining plot developments to an eight-year-old); but unlike an RTD/Tennant episode, missing those lines didn't mean losing the thread – they just feel like a rich seam of optional-extra jewels to be mined next time around.

And then, finally, the sheer audacity of the last minute – the phone-call from Churchill – made me laugh out loud and tingle with anticipation. Fantastic. Literally.

So, actually, it was pretty close to perfect after all?

Yep, seems like it!

Keep it up!

Episode 5.3. *Victory of the Daleks*

[Posted on April 17, 2010]

If *The Eleventh Hour* was very obviously a new start for Doctor Who, and if *The Beast Below* was where the new series hit its stride, then the third episode, *Victory of the Daleks*, represents another new challenge: it's the first episode under the new regime to be written by someone other than showrunner Steven Moffat himself – specifically, Mark Gatiss, previously responsible for Series One's highly regarded *The Unquiet Dead* and Series Two's widely derided *The Idiot's Lantern*. With his previous work varying so wildly, Gatiss still has plenty to prove as a Who writer, and it was brave of Moffat to entrust him with the Doctor's oldest and most iconic enemies, the Daleks.

Did he meet the challenge? I rate the episode a qualified success.

After the tightly plotted construction of *The Beast Below*, *Victory of the Daleks* felt a little more random, had more of the this-happens-then-that-happens quality of some of the RTD-era episodes. It was full of powerful moments and iconic images – my family and I will not swiftly forget the Dalek offering the scientist a nice, hot cup of tea, we loved the Doctor's jammie-dodger bluff to hold the Daleks off from exterminating him on their ship, and the assault on the Dalek ship was gloriously silly – but I could repeat that last phrase again with the emphasis on "silly" rather than "glorious" and it would be equally true. It's hard to escape the notion that the iconic moments were invented first, and then the plot – such as it was – constructed around it afterwards. Is it too much to wish for an episode to both contain profoundly memorable moments *and* make sense?

I don't want to sound too negative here – I thoroughly enjoyed the episode, and expect to enjoy it again, probably more, when I watch it again; it just has the feeling of a good episode that could have been great. It's hard not to wonder how it might have been different had Moffat written it himself rather than delegating; or had it been given to Paul Cornell (*Father's Day / Human Nature*) or indeed Rob Shearman, who wrote Series One's altogether unique *Dalek*. Shearman's episode perhaps benefitted from being much more constrained and claustrophobic than most Dalek stories, and certainly from Christopher Eccleston's very convincing turn as a Doctor going to pieces at being confronted with an enemy who he'd believed was gone forever. That episode, alone of all Dalek stories, took time to consider what it is like to be a Dalek, and perhaps surprisingly that level of introspection lifted what might otherwise have been a competent but mundane story into an altogether higher realm. Thinking of that story has made me realise how rushed all the subsequent New-Who Dalek stories have seemed in comparison, and *Victory* was no exception.

For me, the most powerful part of the episode was probably before the plot kicked in at all – perhaps not coincidentally, the part that took time to stop and breathe, to give us time to taste the atmosphere. The profound *wrongness* of the Daleks' being on the side of the allies in WWII was disturbing. Seeing them gliding serenely and unhindered about the Cabinet War Rooms was an unsettling experience; even the cup-of-tea moment, hilarious though it was, carried with it a disconcerting sense of a nation that had allowed itself to become comfortable with the very thing it was fighting.

A less innovative WWII episode would of course have had the Daleks where they belong – on the side of the Nazis. Subverting that expectation was not just a clever twist but a dark one. What lengths are we prepared to go to? Faced with a war – not a tragicomedy like Bush 2´s "War on Terror" but an actual, no-place-to-run fight for survival – would we go so far as to use Daleks? To be fair, that is not really a choice that the characters in the story had to make, since they had no idea what a Dalek actually is. But I would have liked to see that choice pushed harder: for Churchill to have argued for continuing to use them even after the Doctor had elucidated their true nature. Maybe the production team weren't prepared to risk showing such a beloved historical figure as Churchill in such a light, but no doubt he had to make analogous choices in the real world. One of the things Doctor Who, at its best, can do is to shine a stark, clarifying light on the issues that we can too easily blur over in life. (*The Beast Below*'s Forget and Protest buttons were the clearest example of this choice.) Perhaps not going there in *Victory* was a missed opportunity.

I suppose you could stretch the metaphor a bit and think about the current British government, which is racing helter-skelter towards universal surveillance, mandatory ID cards, a national DNA database and automated email monitoring, all in the name of the War on Terror. (Oh, how I hate that dumb, dumb phrase.) But I don't believe the analogy holds: Brown's government wants to introduce those things for their own sake, and is using the WoT as a pretext; that's very different from, and much less noble than, the situation in *Victory of the Daleks*, in which a country literally on the brink of annihilation is prepared for that reason to consider any measure.

Other things to like in *Victory*: the developing thread of the crack in the universe, and the thought-provoking discovery that Amy does not know what a Dalek is, presumably because she's not lived through *Doomsday* and *The Stolen Earth*. What has happened to our timeline? Surely those episodes can't have un-happened?

Other things to dislike: the sheer implausibility of the attack on the Dalek ship, especially as it seems to have been conceived, designed, arranged and executed all in ten elapsed minutes. Still, I can forgive that because I have been saying for years that X-Wings are clearly Spitfires and TIE Fighters are Messerschmitt Bf 109s (and Y-Wings are of course Hurricanes). It's a delight to see that conception in action, however dumb.

More worrying was the line that Amy used to remind the Dalek-built android of its humanity ("Ever fancied someone you know you shouldn't?"). That, and her sideways glance at that point, does not bode well for the future direction of the series and especially for the companion's arc. If they're going to go raising that spectre again, they'd better actually do something about it – make it work as part of a plot and not just leave it lying around. The best treatment of that theme was back in episode 2.3, *School Reunion*. Unless they have something new to say that is more profound than what was said back then, they'd have been better off leaving well alone.

Checking the schedule, I see that next up is a Moffat two-parter – a sequel, I assume, to *Blink*, which was one of the very best Who episodes of the revival. Fingers crossed that he can keep up his usual standard.

Thoughts in 2013

What looked like entertainment in 2010 feels a lot more disturbing in 2013. Now when I see the WWII allies using Daleks, I'm watching in the light of Edward Snowden's revelations of ubiquitous NSA domestic surveillance, spying on foreign governments that are supposed to be allies of the USA, the use of unmanned drones to carry out assassinations abroad and on occasion to kill children, and the detention of journalists who dare to do their actual jobs by telling the truth about what's being done in our name. When the Good Guys are already using flying killer robots, the Daleks don't look like such a big step any more.

Oh, and by the way ...

[Posted on April 18, 2010]

River Song. Jackson Lake. Amy Pond. Coincidence?

Just saying.

If the next story introduces a character called Adrian Aqueduct, I guess we'll be able to draw our own conclusions.

Thoughts in 2013

Just wanted to include that very short post to point out that I'd spotted the Amy/River connection long, long before *A Good Man Goes to War*.

Episode 5.4. *The Time of Angels*

[Posted on April 24, 2010]

12:12pm – zero minus six hours

I don't plan to make a habit of starting my reviews of Doctor Who Series 5 before the episode airs, as I did with *The Beast Below*. But I wanted to get my thoughts down about the Weeping Angels beforehand, because they worry me. Although I've avoided watching the trailer for this week's episode, it would hardly be possible not to know that it's the first of a two-parter featuring these creatures. Their only previous appearance was in the Tenth Doctor episode *Blink*, also written by showrunner Steven Moffat, which by common consent is among the very best episodes of the revived series. Among other accolades, it won the 2008 Hugo Award for Best Dramatic Presentation, Short Form. I concur with majority opinions here – *Blink* is quite brilliant.

But it achieves that brilliance by being something very different from a normal Doctor Who episode, and I think that would be a very difficult trick to pull off twice – especially if stretched across a two-part story. *Blink* is a tightly woven story, a perfectly constructed machine – a crystalline confection that in some ways is more reminiscent of an Asimov short story or even one of the better Agatha Christie mysteries than it is of Doctor Who. That's not just because the Doctor himself is largely absent from the episode, but because it's put together like a puzzle rather than an adventure. (It also helps that the protagonist, Sally Sparrow, played by Carey Mulligan, is so easy to love. I quickly found myself really wanting things to work out right for her, in a way that I usually don't with one-shot characters.) Every element of *Blink* is not just executed superbly but, well, maybe the word *designed* is what I want. In fact – and this only now occurs to me – one can even imagine an analogy with programming concepts I've been thinking about recently: test-driven and thought-driven development. While most scripts are initially hacked together intuitively, then progressively refined in response to testing them out, you get the sense that *Blink* was thought through in detail before a word was written down, and that it probably changed very little from the submitted script to the final production. (I would love to know whether this imaginary history is actually true – maybe one day Moffat will publish his own *Writer's Tale* – but whether or not it corresponds to the true sequence of events, this origin story gives a flavour of how *Blink* tastes and smells.)

Now here's the point: *Blink* works as it does precisely because the Weeping Angels are not monsters in anything like the conventional sense. They can't talk; they can't be negotiated with (as even the Vashta Nerada, somehow, could); they can't make plans. They follow a more or less predefined course. Their behaviour is predictable. The Doctor catches the notion quite nicely when he describes them as "predators" – in *Blink*, they no more interact with their victims than a lion does with a zebra. That is by no means a weakness of the episode: the simplicity of the Angels themselves is what makes it possible for Moffat to fit such a delightfully complex story in a single 45-minute episode. It's exhilarating to watch the complexities unfold, to see bit by bit how everything that seemed so mysterious actually makes perfect sense, and to enjoy being in the hands of a master.

But it does make me fear for the two-parter that begins tonight, for two reasons. First, I feel that the Weeping Angels have been done: we know what they are, we know how they work, we know what they do to their victims. They are well-defined and tightly constrained. If you like, they are a solved problem. We could write unit tests for them and be pretty sure of passing. That doesn't sound like promising material for a sequel.

And second, I don't see how the Angels can be made deeper or richer without fundamentally changing the nature of what they are – something that not only is hard to imagine being done well, but which also would retroactively rewrite *Blink*. If the Doctor talks to them, figures out their plans, persuades them to change – in short, if he does any of the things that the Doctor does, that make him intrinsically Doctorish – then the Angels would no longer be intrinsically Angelish.

So I'm a bit worried. But I'm not too worried because I trust Moffat in a way that I never trusted RTD. I'm sure he'll have thought of all the same things I've thought of, and much more besides. And I am pretty confident that if he's bringing the Weeping Angels back, it's not just a recapitulate-my-greatest-hits manoeuvre, but it's because he's found a story where they can be used to good effect. I can't see how it's going to be done (though my best guess is that there will be a story involving other people with complex motivations, and the Angels will be an environmental factor that they have to deal with) but I am looking forward to finding out.

Don't let me down, Steven!

8:53pm – intrigued, impressed and a little confused

It's always hard to judge the first half of a two-parter, because you don't know how the mysteries it sets up are going to be resolved. In *The Empty Child*, for example, the mystery of the "Are you my mummy?" boy was established; and as it turned out, it was rather brilliantly resolved in *The Doctor Dances*, in a way that made perfect sense in the programme's own terms. By contrast, the *Daleks in Manhattan* mystery of why the Daleks were turning people into pigs was resolved in *Evolution of the Daleks* as: They Just Are, OK? So seeing *The Doctor Dances* retroactively enhanced the experience of *The Empty Child*, whereas seeing *Evolution of the Daleks* made *Daleks in Manhattan* seem weaker than on first viewing. (*The Doctor Dances* also had the best cliff-hanger resolution of any Doctor Who episode I can think of – "Go to your room!" The contrast with the resolution in, say, *The Age of Steel*, is frankly embarrassing.)

So, with the caveat in mind that we won't really know what to make of *The Time of Angels* until we've seen *Flesh and Stone*, I was impressed. I admired how it handled the problems I discussed in my prologue. I liked how very different the setting was from the mundane, intimate backdrop to Blink, and how the Doctor was thrown into a complex social situation early on. And, being a sucker for time-travel paradoxes, I loved how River Song arranged her rescue from 12,000 years in the past. (Even the casual use of the "12,000 years later ..." caption was an elegant, understated joke, and all the funnier for it.)

I don't think I am giving much away when I say that the Angel is indeed given a way to communicate with the Doctor, and so becomes an actual monster rather than a mere trap. Does this, as I worried above, mean that "the Angels are no longer intrinsically Angelish"? Not really, because the Angel (there is only one, sort of) doesn't communicate by any means as mundane as opening its mouth and speaking. It's artfully done.

Apart from communicating, the Angel seems to have acquired at least three additional powers beyond those seen in *Blink*, which is perhaps not very Occam's Razory. Maybe more like Occam's Potato Peeler. The Doctor passes this off with "The ones on Earth were weakened, just scavengers". Hmm. I'll withhold judgement until I've seen how those powers pan out, but I can't help wondering whether three is too many. So far, only one of them seems to be fundamental to the plot, but maybe in the second half the others will prove to be, too.

It's good to see Moffat making proper use of the two-part format. If single-episode Whos often feel rushed, the same is paradoxically often true of two-parters: for example, *The Sontaran Stratagem/The Poison Sky* felt very much like two separate episodes that merely happened to occur consecutively in the same setting. Everything felt just as rushed and arbitrary as usual, but there was twice as much of it. In contrast, *The Time of Angels* feels much more like the first half a single ninety-minute story. The episode breathes; it takes time to stop and smell the chronovores – which is not at all the same thing as padding. There is a sense that seeds are being sown which will germinate and bloom in the second part. The mysterious man on the ship 12,000 years ago, the very very first sequence in what seems to be parkland(?), the insidious effect that the Angel recording is having on Amy: all of this feels like material that is pointing to something, leading somewhere.

The other way that the episode uses its first-half-fulness is by engaging us in a complex social set-up. The Doctor and Amy are joined very early on by River Song (from *Silence in the Library / Forest of the Dead*) whose relationship with the Doctor is complex to say the least. They are shortly thereafter joined by a military outfit (and it just now occurs to me to wonder how they knew to be there at that time?), and then we have a four-handed game under way. The Doctor seems, unusually, happy to work with the military on this occasion, ostensibly because the threat posed by the Angel is so great, but I wonder whether here, too, there are more surprises bubbling under the surface. Thrown into this stew is a hint of a murky past (or maybe future) for River Song, which the Doctor doesn't know about and wouldn't approve of if he did. It's a rich concoction, and I really, really want to see the second half now, please!

(By the way, I didn't notice an occurrence of the ubiquitous Crack In The Universe that's been in the first three episodes; but that doesn't necessarily mean it wasn't there, unnoticed and uncommented. I'll keep an eye out for it the next time I watch.)

Finally, I would like to know what utter idiot at the BBC thought it would be a good idea to run a cartoon trailer for Over The Rainbow during the climactic moments of the episode. Words fail me as I consider the monumental misjudgement involved here. It's as though Spielberg decided that, just as the shark is bearing down on Roy Schneider with the compressed air cylinder in its mouth, a Bugs Bunny cartoon should run in the corner of the screen. Deeply, deeply wrong and wholly inexplicable.

Famously, a quiet and tense passage in the initial broadcast of *Rose*, the very first episode of revived Who, was ruined by having a fragment of the sound from a Graham Norton show played at the crucial moment. Since Norton is also the host of Over The Rainbow, it looks suspiciously as though he's on a one-man mission to crap all over Doctor Who.

Seriously, BBC. I'm watching Doctor Who, which I paid for with my licence fee. Let me watch Doctor Who. When I am done with that, and only then, you may try to persuade me (though you will be unsuccessful) to watch Over The Rainbow. But NOT DURING THE CLIMAX OF THE PRECEDING SHOW! Arrrgh!

Thoughts in 2013

It's a bit humiliating to see how much of what I wrote there didn't really pan out in the second half. The mysterious man in the ship at the start got dropped on the floor and forgotten; the parkland sequence was – obviously, now I think about it – a hallucination brought on by River Song's lipstick; I was wrong in guessing that the Doctor had a relevant past with the military. These reviews, especially the ones of the two-parters, are going to be full of such misinterpretations and mistakes, distressingly often because I was giving the programme more credit for cleverness than it merited. I won't draw attention to these every time they crop up – you can enjoy spotting them for yourself and feeling superior to me. I won't mind.

Where this is really going to become a problem is in Series 6, which laid down a host of clues that were never satisfactorily picked up. But let's not get ahead of ourselves.

Episode 5.5. *Flesh and Stone*

[Posted on May 2, 2010]

So yesterday evening I watched *Flesh and Stone*, the second half of the two-parter that began with last week's *The Time of Angels*, and the fifth outing for the new Doctor Matt Smith. It had a lot to live up to: a very creepy opening episode featuring an enemy that has quickly become iconic – maybe more so than any Doctor Who creature outside of the Daleks and Cybermen. Did it come up to expectation?

I don't know.

Of all the episodes I've seen, this is the one that I most need to watch again. All the things that I expected to love about it – clever plotting, a resolution that makes sense, frightening monsters – seem a little hazy in my mind now; and I couldn't really say, for example, how I feel about the Angels themselves right now. Does their development make them more interesting or less well-defined? (Well, OK, obviously it does both; but which effect is stronger?)

But the dialogue and the acting, which I'd not particularly expected so much from, were outstanding. Again and again as the episode progressed, I found myself taken by surprise by a clever insight or a moment of undiluted Doctorishness. I laughed out loud a lot of times – not because it was particularly funny, but for the sheer joy of watching. Matt Smith continues to push out ahead of the pack as my favourite Doctor, both fulfilling and transcending established characteristics of the role. He continues to exude a mostly-calm intelligence, and is much more obviously analytical than his predecessor. Much as I liked Tennant, I find I am already beginning to look back on his tenure as a little plasticky, a bit self-parodying; where he was painted in primary colours, Smith's Doctor is subtler and richer.

Amy is also developing as a character (although see below). I've only now realised how rare it is to see one of the Doctor's companions truly scared, as she was last night. And it was good to see: she *should* be scared. Others have commented that Amy has seemed too breezy, too confident; as though she doesn't understand or care what is at stake in her various adventures. Last night, she knew.

As is so often the case in Doctor Who, the frightening parts are not so much the attacks of the monsters as the unexpected ideas – such as people disappearing so thoroughly that they literally never existed. Moffat is particularly strong on this kind of thing: remember Doctor Moon in *Silence in the Library* turning to Cal and telling her that her dreams are real and her real life is not? These ideas, when stated baldly, may not be very spine-tingling; when presented in a coherent fiction, and acted convincingly, they surely are. *Flesh and Stone* gave me several of these moments, and I love it for that – something that is pretty much unique to Who.

Oh, and the epilogue, back on Earth? Put me down as Not A Fan. I hope we're going to see some specific exculpatory reason for Amy's behaviour. I've liked her a lot up till now; I don't want to lose my respect for her. The Doctor's response suggested that something was Wrong there, and I hope it gets laid out for us.

On the positive side, at least Graham Norton wasn't in it this time.

And so on to the rest of the series: the bad news is the Grand Moff himself did not write any the next six episodes; the good news is that he wrote the final two-parter, in which I fully expect to see the Crack In The Universe again, and probably also see River Song killing The Best Man She Has Ever Known. But first: vampires! As always, I avoided seeing the trailer, so all I know is what's in the title – that next week's episode involves vampires and that they're in Venice. It's by Toby Whithouse, whose previous story, *School Reunion*, I thought was pretty brilliant, although I know not everyone agrees on that. I loved its treatment of Sarah Jane on her return, and especially Mickey's realisation that he is the tin dog. Now we'll see what he does with vampires.

Half-term report

Five episodes in, now is a pretty good time to take stock of the new series. Of those five, Moffat has written four (all but *Victory of the Daleks*), and of course has had overall control of the show, including the casting of Smith and Gillan as the Doctor and Amy. How does the half-term report look?

It looks very, very good. If I seem to have damned some of the episodes so far with faint praise – including *Flesh and Stone*, I suppose – it's because I came into this series with very high expectations given Moffat's previous. Those expectations may not have been exceeded, but neither have they been disappointed. The new Doctor is superb in every way, the plots are making more sense than at any previous time since the show was revived, and there are more spine-tingling moments than ever before – not fear exactly, but a sense of being close to something profound.

Most important of all, I am finding myself looking forward to each week's episode with an eagerness I've not felt since 2005 (Christopher Eccleston's series). Each episode feels like an event – something I don't want to miss (even though I know I'll be able to download it within a couple of hours if I do). The countdown to each Saturday's episode is starting around the previous Tuesday. My boys and their friends are playing Weeping Angels. The monsters are iconic again.

There are, always have been, and always will be, things to dislike about Doctor Who. There will always be a segment of the population that just refuses to like it. But the deficiencies are easy to overlook this time around, and the many unique merits of the programme are more apparent than ever. I'm having a great time.

The computer virus was the weakest element of the new series so far; and it's a shame that it was a key plot point in the very first episode. I think it's part of the reason that my initial response to the new series was much less wholeheartedly positive than my reaction to subsequent episodes. It felt a lot more like an RTD idea than a Moffat one ... I almost wonder whether Davies did come up with it, and bequeathed it to his successor, who felt it would be churlish not to use it. The same applies to the Doctor's arrival at the hospital in that episode, by climbing up the fire engine's ladder through the window – it felt knockabout, slapstick, not at all Doctorish.

And, therefore, very different from *Flesh and Stone*. One of the aspects of the new series that I love is that, the first episode aside, the new Doctor is never *frivolous*. Unpredictable, yes, eccentric, yes, but I've never seen him behave as though what's happening doesn't matter – he's never undercut the significance of the unfolding story by treating it as a game. Except in that first episode. So I think it really was transitional.

Episode 5.6. *The Vampires of Venice*

[Posted on May 8, 2010]

Episode six rolls around (and, hey, that was the name of the band that Ian Gillan and Roger Glover were in before they joined Deep Purple): we find out how the Doctor responds to Amy's ill-judged overtures at the end of *Flesh and Stone*, and how he deals with vampires.

It's not the first time that the Doctor has encountered vampires – they featured in both *State of Decay* (Fourth Doctor) and arguably *The Curse of Fenric* (Seventh Doctor), but I've never seen either of those. (I don't count the "haemovore" from *Smith and Jones*, as she exhibits none of the standard vampire attributes.) So this was effectively a first for me.

Vampires are an interesting choice to follow on from the Weeping Angels of *The Time of Angels / Flesh and Stone*, because like the Angels they follow well-established rules. Everyone knows how vampires work: they can't stand daylight, garlic or the sight of a cross, they can only be killed by a stake to the heart, and so on. Because of this, vampire stories – like the first Weeping Angel story, *Blink* – resemble puzzles: the pieces are laid out on the board, their capabilities are known and understood, and we have to figure out a way to check-mate in 45 minutes. Done well, this kind of story can be a tour de force; on the other hand, countless Hammer Horror films show that they can also be hack work of the lowest order, with the Vampire Rules standing in as a shoddy substitute for, rather than the motor of, plot. So, how did *Vampires in Venice* stand up?

[Not wholly relevant aside: for the last week or two, Fiona and I have been watching and enjoying the first series of House, an American hospital drama with elements of comedy, mostly due to Hugh Laurie's impossibly acerbic portrayal of the eponymous lead. Every episode follows much the same pattern: a patient is admitted with a mysterious set of symptoms which cannot be diagnosed. Initial and sometimes subsequent treatments make the illness worse or introduce deleterious side-effects until an insight shows the true cause, and the patient is cured. One of the things that makes this show fun to watch is that around the time that the first unsuccessful treatment causes more problems, I always say, "Oh, I think I know what it is!", and Fiona always – I mean, literally, pretty much *always* – fails to recognise that I am about to say that the cause is: vampires. Seriously. I have done this in every single one of the first eleven episodes, and she has fallen for it on every occasion but one. That is a 91% hit-rate, folks! That is quality wifing.]

It turns out that in *Vampires of Venice*, the vampires are not vampires. They are aliens using perception filters to appear human, and when they exhibit their eating-people tendencies, they appear like vampires. (The Doctor describes the aliens' true form as being "big fish" but they appear more like arthropods. Surely the Doctor can't be one of those appalling pre-cladistic taxonomists who classify organisms according to gross resemblance rather than commonality of descent? I guess not, since there's not even a gross resemblance to any non-tetrapodan gnathostome I've ever seen. Oh well.)

I have mixed feelings about this. It's done well, and makes the premise more science-fictiony (whatever Terry Pratchett might say), which is more in keeping with the Doctor Who approach. But part of me wishes that this episode had had the, oh, what's that Yiddish word?, to stick with actual vampires. Vampires whose strengths and weaknesses we know, and can think through, and reach conclusions. (Oh, yeah: chutzpah. That's what I was thinking of. That's Yiddish, right?)

On the positive side, the not-actual-vampires-ness of the vampires does open the door for a rather neat science-fictional explanation of why they can't be seen in mirrors. It never becomes clear whether a stake through the heart will kill them (though, as Buffy observes in an episode that eludes me for the moment, you'd be amazed at how many kinds of bad guy that works for.)

So what works and what doesn't? I loved Amy's response on first seeing a vampire feeding: she convinces as someone who is genuinely shocked. Seeing this kind of thing makes me retrospectively downgrade all those 1970s episodes where Sarah Jane, bless her, was wholly unable to summon anything resembling a realistic reaction to Sutekh/Styre/Davros/whoever. In terms of acting, the bar has been raised enormously in the last 30 years. (You can also see that in Liz Sladen's own more recent performances in The Sarah Jane Adventures, which by the way I heartily recommend. For one thing, it's about ten times as "adult" as The Dreadful Torchwood.)

I was also pleased to see the Doctor not just brushing over Amy's indiscretion at the end of *Flesh and Stone*, but confronting it head on by bringing Rory to Venice. Rory acquitted himself pretty well, showing enough courage to earn a more protracted stay in the TARDIS; I don't see why Amy thought it was silly of him to try to repel the vampire with the sign of a cross. There's some risk of a Doctor/Rose/Mickey vibe developing in the Doctor/Amy/Rory triangle, but for now let's trust the writers to be aware of that danger, and able to write around it. If Rory's going to stay around, he needs to develop beyond Generic Well-Meaning Buffoon.

And at the risk of sounding like a broken record, I continue to very much like Matt Smith's Doctor. I'm not prepared to install him in the much-coveted position of Best Doctor until I've seen a whole series, but the signs are good. Six episodes in, he has established himself firmly as his own man, and is by some distance the most thoughtful Doctor in recent memory. I particularly enjoyed his anticipation of Amy's plan to infiltrate the vampires' palace, and his reluctant but conclusive recognition that Isabella's father had made his self-destructive decision and wasn't to be dissuaded.

Oh, and by the way: the episode is beautiful to look at. The locations and costumes are gorgeous. Should have mentioned that before.

Here's a thing. By coincidence, it was this very evening that I happened to reach the end of my re-watching the first season of Buffy the Vampire Slayer. I don't want to get too side-tracked by it, but I will just say this: watching *Vampires in Venice* and *Prophecy Girl* on the same evening shows just how much Doctor Who and Buffy differ in their approach. Without ever dragging, Buffy takes the time to stop and look at the characters, and that time is well spent. In that climactic episode of the first series, we are given an opportunity to look at Buffy's quiet courage as she sets her face to confront the Master, knowing that her death is prophesied. There is no big scene; no oh-look-at-me-I'm-so-noble moment; just the gently heartbreaking spectacle of a sixteen-year-old taking on responsibility beyond what she ought to have to carry, and doing her best to shield her friends from even having to know about it, let alone participate. It's masterfully judged: there is nothing heavy-handed about it, but the elemental evil of vampires, the weight of the burden of fighting them and the firmness of spirit that is needed to do so all emerge organically from an episode that has time to breathe.

So I find myself thinking that maybe Doctor Who should rush less. This series certainly rushes less than the David Tennant series did – it's a step in the right direction – but I think that the writers should have the courage to take it a step further. We've seen enough of Matt Smith and Karen Gillan to know that they both have the acting chops to make use of more time – neither of them needs to be running down corridors all the time to stay interesting.

All in all, I rate *Vampires in Venice* a success, but not a resounding one. Comparing with equivalent episodes in previous series, it lacks the weight of Series One's *Dalek*, covers more interesting ground and in more depth than Series Two's *The Idiot's Lantern* or Series Three's *The Lazarus Experiment*, and towers above Series Four's execrable *The Doctor's Daughter*.

I think we're on target for the best Doctor Who series ever.

Episode 5.7. *Amy's Choice*

[Posted on May 24, 2010]

I had a more fundamental problem with *Amy's Choice* than with any other episode in the series so far.

It's a shame that this episode didn't really work, because the premise is replete with opportunity – two alternative realities running in parallel, with the heroes switching between them. Recent Who has dealt with alternative realities a couple of times, both of them very effectively (Donna's realisation that her children are fake in *Forest of the Dead* was the single spine-tingliest moment in all of Who for me, and *Turn Left* was genuinely chilling).

In contrast with those two episodes, this one was set up as a puzzle, very explicitly and pretty early on: The Mysterious Stranger (hereafter TMS) turns up out of nowhere and explains the plot to the Doctor, Amy and Rory: one of the realities is real and the other is fake: they have to choose which is real, knowing that if they die in the fake reality they will simply awake in the other, and TMS will make the danger go away. Stated baldly, this sounds like a transparently contrived dilemma; that it works as well as it does is tribute to good acting on the part of the three principals.

In both realities, things go quickly wrong. The first, set on the Earth a few years in the future, has Amy married to Rory, who is now a Doctor, and she is very pregnant. Idyllic (though maybe more for Rory than for Amy), until the village's aged population turn out to be hosting hostile aliens who eat all the children, and then come after our heroes.

The second reality, set on the TARDIS, shows us a malfunction and loss of power, with the result that the TARDIS is pulled towards a frozen star. It gets progressively colder until the Doctor and co. are threatened with freezing to death.

If you can overlook the artificiality of it all, and TMS's frequent reappearances to act as master of ceremonies and occasional expositor, it's not a bad set-up: how can the heroes figure out which reality is the real one?

And it's here that not one, not two, but three profound problems undercut the episode's effectiveness.

First, nothing actually happens in the cold-star scenario. Nearly all the time is spent in the alien-oldies world, so we're not given a fair chance to compare them for implausibility. What time we do spend in the TARDIS is mostly taken up with TMS's gnomic utterances. To be fair, they are interesting enough – especially when watching for the second time, and knowing what the resolution is going to be – but they don't deliver what the set-up promised.

Second, no-one makes any actual progress towards figuring out which world is real. There is a funny moment when the Doctor waves his hand back and forth in front of his face and says he's looking for video compression artefacts, and he emphasises that Amy and Rory need to be on the lookout for anything unusual (which as Rory points out is difficult given how weird normal life is for them). But none of this leads anywhere. It's a rare example in the Moffat era of a plot line being dropped on the floor and forgotten – and all the more perplexing for its being, at least nominally, the central plot thread.

Third, and most cripplingly, the entire episode is rendered wholly futile when it is revealed that in fact both scenarios are fake. There never was a cold star, there never were alien-infested pensioners – the whole of both scenarios were induced by some kind of alien dream pollen. This means, of course, that it mattered not one jot what happened in either of the worlds: the Doctor and friends could have just sat snugly waiting to be disintegrated by aliens/frozen by the cold star, and stuck their fingers in their ears and sung LA LA LA whenever TMS turned up to emit a plot fragment.

So as I watched and tried to figure out what was going on, I didn't guess that both "realities" were unreal because – well, that would be cheating, wouldn't it? I trusted the programme more than that. It's not that I object to the notion of a twist. If both realities had turned out to be *real*, that would have been good. But when neither is, then (as one of our poets has written), "Nothing really matters, anyone can see, nothing really matters to me".

I said when reviewing the dreadful Buffy movie that any interest I had in proceedings was destroyed by the characters' failure to take their own situation seriously. But *Amy's Choice* turns out to suffer from an even more foundational defect: it's not just that the characters don't believe in their world – it's that they *shouldn't* believe in it. Heck, even the writers don't.

So despite all its fine moments (and I did laugh at times, and I found the final revelation of TMS's identity suitably surprising and thought-provoking), *Amy's Choice* represents a horrible fumbling of the ball. It's not without merit, but the faults lie too deep for any amount of sugar to save it.

It's true that the choice Amy eventually makes does seem to be consciously made by real Amy, not just a part of the dream. In that sense, the dream-worlds are not really like dreams at all, more like role-play settings – they're laid out as internally self-consistent worlds and the player-characters are dumped into them to respond as they would in real life. Which is why Amy's choice, having been made in Upper Leadworth World, remains after the world it happened in has gone. So the game is not, quite, zero-stakes. But the choice still carries a lot less weight than it would have if it had been made in the real world – compare, for example, Zoe's choice between Captain Mal and Wash in the Firefly episode *War Games*.

Shame. Philip K. Dick made an entire career out of stories in which notions of reality were stretched, twisted, inverted and otherwise played with; some of his short stories have left deep impressions on me (his novels, not so much), among which *The Electric Ant, Chains of Air, Web of Aether*, and especially *Faith of Our Fathers* loom large. [Note to self: must write article about how *Faith of Our Fathers* both parallels and utterly contradicts G. K. Chesterton's brilliant novel *The Man Who Was Thursday*.] Given the huge realm of possibilities that this kind of story offers, I didn't expect to see the opportunity fumbled so badly under Moffat's watch.

Episode 5.8. *The Hungry Earth*

[Posted on May 29, 2010]

For various dull reasons, it took me nearly a week to write this review. But I pushed it out just before *Cold Blood* was broadcast, because I wanted to write down my thoughts on the first half of the two-parter before I saw the second. The reason for that is that in many New Who two-parters, the first half is the stronger: think of *The Empty Child* vs. *The Doctor Dances*, *Silence in the Library* vs. *Forest of the Dead*, and arguably *The Time of Angels* vs. *Flesh and Stone*. On the other hand, the second half sometimes lifts the first, casts it in a clearer light and makes it look better than on first impressions – think of how *The Family of Blood* surpassed *Human Nature* (which was already superb).

Either way, I didn't want the second half to bias my impressions of the first, so let's take a moment to think about *The Hungry Earth* as a standalone episode.

I have a soft spot for the Silurians, not only because they were the subject of the first Doctor Who novelisation I ever read (Malcolm Hulke's *Doctor Who and the Cave Monsters*), but because they are an intrinsically interesting enemy for the Doctor: not evil, they were here before us (either 430 million years before, if they are from the Silurian period, or any of a variety of other ages that have been proposed on and off screen if their name is incorrect).

In their original appearance, in the Jon Pertwee story of which *Cave Monsters* was the novelisation, they were accidentally reawakened by a nuclear reactor, and were not so much genocidal as outraged to see their planet overrun by mammals. That story ended with the Brigadier blowing up the cave complex where they lived, to the Doctor's fury. (That's based on my memory of the novel – I've never seen more than fragments of the actual TV story.)

They next appeared in the Peter Davison story *Warriors of the Deep*, alongside their relatives the Sea Devils; but I've never seen that or read a novelisation, so I won't embarrass myself by trying to summarise. And those two stories constitute the whole of the Silurian canon up until *Hungry Earth*.

In Andrew Rilstone's brilliant essay *Is Tolkien Actually Any Good?*, he makes the point that "This is the key to why Tolkien became so very important to me. It wasn't his bad writing, odd pacing, strange characterisation or over-complex history which appealed to me. What I wanted was the idea-of-elves, the idea-of-orcs, the idea-of-caves and the idea-of-dwarves". In other words, the specific plots involving the elves, orcs and dwarves were less important to him (and by extension to other readers) than the archetypes that they embody, and the ages-long romance that they imply. That's how I feel about the Silurians: their sombre history, going back tens of millions of years, is a "long defeat" all its own, diluted only slightly by the fact that they were asleep for nearly all of that time. It's deeply resonant for me, maybe partly because of my work in palaeontology. So I was a bit apprehensive about seeing them on-screen for the first time since 1984. Could they live up to my memory and imagination?

The Hungry Earth begins by sketching some well-drawn subsidiary characters: Nasreen and Tony are inexplicably in charge of a deep drilling operation somewhere in rural Wales; Tony's daughter Ambrose is married to Mo, who also works at the drilling operation, and they have a dyslexic son called Elliot. That's it for the cast, apart from of course the lead trio: The Doctor, Amy and Rory. In a two-parter, five supporting characters is about right: there's enough time to make them separable individuals, people with a bit of depth and motivation beyond stereotypes, and *The Hungry Earth* script does a good job of this. The older two, particularly, are not typical Who-fodder, and they're acted well enough to carry off their slightly idiosyncratic characters. Ambrose is rather more Vanilla Worried Mother, and we've not yet seen much of Mo. Still, these characters are drawn well enough that by the end of the episode, when the Silurian captive says to Tony, Ambrose and Rory that "one of you will kill me, and I know which one", it's a puzzle that feels intriguing and believable rather than just opaque and unguessable.

As for the Silurians themselves: they are, very properly, kept off-stage for most of the episode, and even after they make themselves known we only see one. I didn't realise at first, though – and was rather disappointed when I did – that what we were looking at was a mask. When the Doctor removes it, the reptile-woman beneath looks like, well, a woman who is a reptile.

It's an excellent make-up/prosthetics job, and it does mean that the actor underneath the gloop is able to actually act, but to my mind that advantage is won at too high a price. While the original-series Silurians were rather ponderous and expressionless, they had a certain dignity. More importantly they were very clearly other. (I wanted to say "alien" there, but in the context of Doctor Who everyone assumes that means extraterrestrial.) It was easy to accept them as an unimaginably old elder race, literally and metaphorically seeing things completely differently from how we do, and perhaps with a deep wisdom of their own. By contrast, the new Silurian design is basically a Hot Chick with reptile bits stuck on the back of her head. She can hardly help but come across as a mere human with a rather unfortunate skin condition. Consequently, all her talk of being prepared to "gladly die for my cause" just makes her come across as your regular Brain-Dead Fundamentalist rather than a representative of a profound and ancient civilisation.

It now occurs to me – oh dear – that this might even be deliberate. Could the programme be trying to make some crushingly dull point about fanaticism in our post-9/11 world? It's rarely to Doctor Who's advantage to attempt big-r Relevance – something that any other programme can do just as well or better. It does better when presenting ideas that its science-fictional premise allows but which, say, *Eastenders* would not be able to contain. A reptilian elder-race is such an idea, and it's cheap to throw that away in order to score some exceedingly cheap PC points. After all, it's hardly as though most viewers need to be persuaded that Terrorism Is Bad.

So does this mean a big thumbs down for *The Hungry Earth*?

Strangely, it does not. Despite my reservations about the redesign, and more importantly about what it implies about the Silurian race, I loved almost everything else about the episode. I've already mentioned the rich cast of supporting characters; both Amy and Rory also shine this time around.

But once more (and stop me if this is getting boring) it's Matt Smith's performance as the Doctor that really hits all the right notes. Perhaps I am more attuned than usual to his merits, having recently watched *The Two Doctors* (I know, I know, what was I thinking?), but it really does seem that he can do no wrong at the moment. Even his youth, which initially I objected to, seems to be working in his favour: he so consistently portrays his character as a much older man that the contrast between his face and his soul is powerful in itself. All Doctors have swung between seriousness and levity – it's a signature move of the character – but with this Doctor, it never seems forced.

The classic "Doctor" moments in this episode happened mostly in the brief but intense scene in which he spoke one-on-one with the captive Silurian warrior. I was reminded of the meal shared by Christopher Eccleston's Doctor and Margaret Blaine (aka. Blon Fel-Fotch Pasameer-Day Slitheen) in the otherwise rather lame Series 1 episode *Boom Town*. That episode, near-universally considered the weakest of Eccleston's series, seems to have been conceived and built around that restaurant scene. It feels like a missed opportunity rather than out-and-out failure, as though the writer (Russell T. Davies, natch) thought that with that one brilliant scene written, the rest of the episode would fall into place on its own. By contrast, the at-least-equally-good Doctor/Silurian scene in *The Hungry Earth* is part of a much richer episode, with many other fine moments, not least Amy's slow and inexorable descent into the sinkhole while the Doctor tries, and fails, to rescue her.

Classic moments include:

Silurian captive: I am the last of my species!

Doctor: No. You're really not. Because I'm the last of my species and I know how it sits in a heart. So don't insult me.

and:

Silurian captive: We will wipe the vermin from the surface and reclaim our planet!

Doctor: Do we have to say vermin? They're really very nice.

and of course the closing moment of their dialogue:

Silurian captive: I'll gladly die for my cause, what will you sacrifice for yours?

Doctor: [No words. Just a look of great sadness under control.]

Just writing these lines out doesn't begin to do them justice. The writing is good, yes, but it's Matt Smith's Doctor that brings it to life. Everything I said about not being able to believe in the Silurian as a representative of an ancient race is turned on its head in the Doctor's case: he does make me believe that he is a Time Lord – something none of his predecessors ever really did (with the possible exception of Eccleston).

So: there are plenty of high points in *The Hungry Earth*, and I am inclined to rate it as among the best episodes of this series despite the creature-design miscalculation. I only hope that the second half keeps up the standard "in the small", of both writing and acting, while also working more strongly "in the large" to bring out the poignancy and dignity, as well as the menace, of the Silurian race.

Episode 5.9. *Cold Blood*

[Posted on June 2, 2010]

So, did *Cold Blood* live up to the very promising *The Hungry Earth*, the first half of the two-parter that it concludes? Having watched it only once so far, my answer is a qualified yes. My concerns about the Silurians looking too human were exacerbated when we saw more of them, but since they actually did have noticeably different characters, the ability to read that on their faces was fairly useful.

Eldane, for example, is a statesman – one who wants to broker peace. And you can sort of see that in his face, as compared to the warrior who we saw last week. It's an impressive job of make-up to enable the actors to act through the layers. I still don't think the loss of alienness is a price worth paying, but at least now that I've seen the second part, I can understand why the programme makers did think so.

Part 2 of the Silurian story had a high-concept arc, which I liked a lot: it began with a voiceover from a Silurian, speaking from the future, explaining that this is the story of how understanding was established between *Homo sapiens* and *Homo reptilia*. (Yes, that's what the Doctor calls them: for all his sciencey goodness, he's still an old-fashioned Linnaean taxonomist, and not a particularly good one either if he thinks that synapsid and sauropsid species can be congeneric, but let it pass.) Establishing from the start that peace would somehow be achieved may seem to undercut the drama, but it's not really so. The tension is in seeing *how* something is brought about rather than *whether* it is – trading away the latter is a small loss in exchange for the gain of setting out from the beginning of the episode that the goal is reconciliation rather than conquest.

Unfortunately, the excellent broad-brush-stroke work was not really matched by the detail of the plot, which involved rather more running around, getting captured and last-minute escapes than strictly necessary. Excellent and touching individual moments were rather lost in the rush of forgettable events. We should have been left with a sequence of strong images – not least, the awful moment when Rory had to carry the body of the dead Silurian warrior into what were looking like being successful negotiations. Instead, I was left with a confused blur punctuated by pools of relative stillness where the important stuff happened.

This is part of the problem you get when you take the focus away from the Doctor himself and let subsidiary characters become too important: you lose not just Matt Smith's superb acting, but the outsider's perspective that the Doctor offers – the consistently different approach to solving problems. In his absence, the best that Amy and Mo could come up with was to rush into the execution chamber waving guns: not an approach the Doctor would have taken, or for that matter sanctioned, and one that fails predictably. It would have been much more distinctively Whovian if, for example, Amy and Mo had gained control of the chamber, but the Doctor had then persuaded them to demonstrate their moral level by giving up the weapons by choice. Instead, they were simply overpowered and lined up to be executed themselves. Much less interesting.

More mystifying was the Doctor's choice, in the central conference, to leave the humans' side of negotiation with the Silurians to Amy and Nasreen. Their perspective on the deal to be made was as mundane and selfish as we might have expected (although in fact I expected better from Amy), whereas if the Doctor had been directly involved he would surely have insisted on doing what is right rather than what is expedient.

I can sort of see what the episode might have been trying to do here. Just as the Doctor wants to give the humans more responsibility, and to help them grow to the point where they can run their own planet responsibly, so perhaps the idea was to show us this by allowing him to hand the episode itself over to his human companions. The idea may be noble, but it fails for two reasons.

First, the humans in question are just not big enough to carry the load. Nasreen, played by a woman approaching fifty, might have been expected to have accumulated some wisdom in her half-century, but displays precious little. Amy is of course much younger but has had the benefit of travelling with, and learning, from the Doctor; yet she, too, handles the negotiations with the Silurian leader as a whiny game of what's-in-it-for-us rather than an opportunity to show grace on behalf of the race that she represents. [An aside: speaking of race, it was a nice touch to have the humans' negotiators represented by a Caucasian and an Asian ... though both were of course British, as befits *Doctor Who*, as distinctively British a programme as I've ever seen, however many aliens and spaceships might be involved.]

But the second problem with the Doctor-handing-over-responsibility approach is that it left him with little to do. And that is squandering the series' greatest asset. In stark contrast to his taking control in *The Hungry Earth*, and to the virtuoso moments afforded by the dialogue with the captive Silurian warrior, he spent most of *Cold Blood* doing ... well, not much at all. Blowing up warriors' guns with the sonic screwdriver and running away, mostly.

Ah yes, the sonic screwdriver. It's becoming a real problem again. Russell T. Davies was rightly derided for making it an all-purpose get-out-of-jail-free device, and I can't have been the only person who cheered when it was destroyed part way through *The Eleventh Hour*. Or the only person who headdesked when the TARDIS presented him with a new one at the end of that episode. To be fair, it spent the next few episodes doing only what it is supposed to do, namely open doors. But its functions seem to be expanding again. This is a very bad habit and must be curtailed. It is of course the Doctor's defining characteristic that he never, ever carries a gun (except when he goes to shoot Davros while disguised as a vet, or when he goes to shoot the Master, or on any of the other occasions when he wants to). To use the sonic as an explicitly non-weapony weapon (i.e. one whose function is to destroy other weapons) could be construed as a clever reversal, but for my money it goes much too far towards letting the Doctor solve problems the way an action hero would. And an action hero is the one thing the Doctor must never be.

Still, if I seem to be complaining about all the things that *Cold Blood* did wrong, that's only because it's more interesting that listing what did work. I wouldn't say that it lived up to the standard that its rather spiffing predecessor set, but then neither was it a catastrophic falling away as, for example, *The Sound of Drums/Last of the Time Lords* was after the climactic revelation of *Utopia*. It got the job done. And the clever not-really-resolved ending set the scene nicely for a potential sequel set a thousand years in the future, which I really hope gets made. (Yes, I am still a Silurian fanboy; and good as *Hungry Earth/Cold Blood* was, it's still very much the case that the definitive Silurian story still waits to be written.)

Speaking of writing, I somehow failed to register before watching *The Hungry Earth* who the writer was, so I was astounded to see in the closing credits that it was Chris Chibnall, whose work I generally loathe. (His only previous Doctor Who episode was *42*, which to be fair I need to see again, but he was responsible for the truly appalling Torchwood episode *Countrycide*, as well as the laughably incompetent Torchwood Series 1 finale, *End of Days*.) It's good that I didn't know he'd provided the Silurian scripts or I'd have gone into the first episode prejudiced against it. Instead, he's shown that he can write well when he tries – very well in places – so I can only assume his dreadful Torchwood scripts are done that way on purpose because that's what the show's audience wants. Ugh, it hurts even to think about it. Let's change the subject …

… to Rory!

One of the pleasant surprises over the last four episodes (*Vampires of Venice*, *Amy's Choice* and the Silurian two-parter) has been Rory's swift emergence as a character of perception, wit and courage. Initially I'd been worried that he'd be a retread of Mickey Smith, who took a very long time to develop into the rather heroic version we knew by the end of Series 2. But no: almost immediately, Rory adapted to life on the TARDIS, anticipated the Doctor's explanations, didn't allow himself to be fazed by events. By the end of *Cold Blood*, he had established himself as by some distance the most admirable of the human characters, and one with a great career ahead of him.

Which of course makes what happened to him all the more heartbreaking. To die is one thing; to never have existed is altogether different, and Amy's near-total forgetting of Rory at the end of the episode was pretty darned poignant, I can tell you.

We shall see how this develops. I did see a small clue that points to one possible direction: the engagement ring that he took back to the TARDIS early on in *The Hungry Earth* was still there at the end of *Cold Blood*. What can it mean? With Rory having been so completely excised from history that Amy doesn't even remember that he existed, it seems like an anomaly that the ring should exist at all. My guess is that it was somehow stabilised, protected from the rewriting, by being inside the TARDIS; that perhaps from that tiny fixed point, they will be able to recover Rory. I hope so: usually I hate it when they somehow find a way to bring back people who've been Lost Forever (see: Tyler, Rose), but for Rory I will make an exception.

Of course, losing Rory leaves open the possibility of Amy developing a relationship with Jeff, the good looking one from *The Eleventh Hour*. We weren't shown enough to become interested in him back in that episode, and the idea that Amy might transfer her affections to him is pretty cheap. Though I have to admit that, done right and with our sympathies directed towards Rory, it could be absolutely heartbreaking. But only at the price of greatly diminishing Amy.

—

As usual, I avoided watching the trailer for next week's episode, but I understand it's a sort of comedy historical written by Richard "Blackadder" Curtis. I'm not sure how I feel about this. I do love it that Doctor Who's format lets it veer so wildly between comedy, adventure, profundity and levity; but Curtis seems liable to tip the show too far away from the serious stuff, and that would be a shame. Well. We shall see.

Episode 5.10. *Vincent and the Doctor*

[Posted on June 10, 2010]

Start with a man who sees things different from everyone else. That's an interesting science-fictional premise. Throw in an alien that is invisible – to everyone except the man who sees differently. There's your source of tension, maybe conflict and danger. Make the man one of the best-loved of artists, and you have immediate grounding, the opportunity to show us on film things that we're already familiar with from paintings. And of course add in the Doctor and the freshly Rory-less Amy.

Should be all the ingredients for a classic episode, right?

I truly am not sure. I was distinctly underwhelmed when I first watched this, but having now seen it a second time, I find myself appreciating it much more. While the whole episode doesn't really work, it still contains a lot of delicious little cameos, and I find myself feeling that I'm being churlish if I complain about the core story being rather formulaic and dull and not really making sense.

We start with Amy in the Musée d'Orsay with the Doctor, asking "You're being so nice to me – why are you being so nice to me?" The Doctor is evasive; we know it's because he feels sorrow for her having lost Rory – and maybe some guilt – but he can't say so because she won't understand or believe him. That's disquieting: an unspoken reminder of Rory, whose ghost subtly haunts the entire episode. [Aside: I fear that I use the word "subtly" too often in my reviews. Bad habit. Gotta break it.]

We quickly find ourselves back in 1889, in Provence, and in the company of the eponymous Vincent, namely Vincent Van Gogh (who I am pleased to say gets to have his surname pronounced as we in Britain say it, and not as the American "Van Go"). For reasons that are never explained, or indeed explored, he speaks throughout in a Scottish accent.

There is lots of very enjoyable character work as the Doctor and (especially) Amy simply and frankly enjoy being with such an iconic painter. Van Gogh's eccentricity is drawn in primary colours (appropriately enough) but not over-egged. At one point he raves at the Doctor, waving his arms wildly and crying "It's colour! Colour that holds the key! I can hear the colours ... Listen to them!" I couldn't help giggling at the Doctor's expression – half blankly mystified, half kindly encouraging; patronising without really meaning to be. It brings home yet again what a fine actor Matt Smith is: having recently for some reason subjected myself to *The Two Doctors*, I can't begin to imagine Colin Baker ever bringing off such an expression. (Patrick Troughton might have managed it, though.)

A dead body is found, and a rather pointless fight with the invisible alien ensues. Once it's been driven off, the Doctor asks Vincent to sketch it, then takes the sketch back to the TARDIS and digs out a Seeing Invisible Things And Identifying Things Device (hereafter SITAITD). This is nicely designed, very steampunky, and the way the Doctor half-wore-half-carried it looked terribly familiar to me. It took a long while before I realised what it reminded me of: bagpipes. For such a flagrant plot-engine machine, it's easy to like. (Obviously it takes the Doctor much longer to find the SITAITD than we're shown, as it's night when he enters the TARDIS and daytime again when we comes out.) A rather pointless chase with the invisible alien ensues. One feels that these action sequences were included for no better reason than that someone assumed they had to be there; but actually, they didn't.

The best moments are mostly in dialogue. As the three principals walk along a sunny road together, Vincent says he can see Amy's sadness: "I'm not sad", says she; "Then why are you crying?" asks Vincent. She's not: she goes to wipe a tear away, and there's nothing there; but this is the man who sees what's true rather than merely what is actually there, and he understands instinctively that she has lost Rory, even though she remembers nothing of this. Later, the Doctor accidentally calls Vincent Rory; Amy doesn't bat an eyelid. Like I said: Rory's ghost is always there. Less poignant, but funnier, we then have the Doctor babbling aimlessly as Vincent paints: "I remember watching Michelangelo painting the Sistine Chapel. Wow ..."; a pause, and then: "What a whinger." Completely unexpected. The only time the dialogue clunks is when Vincent is pressed into duty to explain what the invisible alien is doing, which of course is as much for our benefit as for the Doctor's and Amy's. It's pretty clumsy.

We do actually see glimpses of the alien – sometimes for a few seconds from Vincent's perspective, sometimes in a mirror. Eventually we see its whole body, though only in semi-darkness.

It's been widely noted that it seems to have the head of a turkey. I won't disagree with that, but what it really reminded me of was the quilled *Psittacosaurus* specimen described by Mayr et al. (2002).

And here we come to the most disappointing aspect of the episode. I've been carefully referring to an invisible alien so far, but in fact what we have is an invisible monster. In a most un-Wholike way, it doesn't speak or listen – in effect, it's just a big dangerous animal, like a lion or a bear. The Doctor's first hint of the monster's existence came way back in the opening scene, when he saw a hint of its face in one of Van Gogh's paintings, peering out of the window of a church: "I know evil when I see it, and I see it in that window", he says. But it's not really evil – it's just ferocious. And wouldn't it have been more interesting if the Doctor had turned out to be completely mistaken? If the "monster" turned out not to be a monster at all – just a lost creature, causing trouble by accident, unable to make contact with people because its invisibility is actually more a curse than a blessing?

I know it's futile – worse, fanboyish – to try to rewrite episodes, and I will not get into the habit. But just think: that way we could have lost the unconvincing fight and chase scenes; we could have had exploration, investigation and insight; the Doctor could have been Doctorish; and the alien's sense of remoteness from its kind could have been shown to resonate in different ways with Amy's Roryless state, with Vincent's alienation from the townspeople, and of course with the Doctor's position as the last of his kind. There are actually a lot of ways that the

Invisible Monster Who Only Vincent Can See could have been developed: I think Dangerous Animal is possibly the least interesting of them all.

Unusually, the monster is killed long before the end of the episode: the actual plot is over after 33 minutes, leaving a whole nother eleven minutes to fill. It's pretty astonishing that a full quarter of the show's duration is not concerned with the nominal centre of the plot, and I think that at least strongly suggests that the production team knew the monster was a clunker – that the episode's true heart lay elsewhere.

And so it does: those last 11 minutes are filled with scenes that work well. As Vincent, the Doctor and Amy lie on the ground under a night sky, we see the stars swirl, fragment and blur in Vincent's unique vision, as in his painting *The Starry Night*. We see Vincent transported to Paris, 2010, to see an exhibition of his own paintings: the scene is wordless, over music, and his shocked but delighted response is truly moving. The Doctor encourages Bill Nighy's curator character to make a little speech explaining the importance and popularity of Van Gogh, for the benefit of Vincent who is listening in – and even this, which could be mawkish, works well because it's a good speech with actual content and analysis rather than merely adulation; Van Gogh's grateful response is again moving.

Then it's back to 1889 to drop Vincent off.

His goodbye with Amy is genuinely affectionate – there's a bond between them which is hard not to interpret as Amy's displacing her affection for Rory onto the nearest available candidate. That being so, Vincent's earlier despair at the realisation that his new friends are going to leave him is validated all the more strongly: he liked Amy for herself; she perhaps liked him because of his fame and because he was a handy Rory substitute. If Vincent sees this, as he sees so much, he can hardly help but be sad.

As Amy is about to leave, he half-jokingly proposes marriage: "I'm not really the marrying kind", she replies, but of course we know that she was when she had Rory. Only now are we seeing how much he really meant to her – and the irony of course is that she can't see it herself. This is good, clever writing, showing rather than telling, and giving us insights beyond what the characters can know themselves.

In a final post-epilogue (in the never-ending sequence of endings that will be hauntingly familiar to anyone who's seen Peter Jackson's *Return of the King* movie), the Doctor and Amy come back for a third time to the Musée d'Orsay. Amy skips happily away from the TARDIS, keen to see what new paintings Vincent is going to have produced now that his personal history has been rewritten, now that he's been made happy by knowing how great his legacy will be. But it's not to be: when they get to the Van Gogh gallery, they find that even knowing this, he still killed himself at the age of 37. We've seen Amy skipping unselfconsciously away from the TARDIS earlier in the episode, when they first arrived in 19th-century Provence. Then, her carefree attitude turned out to be appropriate: as she'd hoped they would, they do meet and spend time with Van Gogh. This time, the playfulness and optimism that makes her skip is crushed by the reality that depression is not so easily cured. Even the Doctor can't make everyone better.

I think it's "reasonable" within the bounds of the show for the Doctor to find a way to bring Rory back: the way we lost him was science-fictional, so a science-fictional solution is appropriate, and lies within the Doctor's domain of competence. That he was so unable to deal with something outside his competence – depression – was rather touching.

My wife is a music therapist, and works with (among others) depressed people, so I know a little – a very little – about the subject. For me, the amazing thing (if Van Gogh did in fact suffer from depression) is that he found the energy and enthusiasm to paint. I guess that's why *Vincent and the Doctor* portrayed him as bipolar instead.

So.

What we have here is an episode of intriguing ideas, interesting insights and rich characters. But it's brought down badly by an actual story that lacks inspiration, originality and credibility. It's maybe 60 or

70% of a great episode. Could have been so much more.

Oh, but there's one more thing: it looked beautiful. I see it was directed by Jonny Campbell, who also directed *Vampires in Venice*, which, despite its various failings, was also gorgeous to look at. So I hope we'll be seeing more of him.

References

Mayr, Gerald, D. Stefan Peters, Gerhard Plodowski and Olaf Vogel. 2002. Bristle-like integumentary structures at the tail of the horned dinosaur *Psittacosaurus*. *Naturwissenschaften* **89**: 361-365. doi:10.1007/s00114-002-0339-6

Episode 5.11. *The Lodger*

[Posted on June 13, 2010]

The Lodger was written by Gareth Roberts, whose previous on Doctor Who consists of the so-so *Shakespeare Code*, the forgettable and very silly *The Unicorn and the Wasp* and a co-writer credit (with Russell T. Davies) on the truly awful *Planet of the Dead*. So you'll forgive me if I came to *The Lodger* with low expectations.

To my amazement, it's my favourite episode of the series so far. I laughed, I cried, I was scared, I was delighted. I felt caught off guard by this episode in a way that I've not for most of the others. I had no real idea what to expect, so everything took me by surprise.

The Doctor himself is of course the eponymous lodger. Watching him try to lead something like a normal life is hilarious. On paper, this sounds like a similar set-up to Series 3's outstanding *Human Nature / Family of Blood* – unquestionably David Tennant's high-point in his tenure as the Doctor – but the episodes could hardly be more different. The *Human Nature* two-parter was intense and harrowing: the Doctor had literally become human and had little idea how to deal with the threat that presented itself; self-doubt was central; the Doctor felt incomplete, truncated, like half a man. By contrast, in *The Lodger*, the Doctor is fully Time Lord, just playing a role, badly. And it's a set-up that can hardly help but be funny.

As has so often been the case this series, Matt Smith's acting is crucial here: the Doctor slips seamlessly between confident brusqueness and social ineptitude, one moment sensitively deducing the nature of the relationship between his flatmate Craig and his just-good-friend Sophie; the next, he is mucking up that relationship by turning up at inopportune moments and making inappropriate comments. His excellence at football is undermined by his total obliviousness to the effect it's having on Craig. There were four or five laugh-out-loud moments, which is not bad going in a science-fiction/drama programme.

And underlying all this is a sinister mystery in the house where the Doctor is lodging, and a crisis on the TARDIS, where Amy has been inadvertently abandoned. Half the fun is progressively discovering what's going on as the episode progresses. In the part when the Doctor and Craig finally went up the stairs to the upstairs flat, all the hairs on my arms stood up.

How many programs are there on TV that can make you laugh and scare you, all in the same episode? Sometimes even in the same moment? And how many of those programs can also make you think? Well, let's see, there's Doctor Who and ... er ... anything else? I'm struggling.

It's frankly amazing that a programme aimed primarily at children can do all this. More: it's amazing that it even tries to. If I try to analyse why I love Doctor Who in a way that I don't quite love even manifestly superior shows like Veronica Mars, it might come down to its sheer ambition. Even when it fails, it fails because it's tried something great and beautiful that it's not quite been able to carry off. (Well, except for *Planet of the Dead*. That was just plain bad, and come to think of it, so by-the-numbers that it was devoid of the very ambition I'm talking about now.)

What do I mean by ambition? How about trying to make you feel sympathy for a Dalek (*Dalek* in Series 1) or a Cyberman (*Age of Steel* in Series 2)? How about twisting your mind in knots with the implications of time-travel (*Blink* in Series 3)? How about showing you how people can psychologically disintegrate in the face of a threat they don't understand (Series 4's *Midnight*)? How about confronting you with the idea that war pushes you to accept allies you otherwise wouldn't (*Victory of the Daleks* in Series 5)? And remember – all this in a show that has to be comprehensible and appealing to children.

In the end, the great thing about Doctor Who is not regeneration, or the TARDIS, or the Time Lord mythology, or the tin dog, or any of the continuity stuff, or the time-travel paradoxes, or the humour, or the pathos, or the drama. The great thing is that a single show attempts, and in many cases successfully does, *all* of these things. It's a great strength that the Doctor Who format lets you do the hardish sci-fi of *The Hungry Earth/Cold Blood* one week, the historical/psychological romp *Vincent and the Doctor* the next, and the broad comedy/gentle romance of *The Lodger* the week after that. You really never know what you're going to get. In that sense, life is much more like Doctor Who than like a box of chocolates.

One of the fascinating consequences of this wild variation is how dramatically differently reviewers can see specific episodes. I see this all the time, especially with Gavin Burrows, whose reviews all seem to like all the episodes I don't and vice versa – and whose reviews all make points I can't help but agree with. In short, Doctor Who episodes seem to affect different people very differently.

That stands in great contrast to, say, The X-Files, which I've been trying to watch for the last couple of months. I've made it through the first eight episodes, but I'm struggling to find any desire to continue because those episodes are (A) so slow-moving and (B) so very similar to each other. Similarly, who can honestly tell one Star Trek episode apart from another? Even Veronica Mars, for all its unquestionable brilliance, stuck largely to the same formula from episode to episode, bar the finales of the first two seasons.

In fact, the only show I know that comes close to Doctor Who's variety was Buffy, which was able to leaven its usual monster-of-the-week format by throwing in deeply different episodes like *Restless* (the one with the First Slayer in everyone's dreams at the end of Series 4) and *The Body* (Series 5, and I'm not going to spoil it for anyone who doesn't know what it's about). But Buffy had the luxury of aiming squarely at a reasonably mature audience – I guess mid-teens and up – whereas Doctor Who has to work for my seven-year-old son as well as my wife and me.

So: what was meant to be a review of a single episode seems to have turned into a sort of panegyric to the series as a whole. Sorry about that.

It's particularly badly timed, of course, because we now face the last two episodes of the series – the two-part finale by which the rest of the series will stand or fall. (If you doubt that, consider that Series 3, despite its magnificent tenth-Doctor episodes *Human Nature/Family of Blood* and *Blink*, is mostly remembered by the grotesquely misjudged and horribly botched Master story, *The Sound of Drums/Last of the Time Lords*, whereas the generally inferior Series 2 is remembered more fondly because of its Daleks-and-Cybermen climax, *Army of Ghosts/Doomsday*, with its Bad Wolf Bay parting.)

So if *The Pandorica Opens* and *The Big Bang* disappoint, I may regret having written the above. But I'll take my chances – not least because we are back in the hands of the Grand Moff himself for those last two episodes.

The gloves are off now. Come on, Moffmeister – you can do it!

What's in the box?

[Posted on June 17, 2010]

I was so fascinated by last week's trailer for this Saturday's episode, *The Pandorica Opens*, that I've not been able to stop myself thinking about this: what is inside the Pandorica?

As Prisoner Zero told us right back in the first episode, "The universe is cracked. The Pandorica will open. Silence will fall."

Apart from that, we don't have a lot of clues to go on. The relevant parts of the trailer (which is admirably spoiler-free) seem to be these:

Amy: What is it?

River: A box, a cage, a prison?

And this:

Doctor: There was a goblin, or a trickster, or a warrior. Soaked in the blood of a billion galaxies. The most feared being in all the cosmos.

We can probably assume that whatever is inside is related to the Cracks In The Universe theme, and quite possibly to River Song's having killed the best man she ever knew (as told in *Flesh and Stone*). It also seems like a good bet that we've not seen the last of Rory, and that his being written right out of history at the end of *Cold Blood* will somehow be undone. Finally, it seems a given that the events in the final two-parter will involve the Doctor's sudden realisation about Amy, also from the end of *Flesh and Stone*: "And you're getting married in the morning. In the morning ... It's you, it's all about you. Everything. It's about you. Amy Pond; mad, impossible Amy Pond: I don't know why, have no idea, but quite possibly the single most important thing in the history of the universe is that I get you sorted out right now." I've never understood what made the Doctor suddenly launch into that, and I still don't, but presumably it will become clear.

We're invited to assume that the goblin/trickster/warrior is what's inside the box, but I notice that we're not actually told so: all we know from the trailer is that there's something inside, and that there was a goblin/trickster/warrior. Maybe they're not the same?

With those preliminaries out of the way, what could be inside the box? Some possibilities that have occurred to me are:

The Master?

Please, no. That would be so painfully obvious as to be a little bit heartbreaking.

Daleks and/or Davros?

See The Master. Would be a big disappointment. Plus we've already had Daleks coming out of the Genesis Ark in Doomsday, so that would be a retread. My fear is that, having regenerated the Daleks into Extra Big Brightly Coloured Dalektubbies, the programme won't be able to resist using them. But, come on, Moff, be strong!

Cybermen?

Surely not, as they're shown in the trailer. It would be a dreadful anticlimax to see Cybermen gathering for the opening, then have the box open to reveal: more Cybermen. And anyway, Cybermen are just not important enough for this big a gig. Sorry, metal dudes – you know it's true.

The Doctor?

Now we're getting somewhere. We've already seen a manifestation of the Doctor's dark side (in *Amy's Choice*), and it might work well to bring him back in the capacity of Big Bad – especially as his portrayal was so light and harmless-seeming.

Alternatively, the Pandorica could contain a future incarnation of the Doctor, though that would be laying all sorts of continuity/casting traps for the future; or maybe even one of the past incarnations, though it would be hard to explain why the current Doctor doesn't remember these events if that's the case (and no, explanations involving the Blinovitch Limitation Effect do not help).

Could it be another instance of the current Doctor? Not really – not so much for story-internal reasons as because it would be too uncomfortably similar to the two-David-Tennants climax of *Journey's End*.

Bad Wolf?

This is my favourite option – that the Pandorica contains the most powerful sentient being we've seen in New Who, namely Rose Tyler in her Bad Wolf aspect. Bad Wolf actually gone Bad, cut loose from all the ties and bounds of human morality, sweeping aside galaxies like insects, then imprisoned aeons ago.

I'd love this, but I don't think it'll happen for two reasons: first, I doubt the programme makers have the courage and callousness to do that to the Doctor (though I hope I'm wrong on that, and I'm much less sure than I would have been during RTD's reign); second, and I think this is the clincher, if Billie Piper was going to be in it, I'm sure that fact would have leaked and we'd all be spoiled up to the eyeballs by now.

Shame, that. It would have been fascinating.

Satan from *The Impossible Planet*?

Remember at the end of *The Satan Pit* (which was the second part of *The Impossible Planet*), the Satan-creature was possessing Toby when he went zooming off unprotected into the vacuum of space? Toby died, for sure, but it seems unlikely that that could have been the end of the possessing spirit. Could it obtain or manufacture a new body? Or re-inhabit the gigantic end-of-level-boss Chthon-thing that the Doctor had confronted earlier in the episode? Could it be in the Pandorica? I'd be interested in this possibility, because this is one of the very few opponents the Doctor's faced in recent times that he didn't understand. A bit of mystery always helps.

Time and/or Space, or The Void?

Maybe there's not a person or a monster in there at all – maybe it's a thing, or even a concept? Remember that River Song, in the trailer, describes the Pandorica as "a box, a cage, a prison?" It's easy to assume it's a cage or a prison, but maybe the first option is right: it's a box rather than a prison, and it contains something like the very concept of space (which will of course stop functioning once it's released) or time (ditto). Along similar lines, it could contain the Void, which we all remember the Daleks and Cybermen being sucked into at the end of Doomsday – the space between universes.

Nothing?

Maybe everyone's wrong about the Pandorica: maybe it's not a container at all, but an artefact in its own right – a machine created by an ancient race using forgotten technology. Maybe the Time Lords; maybe not.

Left-field guesses

Could it be either Rassilon or Omega, legendary Time Lords from the dawn of history? Or The Other, the mysterious third in the Time Lord historical triumvirate who may be a genetic ancestor of the Doctor?

Could it be a great concentration of Vashta Nerada that sweep across the universe? That would explain the "Darkness will fall" motif.

Could it be the very first Weeping Angel, which gives rise to all the others? That doesn't necessarily make a lot of sense, but I mention it because the Angels seem to be on target to become Moffat's signature recurring monster, and there must be a temptation to use them in the series finale.

Could Rory be in there? How? Why? No idea, really; only a sense that we're not done with him, and of course the Doctor considers his wedding to Amy to be hugely important.

Could it be the thing from *Midnight*, which possessed various people on the tourist shuttle and which was never explained? What is it? A disembodied mind?

Could it be nanogenes, like those that created the empty child, but much more virulent and powerful? And maybe – oh, how about this? – nanogenes that were genetically engineered by Davros to mutate people into Dalek-like creatures?

Could it be The Trickster, from the excellent Sarah Jane stories *Whatever Happened to Sarah Jane?*, *The Temptation of Sarah Jane Smith* and *The Wedding of Sarah Jane Smith*? It would seem odd to pull in a character from a spin-off at this stage, but his shtick is that he messes about with time, which seems to fit with the cracks motif. And of course the Doctor does talk about "a goblin, or a trickster, or a warrior" in the trailer.

My best guess is …

… none of the above.

I think, and hope, that Moffat is a step or three ahead of us, and has something new in store – something that, unlike all the suggestions above, ties together all the unresolved plot threads: the cracks in the universe, Rory's disappearance, his wedding to Amy, River Song's killing of the best man … Oh! Literally as I type that, I ask myself whether the "best man" that River killed was the Best Man at a wedding? Amy's and Rory's, presumably.

So: I don't know where this is headed. I have the strangest conviction that it's going to turn on a choice that someone, probably Amy, has to make, and that *Amy's Choice* will turn out to have been laying the ground for this. But that conviction isn't really based on anything.

All we know for sure is …

The Pandorica is opening!

Thoughts in 2013

I don't think I can be fairly blamed that almost everything I guessed here was wrong – after all, I did make about twenty mutually contradictory guesses. But I'm going to claim a few points for guessing both The Doctor and nothing.

It's disappointing that the Doctor's realisation "it's all about you. Everything. It's about you. Amy Pond; mad, impossible Amy Pond" never did get properly explained. But you can't blame me for thinking it was going to be – Moffat had set it up so that we could hardly expect otherwise.

I'm also awarding myself half a mark for "nanogenes that were genetically engineered by Davros to mutate people into Dalek-like creatures", since that idea did eventually turn up (in *Asylum of the Daleks*).

Episode 5.12. *The Pandorica Opens*

[Posted on June 21, 2010]

So after all the anticipation, the Pandorica opened on Saturday night.

What was my reaction? I can't tell you. Because I don't know.

More than any other New Who episode I can think of, *Pandorica* felt like part one of a two-part story – lots of set-up with little payoff. While an episode like *The Empty Child* obviously finished on a cliff-hanger, and left lots of questions unresolved, to be answered in *The Doctor Dances*, it nevertheless felt like a complete episode in its own right. By contrast, *The Pandorica Opens* feels more like the opening section of an Old Who four-parter: lots of ideas laid out, lots of mysteries depicted, and some hints given; but little in the way of explanations.

It's odd that I feel this way, because when I mentally review what does get explained in this episode, it's actually plenty: the message in the painting, the secret of the Roman soldiers, why it's significant that Pandora's Box was Amy's favourite story when she was growing up, and the truth behind one other important plot point that I thought at first had been completely muffed, but which was actually treated bravely: Rory's otherwise all too convenient and inexplicable reappearance.

So given that, in fact, so many threads were satisfactorily resolved, why did the episode feel disjointed, foundationless, ultimately unsatisfying? Well, it's like this:

Here in rural Gloucestershire, we are currently enjoying the two to three weeks of nice weather that constitutes what we laughingly call "summer", so Fiona and I have been eating outdoors a lot, mostly light salads. Last night, I fancied a seared salmon salad, so I threw something together: a simple green salad base, made with lettuce, cucumber and spring onions with finely sliced sun-dried tomatoes, lightly dressed with a little mayonnaise and some caper vinegar, and with some walnut halves mixed in. On top went the quick-fried cubes of salmon, rare in the middle but slightly burned on the outside, and a few capers.

As Fiona will be the first to tell you, I am not the kind of chap to blow my own trumpet, but I conservatively estimate that it was the single finest salad in the history of western civilisation. The walnuts were a masterstroke, because their texture so perfectly complemented that of the salmon. But what I left out was crucial: celery, for example, and apples, and peppers. Now you can make very fine salads with those ingredients, but they would have been completely wrong for this one. I hope no-one will mistake this for arrogance, but getting that salmon salad right was all about taste, about judgement; about restraint, even.

The opposite of this, of course, is the throw-it-all-in-a-bucket salad, where you just use everything and hope for the best. It pains me to admit it, but a fine example is the pasta salad that Fiona made for herself this evening, which contained both tuna and chicken. And cheese. (Please don't think too harshly of her: in other respects she is the most perfect human being ever to walk on God's green earth, excepting of course that she knows nothing about resource locking.)

Now Russell T. Davies was of course an inveterate Tuna, Chicken and Cheese Salad kind of showrunner, and quite unashamed about it. It was only a fortnight ago that I read him proudly proclaiming exactly this, in this passage from his fascinating book *The Writer's Tale*:

"Instead of all those months of thinking and consideration, rewriting somebody else's script is more like plate-spinning – keeping lots of things in the air, making them look pretty, hoping that they won't crash. In an emergency, I throw lots of things in there – soothsayers, psychic powers, prophecies, funny squares of marble – and hope that I can make a story out of them as I go along, like an improvisation game. [...] The psychic powers are caused by the dust, which is the aliens, and the aliens are thwarted by the volcano erupting, etc, etc, etc. Ram them all into each other. It's [...] a car crash! Fun, though."

– Russell T. Davies, 12 August 2007 (*The Writer's Tale*, p. 177)

Until recently we would all have said that Steven Moffat was a

Seared Salmon Salad guy: most of his stories have been carefully constructed – quite deliberately painted with limited palettes. And, come to think of it, that metaphorical statement has also been reflected literally, in the look of the episodes: *Blink* is a perfectly honed clockwork mechanism built on a superbly conceived "trap" monster, and its look reflects that with cold, hard, dark blues and greys; *The Empty Child/The Doctor Dances* is built on a single, rather brilliant, conceit, and the look of the episode is consistently subdued, gloomy with muted browns.

But maybe it's easier to keep to that kind of disciplined writing when you're only responsible for one story a year. Now that Moffat is in charge of the whole series, and has written six of the thirteen episodes, he seems to have succumbed to at least the early stages of Russell T. Davies Tuna-Chicken-And-Cheese-Salad Syndrome (which I will hereafter abbreviate as RTDTCCSS). *The Pandorica Opens* seems to lose its way not so much because it wanders from the path, as because it's following so many paths at once – something demonstrated most notably in the way that the final scenes set up three simultaneous cliff-hangers for the three protagonists (the Doctor, Amy, and River), who by this point have been separated.

We all know how Davies' sequence of series finales kept turning the volume up louder and louder until we could hardly hear anything. The Series 1 finale had Daleks, so of course Series 2's would be even better if it had Daleks *and* Cybermen. Series 3's would be even *better* if the Master not only threatened to kill millions of people but actually did so (except that they all got better at the end). I thought Davies had missed a trick in not having the Master plan to destroy the whole universe rather than just Earth, but of course the Series 4 finale was *even better* because Davros's plan was to destroy not just the whole universe but all possible universes. As is so often the case when extreme is piled on extreme, the first victim is subtlety (*Journey's End* was like vindaloo sushi), the second is coherence, and the third is memorability. I don't think it's coincidence that I can easily remember pretty much all the key plot beats from *Bad Wolf/Parting the Ways* but almost none from *The Stolen Earth/Journey's End*. (And don't even get me started on *The End of Time*.

Seriously.)

Less Is More is not just an arty sound-bite. Less means that what remains, after the extraneous has been cut away, can be seen, felt, understood, savoured. Adding honey to a pork roast might enhance it, if it's done well; adding honey, raspberry jam, balsamic vinegar and meringue will not.

So, although I was mightily relieved that the Pandorica didn't contain Daleks, I still felt that their inevitable appearance in among the Cast Of Thousands cheapened them, while also obscuring the core issue that was going on at the time. Lots of spaceships are not in themselves more exciting than one spaceship.

Also: I am getting increasingly irritated by the collection of mannerisms that passes as characterisation for River Song. I don't know how much to blame the writing for this, but Alex Kingston's acting is certainly not helping matters. On the positive side, she does help to highlight just what superb performances Karen Gillan is putting in week by week. My goodness, that girl can act. Whatever else critical opinion eventually decides about Series Five, she should most certainly get a BAFTA or six.

Well. All of this is much too harsh on what was at the very least an enjoyable romp, as well as setting up what I hope is going to be a sensational finale. I suppose I am just disappointed because I'd had such very high hopes. And *The Big Bang* has quite a lot of work left to do in order to justify them.

Still, there's a lot to be tied up, and I am already getting impatient to see how it's done: how will the Doctor get out of the Pandorica? Will River regain control over the TARDIS? Is Amy really dead? And whatever happened to the real Rory? Will Jackson Lake have a part to play, as sort-of-predicted a while back?

Update [23 June 2010]

I'm re-watching *The Pandorica Opens* in preparation for *The Big Bang*, and I just noticed something I should have noticed before: when the Doctor and Amy walk into Cleopatra's tent and Cleo turns out to be River Song, she says her "Hello, Sweetie" catch-phrase, and Amy very casually says "River, hi." River doesn't react with "And who might you be" or any other such response – as she ought to, given that this is the first time she has met Amy from her perspective (although of course the second time from Amy's perspective, as The Time of Angels/Flesh and Stone was earlier in her personal timeline). We know that for River the events of *Pandorica* predate those of *Angels*, because at the end of *Flesh and Stone* she looks back on the Pandorica episode.

So: somehow, the River Song in *The Pandorica Opens* is already familiar with Amy. But how? It may of course just be a continuity foul-up, but that would be disappointing and surprising. Could it be that the River Song posing as Cleopatra is from after the *Angels* adventure? But in that case, how did she know about the Pandorica at the end of *Flesh and Stone*?

The only completely consistent explanation would be that River meets Amy a third time, still in Amy's future but, from River's perspective, before either the *Angels* incident or the events of *The Pandorica Opens*. When? Maybe we'll find out next week. I also noticed Amy asking of Stonehenge "How come it isn't new?". Will we see Amy and River back in the far past witnessing the erection of Stonehenge? (Stop sniggering at the back.) Something about Amy's question struck me as significant.

I don't know; but I hope there's a clever solution, i.e. not just They Got It Wrong.

Thoughts in 2013

I'd just like to take a moment to congratulate my 2010 self for correctly spotting that River Song, from the perspective of her own timeline in *The Pandorica Opens*, already had history with Amy – something that we only learned for sure in *A Good Man Goes to War* and *Let's Kill Hitler*. When you make as many incorrect predictions as I've made, you have to celebrate the successes.

Episode 5.13. *The Big Bang*

[Posted on June 26, 2010]

I wanted to blog about *The Big Bang* the moment it finished – I felt electrified, and wanted to let it all pour out – but the way things fell out, Andy Murray's Wimbledon third-round match against Gilles Simon started just as *The Big Bang* ended, then I watched the extra time at the end of the USA-Ghana World Cup match (commiserations to US-based readers, I was supporting you guys). Then I had to reboot my son's iPod (which crashes if you try to play an MPEG layer II file on it, if you can imagine anything so lame), then I had to clear up the detritus of dinner, unload and reload the dishwasher and all. So it's only now – four hours after the end of the programme – that I'm free to write.

Has the glow faded?

Heck, no. I have never enjoyed an episode of Doctor Who so much: never before laughed out loud so many times at the sheer audacity of it, never before marvelled so delightedly at the show's virtuosity. I loved, pretty much literally, every minute. Right now, what I want to do most of all is watch it again (and indeed I'm downloading it in another window as I'm writing this).

Admittedly I'm not 100% sure that it all quite made sense. And some of the deliberate attempts to make us feel the emotion of the moment were perhaps a little ham-fisted. But I can forgive those flaws very easily because of the sheer headlong rush of brilliant moments: not "brilliant" merely in the sense of "very good", but more specifically sparkling, incandescent, glittering; to use a Whedon Word, shiny.

I'll admit that I'm a sucker for a time-travel paradox, always have been: but I've never before seen paradox piled on paradox like this, and never seen them played for laughs in this way. And I don't mean that in a sense that trivialises the weighty matters that the plot concerns – I mean laughs that emerge organically, one might even say spontaneously, from the characters, and most especially the character of the Doctor.

The story didn't develop in at all the way I'd envisaged: the Axis Of Evil that had gathered for the climax of *The Pandorica Opens* wasn't seen again, whereas I'd expected them to play a huge part. This was A Good Thing: going down unexpected routes is always more interesting, and abandoning the actual Bad Guys in favour of a plot-and-paradox episode made this series finale very, very different from those that have gone before. Be honest: don't *The Stolen Earth*, *The End of Time* and *The Last of the Time Lords* sort of blur together in your mind? There's no way anyone's going to be confusing *The Big Bang* with any of them. What we ended up with was a character-driven clockwork plot with added bonus running-down-corridors (albeit much more beautiful corridors than we've been used to seeing): an episode quite unlike any that has gone before, while still fitting perfectly into the series' overall character.

Oh, and so many individual marvellous moments: the absolute shock of surprise when the Pandorica re-opened in the present day, the sequence in which the Doctor repeatedly popped back 2000 years to give instructions to Rory, the reappearance of the Doctor-in-his-jacket scene from *Flesh and Stone*, the world without stars that has an exploding TARDIS for a sun … Really, it was one thing after another.

And perhaps what's most impressive is that, for all the time-travel/rewriting paradoxes, the core strand of the story held enough coherence and momentum to tie it all together – so that, for example, my 12, 10 and 7-year-old sons could all pretty much follow what was going on and why. I'm not going to say that I fully understand all the strands of alternative timelines, and how various changes in the past switched between those various futures: at the moment, I don't. But I understood enough to keep surfing the wave of events.

(And I *will* understand it fully: I'm going to watch again, think it through: and I'm confident that Moffat, just as he did with *Blink*, will have tied it all together in a neat little bow. We're all going to be finding links and in-jokes for some time yet – I am really looking forward to reading other reviews of *The Big Bang* in part for this reason.)

Another reason I'm keen to see other reviews is of course to find out whether the world agrees with me. I can easily see this finale splitting the audience into lovers and haters and not much in between. One of the interesting things about this series is that episodes that some people love seem to get very different responses from others, and vice versa: for example, between us it seems that Gavin Burrows and I have both loved and been unimpressed by pretty much every episode – it's hard to find a single one where our opinions match. (That's within the broader picture of both of us generally being very enthusiastic about the series as a whole.)

In my very positive review of *The Lodger*, I said that "If I try to analyse why I love Doctor Who in a way that I don't quite love even manifestly superior shows like Veronica Mars, it might come down to its sheer ambition". That goes double for this finale episode. It does a hundred things where other shows would do two, or perhaps three. Its scope is both epic and intimate, its lead character is both a fool and a genius, its monsters are both terrifying and comical, and of course it's a show for both children and adults. If most good TV shows are perfectly formed but easily digested, like the Beatles' *She Loves You*, this is more like Genesis's *Supper's Ready* somehow condensed down into a three-minute single: a heady brew, rich, complex, sweet, sour, searing hot and freezing cold. It leaps effortlessly from scenario to scenario and somehow – somehow! – ties it all together into a coherent and consistent whole. Though the stakes were very high, the scope was very narrow – or perhaps I should say tightly focussed.

So farewell to Series 5; and, for now, to Matt Smith's Eleventh Doctor. It's been a wild ride. I am not 100% sure yet that this is my favourite series of the revived series – that honour might still reside with Christopher Eccleston's series, the first – but I can tell you right now that Smith has firmly established himself as my favourite Doctor: thoughtful, insightful, inspired, vulnerable, compassionate, insensitive, endlessly curious: in short, Doctorish to the core.

So The *Big Bang* is an instant classic and a fitting finale.

Special bonus wonderful moment

Rory's rather plaintive realisation, "I'm plastic", very much lost in the aural background during the wedding reception. Loved it. And loved how they just threw that line away.

Series 5 summary and retrospective

Over all, Series 5 was a triumph. With the benefit of hindsight, is absolutely is my favourite single series of Doctor Who, both surpassing its predecessors and setting a level that its successors have not matched. The greatest reason for its success is Matt Smith; but of course Series 6 and 7 also had that advantage, so what made Series 5 better than them? One reason is that Series 5 taken as a whole feels more integrated than previous and subsequent series. Series 1 had an emotional arc (Doctor recovering from Time War PTSD) as well as the Bad Wolf stuff, and that gave it some additional heft. The other series have mostly lacked that, but not so Series 5.

Unfortunately, subsequent events have slightly diminished the shine on Series 5. As I wrote above, "I'm a sucker for a time-travel paradox, always have been: but I've never before seen paradox piled on paradox like this". But three years later, I've seen paradox piled on paradox *many* times, to the point where it's become a Moffat cliché. It's a shame that having done it once to such great effect, he's then proceeded to do it again, repeatedly, with diminishing returns each time. Moffat might do well to remember that *The Empty Child/The Doctor Dances*, arguably still the best of all his stories, achieved its very powerful effect with no messing about with time at all. Timey-wimey is a fine motor for plots, but sometimes it feels as though Moffat thinks it's the *only* motor. It's not, and I'd like to see him head off in a completely different direction in his next set of episodes.

In giving Smith a huge amount of credit for his portrayal of the Doctor, I don't want to overlook Karen Gillan's work as Amy – unquestionably the best actor of all the Doctor's companions. Is she my favourite? Well, of New Who's Big Four – Rose, Martha, Donna, Amy – it's not easy to choose, except to say "definitely not Martha", who was by far the least interesting of the four. (I am ignoring secondary companions like Captain Jack, River Song and Rory, not least because it means I'm less likely to go off on an extended tangential rant about how I loathe Captain Jack.)

Rose completely redefined what it is to be a Doctor Who companion. She's the Beatles of DWCs, and will always be recognised for that. I reacted with absolute horror to the news that Donna was going to be the Series 4 companion, because she was awful in the one-off *Runaway Bride*, but she won me over with an emotional range never so much as hinted at in the shoutfest that had been her debut. As noted, Amy is the best acted of the three, and the only one I've ever seen look genuinely frightened (in *Flesh and Stone*). So they all have their merits. But I think I'm going to stick with Donna, because she was so unexpected and so different from the others.

Christmas 2010: *A Christmas Carol*

[Posted on April 22, 2011]

With the new Series 6 of Doctor Who kicking off in two days' time, we've been watching our way through all the previous Eleventh Doctor episodes. Having finished with Series 5 a few days ago, tonight we watched the Christmas special, *A Christmas Carol*.

And it really is the most extraordinary piece of television. I've rhapsodised about Matt Smith's portrayal of The Doctor enough times now that it won't take anyone by surprise when I say that he absolutely shines through this episode, even when he's bumbling and clueless. His Doctor is much less consumed with his own importance than previous actors have shown him, much more likely to admit that he doesn't really know what he's doing; and yet, paradoxically, he carries more weight. When the Bad Guy says that one of the other characters is "no-one special", The Doctor replies "Blimey, that's amazing. You know that in nine hundred years of time and space and I've never met anybody who wasn't important before." In the hands of certain other Doctors – let's say for example a hypothetical one named Schmavid Schmennant – that line would have been histrionic, overplayed, a big look-at-me moment. Smith plays it very differently: he says it as though he is genuinely puzzled by the idea, and as a result the line is haunting and moving.

It's strange for me now to look back at how outraged I was at Matt Smith's casting when I first heard about it and saw photos of this skinny kid; and to see how reserved I was about him after seeing The Eleventh Hour: "Because his version of the Doctor is so Tennantish, it's hard to make any meaningful assessment of Smith at this stage. I find myself struggling to find much to say about his Doctor that is specific to him." What the heck was I thinking? I certainly was dumb back then.

(An aside: my friend Matt Wedel once observed to me: "About every three or four months I realise that I've spent my entire life up until 'now' being a dumbass; the problem is that 'now' keeps moving and every time I think I've finally got everything figured out, I later determine that I was/am still a moron. I distinctly remember having this feeling for the first time in third grade, age of eight, and I keep hoping it will eventually go away, but that hope seems increasingly unfounded.")

But I wouldn't want to give the impression that Smith leaves the rest of the cast trailing in his wake. He is unquestionably the episode's centre of gravity, but everything that orbits around him is perfectly judged, too: among the supporting cast, Michael Gambon is much more persuasive as Grumpy Old Kazran Sardick than he's ever been as Kindly Old Professor Dumbledore, and Laurence Belcher is genuinely likeable as Young Kazran. Maybe more surprising is that singer Katherine Jenkins is perfectly serviceable in her first acting outing.

The sets and costumes contribute to making a sillier-than-usual planet seem, if not actually believable then at least suspend-disbelievable; and the music (which can sometimes be a weak point in Who) is perfectly judged throughout. The upshot of all this is that a scene like the one in which Katherine Jenkins sings a flying shark to sleep in a cryogenic chamber is truly emotional rather than, as you'd expect, just too silly to work. I expected to laugh a lot during the episode, and wasn't disappointed; but I didn't expect to cry, and I was surprised.

Two of my favourite moments picked from among many: first, when the Doctor tells Old Kazran that he'll be back, and then pops up in the film he's watching – it made me laugh immoderately, so much so that I missed several of the jokes that followed; and second, the way Christmas Future was handled, taking me completely by surprise.

In fact the whole episode surprised me in this sense: that I never expect the Christmas Special to be very interesting. Looking back over the last few years, we had the horribly overblown and incoherent *End of Time* in 2009, the workaday *The Next Doctor* in 2008 (with the silly giant Cyberman at the end), the celebrity guest vehicle *Voyage of the Damned* in 2007 (maybe the low-point among all Davies' episodes), and the much-derided *Runaway Bride* in 2006. You have to go all the way back to the first reboot series in 2005, and David Tennant's debut in *The Christmas Invasion*, for one that stands out – and even then, you have to wonder how much of its appeal was down to Tennant's storming post-rejuvenation scene in the Sycorax hall.

So *A Christmas Carol* is really not what we've come to expect, and it's worth asking why. And at the risk of shooting badgers in a barrel, one can hardly help but notice that all the previous Christmas specials were written by Russell T. Davies. My ambivalence about Davies' writing is on record (see *The Madness of Russell T. Davies*), but I think that Christmas brings out the very worst of his writing. It's been suggested, I think by Andrew Rilstone, that after the very effective *Army of Ghosts/Doomsday* two-parter that ended the Rose era, Davies was basically done with telling the story that he wanted to tell, and was increasingly directionless from then on. I think that idea holds up well, and it's seen most strongly in his concept of what constitutes a "special" episode: sound and fury, signifying nothing. The idea seems generally to have been to pile on more explosions and emotions (or "explotions", if you will). In contrast to Davies' spectacle-for-the-sake-of-spectacle specials, *A Christmas Carol* feels intimate, a chamber piece. You can imagine a very effective adaptation of it for the stage, with Present and Past at stage left and stage right, and the Doctor nipping back and forth between them; now try to imagine a stage adaptation of *Voyage of the Damned*. (On second thoughts, don't.) Less is more: Moffat's big moments feel big compared with what surrounds them; the characters feel important because there are few enough of them that we can care.

So all in all, I rate *A Christmas Carol* a triumph, despite its intrinsic silliness, and to my enormous surprise it's near the top of my all-time favourite episodes. For all the flying-shark accoutrements, it's essentially the tale of a shrivelled, withered heart being awoken, against its will, by love and shame and the desire to be something better. Now that is a *story*. And not one that we expect a Christmas Special of the kids' sci-fi show to tell us.

Thoughts in 2013

Sheesh. Doesn't this praise read completely differently three years later? "Less is more: Moffat's big moments feel big compared with what surrounds them; the characters feel important because there are few enough of them that we can care." If only Moff himself had read this and kept it in mind throughout Series 6 and 7. More little stories in Series 8, please!

Series 6

By the end of Series 5, Moffat, Smith and Gillan were all firmly established in their roles. With a superb Christmas special also under their belts, Series 6 represented That Difficult Second Album, but circumstances were all ideal: the core cast was intact, including Rory and River, and Moffat had earned the necessary critical space to take the series off in whatever direction he wanted. No-one was going to tell him "you can't do that, it's too complicated".

And then, this happened:

Episode 6.1. *The Impossible Astronaut*

[Posted on April 23, 2011]

Well, I certainly didn't expect that.

I wanted to post within minutes of the end of the episode. I was going to entitle my article "*The Impossible Astronaut*: First Impressions", and the entire article would consist of the following:

"What?"

I don't think I have ever felt so at sea during a Doctor Who, certainly not a series opener. With *Rose, New Earth, Smith and Jones, Partners in Crime* and indeed *The Eleventh Hour*, we got nice, simple, self-contained stories that anyone coming in cold would be able to easily follow. Not so this time: it was hugely complicated, multi-stranded, truly frightening in places, and absolutely not self-contained. It's not just that it's the first half of a two-parter, but one that leaves many, many questions unresolved.

I'm not quite sure what I think about that. It's certainly courageous, but is it so in the vanilla sense of the word or in Sir Humphrey Appleby's sense? Can it be wise to throw new viewers straight into so deep a deep end? Or are we now working on the assumption that there won't be a lot of new viewers by this stage, that the programme's captured everyone it's going to? If nothing else, it does indicate a huge degree of confidence on the part of the programme makers: both self-confidence, that they believe they can pull it off, and maybe more importantly confidence in their audience, that they can cope. That, I like. And there is, to be fair, something invigorating about awaiting the second half of a story and having almost no idea what it's going to contain.

So while I wait for the actual story to settle down and start making sense next week, what I am left with this week is a blur of individual moments, most of them delicious. If the episode is more of a smörgåsbord than a square meal, it's a good smörgåsbord. More than once in reviewing Series 5, I used the word "audacity" (*The Beast Below*, *The Big Bang*), and I've found myself coming back to that property of the programme again and again while discussing it with people. It's a quality that seemed to increase throughout Series 5 and continue into the Christmas special, and it's certainly not fading away as we begin on Series 6.

I'll just mention a couple of instances.

— The Casanova introduction, surely a knowing nod to predecessor David Tennant's earlier role as that character.

— The Doctor waving cheerfully at Amy and Rory, unnoticed, from a Laurel and Hardy film.

— "I wear a Stetson now. Stetsons are cool." Would have been funny even without the fez line from *The Big Bang*.

— Rory's rueful resignation to his job of baby-sitting Canton Delaware through his first-time-in-the-TARDIS culture-shock.

— The Doctor silently gesturing for Nixon and Delaware to continue their discussion when they finally turn to notice him there, assiduously taking notes.

What does all this mean for the series? It's hard to tell this early, but one thing is clear: Doctor Who is not out to dumb things down for its viewers. I imagine editorial meetings where Moffat outlined the plans, people told him "That's too complicated, people won't follow", and he just refused to accept it. Right or wrong? In the Big Brother/X-Factor/Who Wants To Be A Millionaire? era, for my money it's better to err on the side of asking too much of an audience than too little. I like it that Doctor Who is throwing so very much at the wall and seeing what sticks, and I love it that it trusts us enough to make sense of it all.

Special bonus observation

The moment I saw the scene where the Doctor meets the eponymous astronaut, it hit me like a truck that I was looking at a re-creation of the cover art from Pink Floyd's awesome *Wish You Were Here* album. If you're not familiar with that album then (A) what the heck have you been listening to all your life? And (B) take a moment to google for the front cover, with the two men in lateral view shaking hands, and the back cover with the lake:

I wonder whether it's deliberate? A quick bit of googling suggests that no-one else has yet picked up on it, so maybe it's just a coincidence. But for me, loving that album as I do, the visual allusion introduced another layer of poignancy to what was already a very surreal scene.

Who killed the Doctor?

[Posted on April 29, 2011]

I want to briefly consider the core question about last Saturday's Doctor Who episode, *The Impossible Astronaut*. Who killed the Doctor?

I mean, we already know that an impossible astronaut did it (clue's in the question), but since the astronaut suit completely covers the actual perpetrator, we don't know who did it. So who was in the suit? Who are the candidates?

The Doctor?

This perhaps makes most sense dramatically, and fits in well with Moffat's wibbly-wobbly timey-wimey approach. It seems that the new series has cheerfully cast aside the Blinovitch Limitation Effect, so the idea of the Doctor meeting himself is not a deal breaker. (Not that it ever stopped Old Who from staging stories like *The Three Doctors*, *The Five Doctors*, *The Six And A Half Doctors*, etc.)

Does the Doctor have a motive? Not clear: the killer would obviously need to be from earlier in his own timeline than the version that he killed, which would of course mean that the 1100-year-old Doctor who we met first in TIA knew what was going to happen because he did it himself. But why? (Motive is going to be a problem for pretty much all the candidates.) Could it be that in the missing 200 years the Doctor got split somewhere, as in *Journey's End*, and that one of them needed to be disposed of to restore normality? That would be a little cold.

River Song?

Ah, River bleedin' Song. I am in general a big, big Moffat fan, but I do not understand what he sees in this collection of mannerisms passing as a woman. Who knows why she ever does anything? Or in what order? I don't know whether it's the writing or the casting, but River is one character who just doesn't work for me.

Anyway, she is the logical front-runner because we already know that

"I killed the best man I ever knew", and that's why she was imprisoned.

Amy?

Why why why? I am pretty sure that the girl in the space-suit at the end of the first episode was not Young Amy (or Amelia, as we call her), so there's nothing to tie her to the eponymous I.A. And yet something in me feels a sort of inevitability that it will turn out to be Amy simply because she, of all the supporting cast, felt it most strongly when the Doctor was killed. It would hurt her more to do it than it would hurt the others, and I think Moffat is a sadist in that way.

Rory?

I only mention Rory because he's on the scene and it would be remiss to overlook him. Of all the supporting cast, Rory is the one who, were I the Doctor, I would most trust to Do The Right Thing however much he didn't want to; and so, if I were the Doctor and needed someone to kill me, Rory is perhaps the person I would ask to do it.

Canton Delaware?

So far, it's not clear what his role is in all this, but we know that many years later, the Doctor will send him to the place of his death to supply the fuel for his cremation, so at some point he is definitely going to be a part of it. Could he be both the killer and the immolator? And again: why?

The little girl?

She turned up only at the very end, in the space-suit. We don't know who she is (unless I misread her face and she is Amelia), nor what her involvement is. We don't know why or how she's been phoning the president directly every night. And since we also don't know what the deal is with the see-them-then-forget-them aliens, we might speculate that she is something to do with them.

The Master?

Please, no.

What does it all mean?

You know, I really have no idea. Back when I surveyed the possible contents of the Pandorica, most of the possible answers made some kind of sense to me. And back when David Tennant broke off his two-parter in mid-regeneration at the end of *The Stolen Earth*, Andrew Rilstone listed six possible explanations for what was happening (none of which turned out to be true, naturally).

But this time I am at a loss to come up with a single explanation of it all that makes sense, that ties together the Doctor's death, Amy's pregnancy, the Immediately Forgettable Aliens, Canton Delaware, the girl in the space-suit, and so on. Usually the puzzle set by two-parters is: which of the candidate solutions will turn out to be the right one? But this time, Moffat is asking us, and himself, a harder question: is there *any* solution?

I can only assume that the answer is yes; I hope, I really hope, that when it comes, it makes sense.

Episode 6.2. *Day of the Moon*

[Posted on May 1, 2011]

Writing about *The Impossible Astronaut* last week, I noted that I was going to entitle my article "*The Impossible Astronaut*: First Impressions", and the entire article would consist of the following: "What?"

So, predictably, here are my first impressions of *Day of the Moon*:

"What?"

Well, then. What do we still not know?

— Why was "Get out" written all over the orphanage? If Amy wrote it, she would have recognised her own handwriting, so I don't think this can be a Sally Sparrow retread. Who closed and locked the door when she was in the room with the sleeping Silence? Why? Who unlocked it? Why?

— Who was the woman with the eye-patch, who Amy saw through the window in the door to the little girl's room? Why was the hatch there and why did it vanish? Why did the woman say "No, I think she's just dreaming"? Who did she say it to?

— Now that we know the alien race who can't be remembered are called the Silence, what does Series 5's repeated threat "Silence will fall" mean?

— Why did the Silence have a TARDIS-like console room identical to the one in *The Lodger*? Wikipedia, rather disappointingly, says that "the control room set used from The Lodger was used again for this episode. Moffat wanted the set to be used again, feeling it would be a suitable Silence base. The set was adapted to give it a darker, evil feel." But surely we can hope for a story-internal reason. Was *The Lodger*'s ship actually the Silence's?

— The Doctor reasoned that the Silence incubated the Apollo programme as a way of causing a space suit to be made – but why did they want one?

— Why did the Silence Kidnap Amy? What was their plan for her? They tell her "We do you honour; you will bring the silence", but what does that mean? They *are* the Silence? Is that different from the silence?

— Is Amy in fact pregnant? Why doesn't the TARDIS know? It seems that its built-in pregnancy scanner is trying to tell us that Amy's uterus is in a superimposition of quantum states. How will the midwife cope? (And will the baby have a time-head? I loved that.)

— Who is the little girl that we first saw in the suit at the end of episode 1? Is she, as the photo in her room invites us to believe, Amy's daughter? If so, with whom? If Rory, then how was she able to regenerate at the end of the episode? If not Amy's daughter, is she River's? With the Doctor? That would explain the regeneration. Or could she be The Doctor's Daughter, from the terrible episode of the same name?

— How did the little girl get into the space-suit at the end of the last episode and during this? Did it "eat her", as suggested? How did she get out, after Amy saw her?

— We are still no closer to answering the long-running question: who actually is River Song? Could it be that the girl in the space suit is River? Why is River in prison? Who is the "best man I ever knew" that she killed?

— And we are also no closer to knowing who killed the Doctor, despite having thought about that in detail last week. Will he continue to have been killed?

— What else might the Silence have done that no-one remembers? Did they impregnate Amy? Ugh. Would Moffat go there?

— And finally, most important of all: is a review a review if it consists of nothing but questions?

I'll close with a few observations.

We saw that River is an excellent shot – she took out all of the Silence in the control room – but we know that Amy is a very bad shot, having missed the astronaut at the end of the last episode from point-blank range. This is hardly conclusive, but does seem to gently suggest that they are not related.

The Silence look kind of like The Gentlemen from the classic Buffy Season 4 episode *Hush* – the one where everyone's voices are taken away. They share the same formal elegance, unhurried menace, and distorted, shiny heads. And of course the name of the alien race called the Silence chimes (har!) with the modus operandi of The Gentlemen. I doubt that has any plot significance, but I wonder whether it's a deliberate homage.

Finally – where now? As usual I avoided the trailer for next week, but from what I've not been able to avoid finding out, it seems that it will be much more of a self-contained romp, and so we shouldn't expect much in the way of resolution of any of the issues raised last week and this. I love a good, provocative mystery or six, but is Moffat pushing it too far? One insightful commentator noted, "I think Steven Moffat's audience is going to start getting a bit frustrated if we don't start getting some answers soon – it's just too much to hold."

Come on, Moff. Give us some answers.

Not all of them. But some.

Thoughts in 2013

Re-reading this review is a very depressing experience. It may not be apparent from what I wrote, but at this stage in Series 6 I was extremely excited – delighted that such a complex, demanding plot was under way, and fascinated to know how all the answers tied together. But looking back now, nearly two complete series later, *lots* of those questions never did get answered:

— Why was "Get out" written all over the orphanage? Who closed and locked the door when she was in the room with the sleeping Silence? Why? Who unlocked it? Why? After watching the episode several times, still none of this makes sense.

— What does Series 5's repeated threat "Silence will fall" mean? We never did find out, unless we tie it via the Fields of Trenzalore stuff to the bit where the Great Intelligence goes into the Doctor's time vortex. But that hardly seems related to this material at all.

— Why did the Silence have a TARDIS-like console room identical to the one in *The Lodger*? That seems to have been completely dropped on the floor, and Wikipedia's answer that they just wanted to re-use the set seems to be correct.

— Why did the Silence want an Apollo programme? No idea.

— How did the little girl get into the space-suit? Did it "eat her", as suggested? How did she get out, after Amy saw her?

I'll give it this, though: the questions about Eye-Patch Woman *were* satisfactorily answered, along with the stuff about the Silence kidnapping Amy, Amy's is-she-isn't-she pregnancy, and of course the identity of both the little girl in the space-suit and River Song. All five mysteries had the same resolution, and it turned out to be a rather satisfying one (if not particularly well executed). Although "We do you honour; you will bring the silence" still makes no sense.

I don't want to get too ahead of myself, but … Oh, Series 6. So near to utterly brilliance, yet so far.

Episode 6.3. *The Curse of the Black Spot*

[Posted on May 8, 2011]

They're all the ingredients you need for a classic Doctor Who episode. Set it during a classic, resonant period of British history. Present the Doctor with a terrifying threat, one that takes people with a seeming inevitability, and that plays on deep fears. Have the threat inflict a mysterious physical mark on those affected (though the mark will be explained later). Bring in a captain with a past: a loveable rogue, someone who's deserted the respected organisation he used to work for and gone renegade, but who still retains a heart of gold. Rack up the fear by making the threat appear increasingly powerful and implacable. Then pull the rug away, and reveal that all along it was trying to help – that it was an alien medical programme that went off the rails when trying to deal with humans. In the end, it turns out that the key to resolving everything that's gone wrong is to willingly touch the threat – which isn't a monster after all – even though up till now, avoiding touching it has been paramount. With the Doctor's insight, the alien medic can be made a threat no longer, the damage it's done can be reversed; and, just this once, everybody lives!

But enough about *The Empty Child*. Let's talk about *The Curse of the Black Spot* instead.

It's pretty clear that the brief this time around was to keep it self-contained and comprehensible – in contrast to the whirlwind impenetrability of the opening two-parter, *The Impossible Astronaut/Day of the Moon*. "Give us pirates", the writer was presumably told, "and plenty of 'em". All the classic tropes are there – the stowaway, the mutiny, the fatal love of treasure, the captain who is not quite beyond redemption, the eponymous black spot, and of course walking the plank. (Did real pirates ever make their victims walk the plank? You'll often hear that it's a baseless myth, but it seems that it did sometimes happen.) The threat in this case is provided by the siren, a mythical being that sings sailors to their deaths. A bit of a mix of mythologies, but there you go.

Can all those elements be tied together into a coherent whole? And is that whole a Doctor Who story? With reservations, yes to the first question; without reservations, yes to the second. It does feel as though there's slightly too much going on for forty-five minutes, though, and as a result the mutiny subplot feels rushed and doesn't really go anywhere. One of the two mutineers (yes, it's a very small mutiny) never leaves the gunpowder room, so far as I can tell, and is still there as the story ends, with The Doctor, Amy and Rory in the TARDIS and the captain and his son and crew on the alien ship. Presumably he just stays there till he dies of thirst. (Or did I miss something?)

That is one of only two gaps in the plot — and the less important of the two, since it's not really relevant to anything else that goes on. The more significant one, which does bother me, is this: why do the Doctor, Amy and the captain appear unfettered and upright on the alien ship? Everyone who's been taken before them appears immobile, wired into the alien life-support system. That seems just careless to me: it wouldn't have been too hard to have the Doctor produce some explanation along the lines that the ship treated them differently because they admitted themselves voluntarily, but if it was in there then I missed it.

(I'm just being polite when I say that. It *wasn't* in there, and I didn't miss it, but I somehow feel it would be a bit brusque to just come right out and say that.)

I'm not sure how much I resent that plot-hole. I wonder whether the RTD era accustomed us so thoroughly to the idea that Doctor Who didn't have to make sense that now we think it's good if an episode *mostly* makes sense. That can't be healthy, can it? Surely it's not too much to ask that every episode should make perfect sense? Or, to be more precise for a serial, that everything unexplained in a given episode should be explained by the end of the series? I often say that the worst thing Bill Gates ever did to the world is habituate people to the idea that Computers Are Unreliable And That's Just How It Is — that a daily reboot and a yearly reinstall are part of the nature of the universe. I'd hate to think that Russell has similarly made me think that two or three

Hey Wait That Doesn't Make Sense moments per episode are par for the course in Who. Back in the days when we didn't know who Steven Moffat was, I remember being delighted by the plotting of *The Empty Child* – that a mystery so obscure turned out to have a resolution that, in story terms, made such sense, was so neat. Now that he's the Who Supremo (or Whopremo, if you will), I want him to hold all the scripts to that standard. And it would have been so easy to fix this one so that it did.

Well. Now I'm whining. Which isn't really fair. I thoroughly enjoyed *Black Spot*, especially the Doctor's (very proper and scientific) readiness to abandon his previous hypotheses as soon as they were shown to be wrong. It was certainly a much better introduction to the show than either of the previous episodes would have been for a newcomer. And yet, already I find myself longing for the greater reach, if not grasp, of those first two episodes, which I am liking more as they continue to percolate through my mind. I like the idea that, hey, this is Doctor Who, we could go *anywhere*, do *anything*. It's a wonderful thing that the show can encompass huge sprawling half-resolved epics like those and little self-contained chamber episodes like *Black Spot*. It needs both, and this was a good example of the latter done well.

A final thought, apropos of nothing. We know that River Song is going to kill the best man she ever knew. You know who's a good man? Rory. Just saying.

Episode 6.4. *The Doctor's Wife*

[Posted on May 15, 2011]

"Doctor Who continues to exhaust superlatives", Andrew Rilstone wrote back in the far-off days of Series 2 (although I am not sure he meant this altogether positively). Five years on, I can only echo the quote, if not the ambivalent sentiment behind it. More and more it feels to me as though Series 6 is a qualitative step up from what's gone before. Which, given how much I loved Series 5, is high praise.

Like most people (everyone?) I assumed that the eponymous wife was going to be River Bleedin' Song, and I was completely wrong-footed by her not even appearing in the episode. (Of course, she'd been dropped off back at the Storm Cage at the end of *Day of the Moon*, so she wasn't travelling in the TARDIS with Amy and Rory.)

So who is the Doctor's wife? As with all the best mysteries, the answer is near-impossible to guess, but feels obvious once you're told it. We've known for a long time that the TARDIS is sentient – that it's exerted more control over its own navigation than the Doctor has, for example, so that a long-held fan theory argues that the Doctor's habit of landing in the middle of invasions and suchlike has the story-internal explanation that the TARDIS takes him where he's needed. And the Doctor loves the TARDIS. We've seen that many times.

So when the TARDIS's life is put into a human body, it makes perfect sense that she is his "wife" – his most faithful and long-running companion, the one who shares not only his experiences but his essence. And this is by way of being a wish-fulfilment thing, isn't it? Plenty of people love their cars, or their bikes, or boats, and think of them (however misguidedly) as sort of human. If *The Lodger* was the "what if the Doctor came to stay at my house?" fantasy, then *The Doctor's Wife* is the "what if my car/bike/boat was really alive?" fantasy.

Except of course it can't last. The body has eighteen minutes to live.

Well, of course.

It's interesting to compare *The Doctor's Wife* with Series 4's *The Doctor's Daughter*. The episodes have in common that (A) they both "cheat" in that the eponymous character is not literally what the title suggests; (B) they both contain a character called "the Doctor". Beyond that, you'd hardly believe they are part of the same show. *Daughter* gave us a plot that made no sense, resolved by somersaulting through laser beams and releasing Magic Pixie Dust from a goldfish bowl. In a very uneven series, it was (along with *The Unicorn and the Wasp*) one of the two least engaging episodes. In contrast, *Wife* gives us a promise of surviving Time Lords outside the universe, the all too believable breaking of that promise, a Doctor who figures things out as he goes along instead of Releasing Pixie Dust, a clockwork plot that ties itself together coherently, and (maybe most striking of all) a moment at the end when the Doctor is genuinely distraught. As usual with Matt Smith, the moment is underplayed, more implied that stated, and without the funny-shaped-mouth shouty thing that David Tennant ended up doing pretty much every episode as he gradually became a parody of himself.

Please understand me. It's not my intention to say that David Tennant was a *bad* Doctor. He was very good — he makes it into my top four. And yet there is a great gulf between his pantomime Doctor and Matt Smith's much more subtle, nuanced portrayal. It's as though Tennant was acting for theatre (but being filmed), whereas Smith is acting for film and trusts the camera to pick up the details. Although he is in a 28-year-old body, he is convincing as a man who has been alive for nine hundred years and seen things he should never have seen. The Horde of Travesties, the Nightmare Child, the Could-Have-Been King. They're all there, lurking beneath his face, just below the surface. It's a superb performance every single week.

Of course, it helps that the recent scripts have all given him rich seams of quintessentially Doctorish moments to work with. "I'm up here being clever and there's no one standing around looking impressed", from *The Impossible Astronaut*, is particularly memorable, but each episode seems to be throwing up half a dozen of these moments. Recent Doctor Who episodes are making me laugh out loud a lot — and not always because they are funny. More often it's the sheer audacity that makes me laugh (yes, it's that word again). Against this backdrop, the Doctor's occasional moments of vulnerability are all the more poignant. "You want to be forgiven", says Amy when the Doctor is excited about finding other Time Lords. Pause. "Don't we all?", he replies. The writing is good, but it's the acting that makes it sing.

And in among all this, there is so much that you miss the first time through an episode. For example, there's the conversation that the Doctor and his TARDIS-wife have around the jury-rigged console as it pursues the TARDIS proper. We'll land in one of the old control rooms, she tells him. But I deleted them all, he replies. I backed them up, she says, I have about thirty. But I've only changed the desktop about a dozen times, he protests. "So far", says she. Idea layered upon idea. It's scintillating dialogue, and in context it's sort of thrown away, like all those gorgeous fragments of melody in a Sondheim musical that he never returns to and develops. (I am thinking, for example, of the "and maybe they're really magic, who knows?" line in *Into the Woods*.) That whole conversation is hard to make out against the background sound-effects, and with so much else going on at the same time. It's there for when you go back and watch again. And I think this must be deliberate – it's happening a lot in this series. Moffat and co are deliberately throwing too much at us at once, to make re-watching a rewarding experience. They're making TV, in other words, that is *meant* to be watched twice or three times, not just once. That's ambitious. And I always respect ambition.

By coincidence, I re-read *The Doll's House*, volume 2 of Neil Gaiman's classic comic-book series *Sandman*, last week. It's justly renowned – rich in images, particularly, and it leaves a strong impression in the imagination. It also runs half a dozen plot threads in parallel, expects the reader to do some work, and amply repays invested effort, as all the threads come together at the end. As I read it last week, I found myself thinking how much Series 6 so far resembles *Sandman*, if not in content or tone then in approach. Imagine my surprise when I found that the very same Neil Gaiman was the writer of this week's episode. I guess this comes under the heading of Celebrity Writer, but he's actually a perfect choice for Series 6, because what he naturally does fits so well with the way the series is going.

Mind you, this week's episode didn't do much to advance the overarching plot of this series. All the same questions remain open, but we have a couple more options for answering them. Who is River Song? Who is the regenerating girl in the space-suit? We have another candidate for both roles: the TARDIS, manifesting as a human again. Is River the TARDIS from the future? Is the girl? Are they both?

Thoughts in 2013

In retrospect, this was probably the high-water mark for New Who. On the back of the superb Series 5, the new series was starting out even better, laying out a rich tapestry of ideas that I trusted would all come together in a coherent and satisfying way. I was actively enjoying being lost, for the moment, in the series-long arc, and loving the individual episodes.

From here onwards, there was always still a lot to love. But the quality slipped a bit from this high-point into the two-parter that followed; and then the proliferation of concepts gradually came to look less like a master-plan and more like an exercise in excess for its own sake.

Episode 6.5. *The Rebel Flesh*

[Posted on May 27, 2011]

"We have met the enemy, and they are ours" – General William Henry Harrison.

"We have met the enemy and he is us" – Walt Kelly.

The Rebel Flesh is old-school base-under-siege Doctor Who. But this time, the enemy is us. The bad guys are the same people as the good guys. Not in the mundane figurative sense that we all erect barriers against ourselves and work against our own self-interest, but in the distinctively Whovian literal sense that the bad guys are duplicates of the good guys – such perfect duplicates that you can't tell who's who.

That is, you can't tell who's a duplicate and who's real.

And you can't tell who's a good guy and who's a bad guy. Not even if you know who's a duplicate.

This ambiguity is ground that we've trodden before, and less than a year ago: in the Silurian two-parter *The Hungry Earth/Cold Blood*, it was made very clear that the Silurians were not merely Bad Guys (although their species certainly included some). They were people, albeit non-human ones; and the same is obviously true of the duplicates in *The Rebel Flesh*, even before the Doctor spells it out. And also as in Series 5's Silurian story, it's an angry woman acting alone who spoils the chance of the peace that the Doctor is trying to broker, by killing one of the apparent enemy. The difference is that last time around, she was angry because she was frightened – because she'd lost her son and was out of control. But this time, the villain of the piece, Cleaves, is angry mostly because her authority has been challenged – because she can't bear the idea of not being in control. Her anger is as much towards the Doctor as towards the duplicates.

Is the character name Cleaves telling us something? "Cleave" is an interesting word – one that has two opposite meanings. An axe can cleave a skull, dividing it in two; but a bride can cleave to her husband, joining the two into one. Early in the episode, the "real" Cleaves, like the other staff of the base, is split in two – one real person, one duplicate; could it be that she will somehow be reintegrated with her duplicate by the end? Or am I reading too much into a name?

I am, aren't I?

The Doctor's reaction to the killing is telling, and emblematic of the differences between the previous regime and the current one. David Tennant, in the Russell T. Davies era, would have been filled with righteous anger – he'd have gone shouty and square-mouthed and given a long speech about the uniqueness and dignity of all life. There is some of that in Smith's reaction, for sure, but the overwhelming impression is very different: it's of shock, horror, disappointment and plain sadness. When he shouts, it's not because he's declaiming from a soapbox, but because he's taken by surprise at how terribly disappointing people can be and how catastrophic the consequences are.

At moments like this, you forget that the Doctor is played by someone only 28 years old; he looks like a very, very old man.

My eldest son Daniel, on watching this episode, mentioned how much more it hurts when one of his teachers is disappointed in him than when one is angry. It's a different and deeper hurt. Playing the Doctor's reaction this way is very effective, and lends gravity to a scene that otherwise is perhaps a little hackneyed.

And yet, and yet ...

Fiona pointed out that in this episode, for the first time, we see Matt Smith looking like he's acting. Not in this killing sequence, but at the various times when he's wacky. When he's being The Wacky Doctor.

Is it a failure of acting? I doubt that suddenly, now, after eighteen pitch-perfect episodes, Smith has fallen off the narrow path. I think the Doctor is acting. He's trying too hard to be his normal self, to avoid thinking about Amy's pregnancy, to keep his own mind off knowing that the three people he trusts most are keeping a great and terrible secret from him. We're used to seeing this Doctor either in control of the situation, or cheerfully unconcerned that he isn't. But now the mask is beginning to slip; we're seeing the cracks. He's worried, and overcompensating.

Speaking of acting, can I just give a shout-out to Arthur Darvill's superbly consistent and nuanced portrayal of Rory? He does this week in, week out, absolutely convincing every time, and gently funny. My favourite moment this week: the TARDIS has just landed, the Doctor runs enthusiastically into the monastery and Amy runs after him; there is a momentary pause before Rory follows, and when he does it's a strangely reluctant run. It's extraordinary that he can get such complexity into so simple an act as running, but it gave me the impression that he was trying to appear to be running more enthusiastically than he actually felt. He's a pro.

The setting worked well. The whole episode uses a very consistent palette of dark blues and browns, and that contributes to the growing sense of claustrophobia (which it just now occurs to me should be defined as "the fear of Father Christmas").

The one place where I felt this episode really let itself down was the brief moment when Jen's duplicate emerged in snake-like form. It's not just that the effect wasn't convincing: it's that it was the wrong effect. The story doesn't want or need to go there — we don't need weird body-shaping powers for the duplicates. The thing about them that makes them interesting is that they are people — precisely *not* that they are monsters. (Thankfully this section was very short, and not repeated.)

In the end, the episode turns on the original people's conviction that they are real, and that the duplicates are not. (Though part of me wonders whether in the end, all the people will discover that they are duplicates, and that the *real* real people are all safely on the mainland, far from the acid factory.) But in essentials, the originals and duplicates are the same: they are indistinguishable physically, and they share the same memories: they are perfect and complete enough copies that a duplicate can believe it's an original. (This is why the snake-neck moment was such a misstep – the episode needs to be emphasising how similar duplicates are to originals, not inventing new differences.)

So what does the originals' conviction of superiority rest on? Just that they were there first? That's thin. Then, presumably, on how they came to be – by being grown in a womb rather than in a vat. Stated baldly, that is also pretty unconvincing. It seems inevitable that there will be an original-and-duplicate reconciliation in *The Almost People*; the question is how it will be brought about, and whether it can avoid clichés such as a duplicate saving the life of his original.

I leave you with a speculation on where Part 2 might be going. The duplicates may feel like they are half Auton, half Silurian, but I think they may turn out to be related to a completely different Who beast. When I saw the silhouette shot from very early in the episode, before we've met any of the people, my gut reaction was: Sontarans.

Was I just misreading the shot, or was it planted deliberately as a resonance, a clue? There are other reasons to suspect there might be a connection. We know that the Sontarans are a clone race, that they are grown in vats. We know from a couple of throwaway remarks that the Doctor has not only seen this technology before, but is familiar with a more advanced version of it. Could we be seeing the Sontaran origin story?

Thoughts in 2013

"Am I reading too much into a name? I am, aren't I?"

I was.

"Is it a failure of acting? I doubt that."

It was.

"Could we be seeing the Sontaran origin story?"

We weren't.

Episode 6.6. *The Almost People*

[Posted on May 30, 2011]

It's part of the essence of Doctor Who that it drops bombshells on us. It's a show where things are not always as they seem, and where trying to figure out exactly what's going on is an important part of the fun. Back in the day, we were shocked by the revelation in *The End of the World* that the Time Lords were gone; we all guessed wrongly at the identity of The Doctor's Wife; we were chilled by the sight of Daleks on our side in *Victory of the Daleks*.

The one constant that makes these constant twists and turns work is that the character of the Doctor himself is reliable and consistent, even as his personality changes between incarnations. He himself is the bedrock against which all the waves of the universe break, the ground against which we evaluate the changing figures.

And then the Doctor killed Amy.

The Doctor. Killed. Amy.

She was alive; and then he shot her with the sonic screwdriver, which as it turns out *is* a gun; and then she wasn't alive any more.

And whatever else happened in the episode, that is what we'll remember.

I'm not fond of hyperbolic reviews that say things like "That wasn't Doctor Who", but if I were ever to write one, this would be the time. This is not the kind of thing the Doctor does. It just isn't.

Yes, the Amy in question was a ganger, not the "real" Amy. But, come *on*, we've just spent two whole episodes establishing that the ur-flesh from which gangers are made is alive; not alive like moss, but sentient. Establishing that gangers are *people*, dammit. So what can the Doctor possibly have been thinking in killing one? Even if we say that this particular ganger did not have an independent life, and was only functioning as a prosthesis for Real Amy – it seems we are supposed to conclude this, from the sight of Real Amy waking up – what's the urgent cause for what he did? Even if you can persuade yourself, contra everything the Doctor told us last time, that the ganger is not "really" alive, then all the ganger-termination has achieved is to restore consciousness to "real" Amy, alone and trapped in an alien world, giving birth to the baby she knows nothing about, terrified out of her wits. If Ganger Amy truly needs to be disposed of for Original Amy to regain consciousness, why not wait until Real Amy has been found first?

There's much more that could be said about *The Almost People*. Some of it's good, but much of it is bad. Most seriously, it muffed most of the issues raised by *The Rebel Flesh*, treating the gangers as plain-and-simple Bad Guys for most of the episode. I could quibble with the stupid scene with the eyes in the wall, which didn't connect with anything else and would have been meaningless even if the effects had been convincing. But I'm not going to bother going there. All of that seems an irrelevance in light of the utter lack of humanity that pervaded the whole episode.

The *whole* episode? Yes, not just the coda with Amy. Throughout, people were dropping like flies, and the Doctor seemed bizarrely unconcerned. Even if we assume his position on the humanity of gangers had flipped 180° since last week, his completely casual response to the death of Real Jen, and near-total lack of engagement with Real Jimmy's acid-through-the-heart death scene, didn't chime with the way I have always thought of the Doctor – far less, the way Matt Smith has always played him. And the utter disregard for the deaths of gangers ignores the whole of last week's episode.

So I will leave everything else unsaid this time, and leave it at that. I'm very disappointed. I rate this by far the most unsatisfying episode of Series 6, and below any Series 5 episode.

So now, after such an excellent start, we find ourselves relying on Moffat himself to redeem the first half of Series 6, with his mid-series finale *A Good Man Goes to War*.

Come on, Moff. You can do it.

Can't you?

I can see I am going to have to make a follow-up post on this subject, if only to figure out what my own thoughts are. ("How do I know what I think until I see what I say?" – E. M. Forster.)

The Almost People, redux: let's see if we can sort this out

[Posted on June 1, 2011]

A few days have passed since I watched *The Almost People*, and I have calmed down a bit — just a little bit. I am sure it wasn't Moffat's or Graham's intention to have the Doctor commit murder. So what was going on?

The first thing to say is that this was by no means the only moral problem with *The Almost People*. Even if we can explain away the Doctor's actions at the end of the episode — and we probably can, just — it still leaves deep problems with the trail of bodies along the way.

To recap: we have an unusually large cast of fifteen:

— The Doctor, Amy and Rory

— Ganger Doctor

— The factory staff: Cleaves, Jen, Jimmy, Buzzer and Dicken

— The ganger versions of Cleaves, Jen, Jimmy, Buzzer and Dicken

— The second Ganger Jen

At the end of the episode, six of these have survived: The Doctor, Amy (let's be generous and count her), Rory, Cleaves, Ganger Jimmy and Ganger Dicken. So we have a proportionally huge body-count of nine — 60% of the cast. In itself that would not make the episode a disaster, but the Doctor's complete lack of concern is appallingly out of character. He even goes so far as to describe the 40% survival rate as a "happy ending". It's not exactly "Everyone lives!"

Let's review the deaths. In chronological order:

— **Ganger Buzzer** electrocuted by Cleaves in *The Rebel Flesh*

— **Second Ganger Jen** thrown into acid by Ganger Jen

— **Real Jen** found lying outside, having died literally one or two seconds before the Doctor reached her

— **Real Buzzer** eaten by Ganger Jen

— **Real Jimmy** killed by acid burning through to his heart

— **Real Dicken** killed by Mutant Ganger Jen

— **Ganger Jen** exploded by the sonic screwdriver

— **Ganger Doctor** and **Ganger Cleaves** dissolved by the sonic screwdriver, apparently as a side-effect of exploding Ganger Jen.

(It's notable that the only one of the Real factory staff to survive is Cleaves, who is the one responsible for all the carnage in the first place.)

To give the Doctor due credit, he is horrified by the first of these deaths, and not present for the second and fourth. But for all the others, he's there, he knows exactly what's happened and why, and *he knows that all those who died are people*, as he so clearly expressed when Cleaves cattle-prodded Ganger Buzzer into oblivion. Yet there is no reaction. Not even a "Darn it, we arrived too late" for Jen.

I don't get it. Why did the Doctor not make even a token attempt at preventing Real Dicken's completely pointless sacrifice as he stupidly tried to close the door from the outside? Why did he allow his own ganger and Cleaves's to throw away their lives sonicing Mutant Ganger Jen when he, as a non-ganger, could safely have done it with no side-effects? What happened to the relentless respect for life and sentience that has always characterised the Doctor?

So although I started this article thinking I was going to try to defend him against the charge of murdering Amy, I find that instead I am condemning him for everything else that happened.

Still, let's try and get the Doctor off the hook for the bit where he kills Amy.

We can say that Ganger Amy is not independently sentient, as the gangers of the factory staff are; that her ganger is merely a meat puppet that is being controlled (unwittingly) by Real Amy, off in her maternity ward somewhere. I suppose in retrospect, this was part of the purpose of the opening scene of *The Rebel Flesh*, where a ganger of Buzzer casually dissolves in a vat of acid and is unconcerned about it: to establish that ordinary gangers, having not been activated by a solar tsunami, do not have independent life.

(Let's pretend for the moment that we've forgotten about the Doctor's insistence that the Flesh itself is alive, the pool of half-dissolved gangers, the wall of eyes, and Ganger Jen's insistence that she remembers every single time that another instance of herself was killed; let's imagine that those scenes never happened, and that Graham gave us a good, consistent model of what a ganger is.)

All right then: so why did the Doctor have to dissolve Ganger Amy? To "break the link" and so allow Real Amy to control her own body again, I suppose. But that makes no sense, either: she's much happier in the TARDIS with the Doctor and Amy than alone in an alien maternity ward, so why not just leave her there until they find her?

Well, let's say that the Doctor somehow knows that Real Amy won't be able to give birth successfully unless she's conscious of the body that's doing it. *How* does he know that, you ask? Never mind, we're trying to cut him some slack here, remember?

All right, then: why not *explain* that to Amy? Instead of having her suddenly appear in a pregnant body, frightened out of her wits, giving birth and not knowing how or why or where, why not *tell her* what's happened and why it's necessary to break the link?

Come *on*.

"Amy, I'm sorry about this, but your real body is far away, about to give birth. Unless you go back to it, you will die in childbirth. To save you, I have to break the link, which will dissolve this body, but don't worry because unlike those other gangers, it's not conscious itself, despite what I told you right back when we first saw the Flesh in the previous episode."

That wasn't so hard, was it?

Why am I so upset about this?

It's because clearly the real reason that the Doctor. Murdered. Amy. instead of sitting her down and explaining it all was just because It Makes A Smashing Cliff-hanger. And that won't do. That is a reason why Moffat/Graham did it, but not a reason why the Doctor did it. And we want and need and deserve story-internal explanations for everything that happens.

And that is the real problem with *The Almost People*. In trying to wrap my head around what happened and why, I've been rudely jerked out of the world of Doctor Who, and into the world of the BBC's Light Entertainment Ratings Generator department. When I watch Who – or anything, for that matter – I want to be thinking about the character, not the author. And there is *no* story-internal reason why the Doctor behaved the way he did, either towards Amy or towards all the corpses earlier in the episode.

The bottom line is that the Doctor in *The Almost People* feels like a character who's wandered in from a completely different story. The casual disregard for death is appropriate for Bruce Willis's character in *Die Hard*, or Arnie's in *Terminator*, but absolutely not for the Doctor.

It just isn't.

It won't do.

Episode 6.7. *A Good Man Goes to War*

[Posted on August 10, 2011]

It's been just over two months since the first time I watched *A Good Man Goes to War*, the finale of the first half of Series 6. At the time, I wasn't quite sure what I made of it, so I didn't write my review straight away, wanting to give it time to sink in, and also planning to watch it a second time. Now, with the second half of the series scheduled to start in less than three weeks, the time has come for the reassessment.

So I watched it again tonight, and the verdict is in.

There are plenty of things to complain about, if you're so inclined. There's no doubt that Moffat falls into the Greatest Hits trap that also tripped him up in *The Pandorica Opens* – that the blink-and-you-miss-it appearance of the Judoon really added nothing, and the reappearance of The Pirate No-One Particularly Wanted To See Again from *Curse of the Black Spot* bought the episode nothing at all. Worse, the villains do not seem to have good motivation – at least, not yet, though that may change when we've seen part 2. (The implication is there that they are the Doctor's enemies because of something he *will* do rather than something he has done.)

But it turns out that I just don't care too much about any of that. In this episode, Moffat throws a hundred things at the wall, and if 10% of them don't stick, that still leaves ninety wonderful things. On my second watch through, I laughed out loud at least half a dozen times, which is good going for a basically serious drama. The Sontaran nurse Strax was fertile comic ground ("Give her to me, human fools, she needs changing!") and also strangely poignant in the end ("Rory. I'm a nurse.") Rory's attempt to be cool on finally meeting up once more with Amy – superb acting, very believable. And, needless to say, the Doctor himself, brimming with lines that simply could not work from any other character ("Amelia Pond, get your coat!"; "I want you to tell them to run away").

So what is going on here? Is it OK to make an episode where you merely try lots of things, and some of them are cool and some are dumb? Can Doctor Who episodes be just variety shows? You may not enjoy the stand-up comedian, but if you hang around for the while there's a juggler or a singer or a ventriloquist who you might like. Is that good enough? And is that, in fact, all that Moffat is doing here?

No, and no. It wouldn't be good enough, but that's hypothetical because it's not all he's doing. Over a series and half, he's built up three characters that we have learned to care about (four if you count River Song, but she's never worked for me). Amy and Rory are, for me, the most successful companions the Doctor's ever had because their relationship is convincing and they are both, well, likeable. I care that things work out right for them in a way that I never did for, say, Martha. If Rose was the first companion who we could imagine having a life outside the TARDIS, Amy and Rory are the first whose outside-the-TARDIS life we could actually care about.

So what's going on? Is it OK to make Doctor Who a character-based drama about how ordinary people respond to the extraordinary? And is that, in fact, all that Moffat is doing here?

No, and no. That alone wouldn't be good enough, but that's hypothetical because it's not all he's doing. Because Doctor Who, both traditionally and especially since the 2005 re-launch – and especially since Moffat took over – is most of all a programme about ideas. Moffat's predilection for timey-wimey is well documented, and I do enjoy the challenges that time paradoxes present, but they are really only the tip of the iceberg. This series has offered questions about perception (The Silence in *The Impossible Astronaut/Day of the Moon*), a meditation on the qualities we ascribe to our loved possessions (*The Doctor's Wife*) and a debate on what it is to be human (*The Rebel Flesh*, albeit one that was muffed in *The Almost People*). Its reach may exceed its grasp sometimes, but that's because it's reaching so very far.

In the end, then, what makes Doctor Who such a delight is not any single aspect of the programme, but the collision of genres – variety show, soap opera, psychological investigation – all happening at once, all set in the context of a sci-fi plot, and all somehow, miraculously, tied together into a unity. It's not just a *collision* of genres, it's a *synthesis*.

So, what next? One of my many laugh-out-loud moments on watching *AGMGTW* was right at the very end, seeing the title of episode that's coming up: *Let's Kill Hitler*. That is just perfect: audacious, historical, science-fictional, timey-wimey if you will, and just plain enthusiastic. If I had to pick three words to sum up Doctor Who to someone who didn't know it, I think *Let's Kill Hitler* might be them. But that episode is the second half of the two-parter of which *AGMGTW* was the first. So it has a lot of answers to provide. (We've been saying this about every episode since the series started, mind you.) Most urgently, what does River mean when she says that the Doctor "will fall so much further than ever before"? And (probably related) why does everyone think the Doctor is a warrior now? Plus we still have all our running mysteries from the first two episodes: who is the girl in the space-suit? (River?) How is she able to regenerate? Why was the Doctor killed? By whom? Is he only Mostly Dead? And what are The Silence up to? Come to that, who was responsible for the universe exploding at the end of Series 5?

Many questions. There is an element of frustration, to be sure, in not knowing exactly what's going on. But at the same time, it's exhilarating – like a roller-coaster, or skiing down a black run that you're not really good enough for. The sense of not being fully in control, or even fully understanding what is happening, has its own magic.

I'm on board.

P.S. "Rory wasn't even there at the beginning. And then he was dead, then he didn't exist, then he was plastic, then I had to reboot the universe – long story." Best. Line. Ever.

Thoughts in 2013

Well? What *did* River mean when she said that the Doctor "will fall so much further than ever before"?

We never found out, did we?

Episode 6.8. *Let's Kill Hitler*

[Posted on August 29, 2011]

Oh, I have been looking forward to this for so long ... The title alone had me salivating: the juxtaposition of the causal "Let's" with the history-changing "Kill Hitler" is pure Who, capturing in three words the programme's unique blend of the light-hearted and the profound. Only Doctor Who can switch between the two so constantly, seamlessly and effortlessly.

In a conventional novel – Jane Austen's justly revered classic *Pride and Prejudice*, say – events follow one another in chronological order. Causes precede effects. Elizabeth rejects Collins; both subsequently and consequently, he proposes to Charlotte instead. Lydia elopes with Wickham; both subsequently and consequently, Darcy goes off to find them in London. This makes for a comfortable reading experience, and is quite understandably the most common approach taken in fiction. Many, probably most, great works of literature work this way.

More modern novels often make extensive use of flashbacks. For example, Fred Pohl's *Gateway*, also a classic in its way, tells the story of the protagonist's psychoanalysis interspersed with flashback accounts of the events on the Gateway space station that resulted in his being in the state that requires the analysis. The back-story unfolds in parallel through the flashback exposition and the present discussion. Here we see some effects before their causes, but within each of the two threads, chronology and strict causality is followed. It's a structure that lends a level of richness not available to traditional novels because interleaving of the past and present strands allow us to watch a past event happening more or less simultaneously as we see the developing psychological effects of that event in the present.

Then there are more adventurous structures like that of Christopher Nolan's movie *Memento*. Here almost the whole story is told backwards, in segments of maybe five minutes, each taking place earlier than the one before. To make things even more confusing, the lead character is unable to form long-term memories, so in any given segment he can't remember what is going to have happened in the subsequent (for us) segments. As the film progresses, we discover not *what* happens, but *why* what we have already seen happen, happened in the way it did: what led to it. It works, and it's rather brilliant, but it's hard to imagine this approach being adopted more widely – it feels more like a gimmick than a natural alternative approach to storytelling, and the Philadelphia Weekly's summary of the film as "an ice-cold feat of intellectual gamesmanship" seems reasonable.

[Also, the lead character looks so much like Dennis Bergkamp that I kept expecting him to sneakily elbow a defender in the throat before casually scoring a goal of such astonishing technical quality that one can only laugh.]

And then there is Series 6 of Doctor Who.

It's hardly a secret that I loved Series 5, the first with Steven Moffat at the helm. It played with the concept of the story arc in a way that the previous four series under Russell T. Davies never did, dropping bits of the overarching story in here and there in a way that constantly changed the game and kept us guessing. Although I enjoyed all the Bad Wolf sightings back in the day, all of that seems terribly amateurish and half-hearted in retrospect: the RTD series feel like what they were: anthologies.

Not that there is anything wrong with that. Back in the day, Who Classic spent nearly all of its time quite free of anything that we would now recognise as an arc, the only real exceptions being the very loosely coupled *Key to Time* compilation and universally derided *Trial of a Time Lord*. (Has there ever been a lamer story title than *The Mysterious Planet*?) All the great stories of Classic Who were stand-alones, from *Tomb of the Cybermen* through *Spearhead From Space* to *Genesis of the Daleks*. And that was fine: one the great strengths of Doctor Who has always been its freedom to leap from story to story, sci-fi or historical, Earthbound or extraterrestrial.

And yet, things have changed. We can't really ignore the fact that we now live in a world where we discovered only over an extended period why Buffy suddenly had a sister that we'd never seen before, where it took us 22 episodes of *Veronica Mars* to figure out who killed Lily Kane, and where we only really understood what had been done to River Tam *after* the end of the one series of *Firefly*. [Side-note: I really must write properly about *Firefly* some time. Until then, the short version is: utterly brilliant.]

So here we are in a post-*Buffy*, post-*Veronica*, post-*Firefly* world where audiences have been trained to work harder, to think through what they're watching, to weigh possibilities over weeks or months, to try to outguess the series creators. The game has been upped since the old days of Tom Baker and his tin dog, and although series 1–4 of New Who were in many respects outstanding, there is also a real sense in which they are rather quaint and old-fashioned, paying only lip-service to the notion of a plot arc and really being 97% Alien Invasion Of The Week.

Series 5 of New Who changed that, bringing everyone's favourite 48-year-old sci-fi TV series right into the 21st century. And it's increasingly apparent that Series 6 is seeing the 21st century's stake and raising it. This is arc with extra arc on top. And it's playing out at dizzying speed in apparently random order. It's *hard*. Moffat expects us to work. He expects us to think. And he trusts us to do it. At a time when TV is mostly dumbing down just as fast as it can, isn't that refreshing?

It's almost become a truism this series to say that concept is piled relentlessly on concept, and that was true yet again in *LKH*, with the Führer himself complemented by shape-changing assassin robots, shape-changing assassin *people* and The Doctor on the very brink of death yet again. I love the way that Hitler himself was almost thrown away. "Shut up, Hitler", says Rory, in one of the most perfectly deadpan lines you'll ever see. Into a cupboard he goes – thereafter to be ignored as the story goes spinning off in a completely different direction. I like to imagine him sitting in the cupboard still, waiting for the world to recommence turning around him; but it doesn't. Not this world. It turns around the Doctor, and Amy and Rory, and River.

Does it all work? Somehow, yes: it makes at least enough sense to let sheer momentum carry it along. Plus there were some actual answers thrown into the mix: about time, you might say, after the masses of questions thrown up by the early episodes of Series 6. (I'll summarise some of these near the end.)

But the overwhelming sense, for me at least, is that Moffat is doing two things. He's playing a game with us – a complex, cryptic one where we don't know all the rules; and in some sense he's treating us as equals. What I mean is that even in the best of the RTD episodes I had a sense that he was holding back, that he wanted to make sure that he kept it simple enough for us, that he didn't trust us to follow if he suddenly went flying off at right angles to reality. Whereas under Moffat, I feel that anything could happen, and he's constantly challenging us to keep up. It's unsettling, but in the best sense.

Which is why I loved *Let's Kill Hitler*, and all the wibbly-wobbly timey-wimey that was involved in the story of Amy and Rory, Amy's best friend, her daughter, the reason that River in *Silence in the Library* knew the Doctor's true name, and the various deaths. Yes, it needed a little bit of Sit Down And Think after the episode ended to get it all straight, but that is part of the appeal for me. I can see why it might not be everyone's cup of tea, but those who love it will *really* love it.

And then you have those who don't. Jim Shelley, writing in the downmarket tabloid *The Daily Mirror* was much less impressed – "Personally, I was perfectly happy when Doctor Who was a series about The Doctor, a foxy female sidekick and her gormless mate fighting creatures from space." But I can't go worrying about that. If Jim Shelley lacks the mental agility to follow the Grand Moff's elaborately improvised dance through a maze of twisty little tunnels, some of them all alike and others all different, then that's his lookout. Me? I'll be dancing along as closely behind as I can manage.

Of course, that's not to say that it was perfect. While Karen Gillan, Arthur Darvill and most of all Matt Smith continue to give utterly believable performances, the character of River Song is, as usual, undermined by the horribly mannered performance of Alex Kingston, and I can't help wondering how much better yet Who might be had someone else been cast in the increasingly crucial role of River. Actually that Jim Shelley review says it just right: "Whereas the rest of the cast play their parts perfectly naturally [...] you can see Kingston acting." Worse, she seems to think she's in pantomime.

That's a shame. But it's not enough to seriously spoil the overall effect. (And her stilted delivery paid off in a big way when I heard the Doctor's response to her question "Who's River Song?" A wonderful moment.)

Time to review what we now know.

— We know now that the little girl in the space-suit from *The Impossible Astronaut* and *Day of the Moon* really is – as we suspected – Melody Pond/River Song, who is in turn Amy's daughter. (We know because she spoke about the last time she regenerated in New York as a child – a scene that we've already seen).

— We know that the newly introduced and irritatingly River-like character "Mels" actually *is* River, so that Amy's best friend as she was growing up was in fact her own daughter. (And so Amy named her daughter after her daughter. Sweet.)

— We know that River is considered a criminal by, well, we don't know who, but the people piloting the shape-shifting robot. And that the reason for this is that she killed the Doctor.

— We know that the Doctor's death by Lake Silencio in Utah in April 2011 is known to the shape-shifting robot pilots, and that it is one of those Fixed Points In Time And Space.

We are being *invited* to believe that the person in the space-suit who killed the Doctor back in April was River, but actually we don't *know* that. We know that River was imprisoned because she killed "the best man she ever knew", but we don't know that that was the Doctor (I still have a sneaking suspicion that it might be Rory); and even if it was the Doctor, we don't know that it was by Lake Silencio. And if it *was* by Lake Silencio, we don't know whether it was Girl River, who we later saw in the suit, or Adult River. Again, we were invited to assume the former, but the latter would make more sense – otherwise the adult River who we saw in *LKH* would not still have felt a need to kill the Doctor, having already done so earlier in her life (though later in his).

Back when *The Impossible Astronaut* aired, Allyn Gibson wrote that "There was no resolution, though as the first part of a two-parter that's largely to be expected." But it's increasingly apparent that he was wrong: *TIA* was actually the first part of a *thirteen*-parter. It all ties together. But can it make sense? Can the Moff pull it off?

That's what's so great here: YES! Yes, he can! We've seen it done before, in the small in *Blink*, over the slightly longer spans of the two-parter *The Empty Child*, which made more sense than any other Who story I can remember, and over the yet longer span of series 5. (The moment in *The Big Bang* when we discover that the Doctor's jacket in *Flesh and Stone* was not just a continuity error still sends shivers up and down my spine when I think about it.) Bottom line, I trust Moffat to make it fly.

Don't let me down, Steven!

Episode 6.9. *Night Terrors*

[Posted on September 11, 2011]

When Series 6's complex and demanding opening two-parter *Impossible Astronaut/Day of the Moon* was followed by the relatively straightforward third episode, *Curse of the Black Spot*, I couldn't help but feel a little underwhelmed by comparison. It had a lot to recommend it (in fact I really must go back and watch it again), but set against the sprawling ambitious of the opening gambit it seemed somehow mundane. That's harsh, but based on a true story.

Night Terrors had the similarly difficult job of following on from Moffat's mid-series two-parter *A Good Man Goes to War/Let's Kill Hitler*; but would it be substantial enough to stand up against those very rich episodes?

Sadly, the answer is "nearly but not quite". The ingredients are all lined up: the stuff that classic Who is made of. The frightened child, the spooky old lady, something weird happening to the companions while separated from the Doctor. And yet while there's plenty to like, the episode somehow never really sings. Given that it was very deliberately designed to be frightening, it didn't really achieve that goal – at least, nowhere near as well as *The Empty Child* or *Silence in the Library*. And I think there were three main reasons for that.

First, the frightened child himself. We've been spoiled for child actors in recent years. I've seen Haley Joel Osment in two films, for example, *The Sixth Sense* and the very demanding *A.I.*, and he was absolutely convincing in both of them. Closer to home, Caitlin Blackwood did a fine job of portraying Amelia Pond in Series 5 of Who. The result has been that I had more or less forgotten how excruciatingly bad child actors can be – as for example, the pair of Cute Kids in *Chitty Chitty Bang Bang*. George is nowhere near down at that level, but the poor kid is not *quite* good enough to be convincing. And in a story like this, that's crippling.

Second, the characterisation of the Doctor seemed somehow a bit off. There were delightful moments as usual – notably the don't-open-the-cupboard/do-open-the-cupboard sequence. But there is usually an intensity to this Doctor that's apparent beneath the surface in even the more tranquil scenes – a sense that wheels are spinning somewhere inside. In *Night Terrors*, for the first time in a long while, there were times when it seemed as though the Doctor just didn't have much idea where he was headed or why.

And third, the plotting wasn't as tight as I'd hoped. For example, very early on George's mother just drops silently out of the story. That seemed like it should be relevant, especially once it became apparent that Alex's memory was unreliable – could it be that she didn't really exist, and was a figment of George's imagination? No, it turns out, she had just popped out for a bun or something, and returned for the Happy Ending. Meanwhile, we were introduced to a couple of extras: the Threatening Landlord and the Creepy Old Lady. But as it turns out, neither of them really had anything to do with anything: they became victims of the Scary, sure, but that fact didn't play into anything else that happened. It would have been perfectly possible to snip out one or both of those characters and use the time to develop George's mum.

None of this makes the episode bad, of course. There's a lot to like about it. Had it cropped up in a Tennant-era series, I would probably have classed it as one of the better ones. But my sense is that Who has shifted up a couple of gears since then, and is aiming for more. In that context, *Night Terrors* feels a bit like treading water. It isn't just a matter of its being a non-arc episode, or of Moffat-vs.-the-rest, because *The Doctor's Wife* took wings and flew in a way that this didn't, quite.

Here's how it feels to me. When Moffat writes an episode, especially since he took over as show-runner, it feels to me as though he's got behind the wheel of a powerful sports car that he's lusted after since he was a child. And he's thinking, "All right, let's see how fast this baby can go!", and flinging it round the corners for the sheer delight of doing it. He seems to be surfing on the edge of the possible. Whereas Mark Gatiss's writing, in *Night Terrors*, seems altogether more sober and, well, cautious. It could have jumped in much deeper, but it was content to stay, if not paddling in the shallow end, then at least not going out of its depth.

And that's all I have to say about that.

Episode 6.10. *The Girl Who Waited*

[Posted on September 22, 2011]

Waiting has been a recurring theme in New Who. Sarah Jane waited thirty years (in real time!) to see the Doctor again after *The Hand of Fear*. Captain Jack waited in Cardiff for somewhere north of a hundred years before finding the Doctor in *Utopia*. Amy waited twelve years for the Doctor within a single episode (*The Eleventh Hour*), and then for another two years later in the same episode! Rory waited two thousand years for Amy to emerge from the Pandorica in *The Big Bang*. (It's part of Rory's charm that he is the only one of these to have waited for anyone other than the Doctor. Amy means more to him than the Doctor does.)

What happened to these people while they waited? Sarah Jane got on with her life, on the whole rather successfully. Nothing of the remotest importance happened to Jack because of his convenient Never Dying Or Ageing Or Anything superpower. Nothing happened to Rory, either, because he was plastic. But Amy, alone of the four of them, felt it. We're left in no doubt that her encounter with the Doctor at age seven shaped the whole of the rest of her childhood, adolescence and early adulthood. All those Raggedy Doctor dolls, and the four psychiatrists tell a story. Amy was damaged. Her twelve-year wait for New Who was as painful for her as the most obsessed fanboy felt the sixteen-year wait from 1989 to 2005.

So it was particularly cruel to make her wait another 36 years – time spent isolated from both Rory *and* the Doctor, and indeed any other person. If 36-years-in-the-future Amy was not quite the same person we know, she can be forgiven for having gone slightly round the twist. I've been unapologetically a Karen Gillan fan since her earliest performances as Amy, and she was excellent again in the difficult double role of Young Amy and Old Amy – the latter role apparently initially intended for a different actress, but given to Gillan on her own request.

It's a truly extraordinary make-up job. Amy is very recognisably Amy, but also absolutely convincing as twenty years older. (A shame, then, that the story says she's 36 years older – she does not look 58, which is the absolute youngest she can be. Maybe that duration was a hangover from when a different actress was envisaged, but it would have been so easy to fix.)

But all the make-up in the world can't overcome an inadequate performance, so it all hung on Gillan's ability to walk, talk, and even appear to think like a different person – like someone 36 years older, in fact. Apparently she worked extensively on this. The result was a subtle performance in which the two Amys were rather different but not dramatically so. Part of me thinks that in terms of Oscar Clip Potential, this is a bit of a missed opportunity – she could have gone further with the differences. But at the time I watched it, it seemed appropriate, and on mature reflection I realise that I was right the first time. We don't need Oscar Clip stuff here, we need acting that serves the story – just as George Harrison's solo in *Something* serves the song rather than drawing attention to itself as a more technically impressive solo would have.

Visually it's a beautiful episode, switching between three very different kinds of environment: the sterile, minimalist rooms of the main complex, the grimy industrial underbelly where Old Amy lives, and the gorgeous stately home and gardens outside. As a design choice it's striking, and the sudden transitions between the three environments serve to highlight the sense of disconnection in Amy's life.

So all of this is good: the make-up, the acting, the sets. But the real question is, does it work? Yes, it's yet another time-travel story, but it's resolutely not timey-wimey. (I can't believe that's a thing now, but it is.) In fact, it's very linear, and the questions it raises are more moral and emotional than causal. The fact that Old Amy makes a choice that contradicts her own memory of that choice from long ago is casually thrown away, because that's not the focus. The *making* of that choice is the point, not its consequences.

And yet ... There *are* consequences, and they are hard to think about. It's strange to think of how time-travel, as well as its other paradoxes, provides a simple way to make multiple instances of the same person. If I step into the TARDIS, the Doctor takes me back sixty seconds and I step back out, then I meet my sixty-seconds-younger self. Now the Doctor can dematerialise and never return, but there are two of me. That's strange, isn't it? Which one is real? Surely both. Why shouldn't both continue to live? In the case of the two Amys there is a further problem of course: who gets Rory? But the solution seems obvious. Drop off one of the Amys on a nice planet, then once she's settled in, travel back sixty seconds to make a duplicate Rory for her.

It can't be that easy, can it?

But why not, exactly?

I suppose this is just a special case of the classic narrative difficulty of time travel: that you can use it to solve any problem, taking as many attempts as you need. In the past, Doctor Who simply ignored this, eventually coming up with the Blinovitch Limitation Effect as a technobabble rationalisation. But since New Who has played fast and loose with the timey-wimey, especially in the Moffat era, these may be issues it has to confront sooner or later.

Well. That's a problem for Moffat. For some unaccountable reason, I have never been invited to write *any* episodes, so I'm not going to let it bother me too much.

I leave you with the observation that in this episode the Doctor is not merely largely absent, but rather ineffective when he's around. If Amy's own carelessness gets her onto a different timeline from him, it's his mistake that locks her there. It's been a frequent criticism of the last few series that the Doctor is becoming an increasingly mythologised character, known and feared through the universe. But we know from this episode and others that he is very fallible. What might the consequences of that be next time out?

There is a plan.

Episode 6.11. *The God Complex*

[Posted on September 24, 2011]

… And then there are the times when Doctor Who just gets it all so perfectly right that you feel you never need to watch anything else ever again.

There's so much that could be said about *The God Complex* – about the careful selection of one-shot companions; about the craftsmanship with which they're given separate and interesting characters so that in the space of 45 minutes we come to care about who makes it and who doesn't; about the nightmarish nature of the hotel's corridors and staircases, before we even get into the individual rooms; and about how the nature of what the monster is doing turns out to be different from what we all assumed. But that's not the point.

The point is, as so often with Doctor Who, about three people who we've grown to love, and whose relationships are not quite straightforward; and about how those three people come through when they're thrown into situations that are bizarre, terrifying or puzzling. Or, in this case, all three. For most of the last three series, Doctor Who has been a programme about one person, the Doctor, who takes some friends along for the ride. But now it's very much about three people: the Doctor, Amy and Rory.

Back in 2005, I think we were all taken by surprise by how central Rose made herself to the story, how indispensable she became, so that when the was stranded in another universe at the end of *Doomsday*, losing her felt like losing a Doctor. Perhaps it was even a bigger upheaval than Doctor Chris's regeneration into Doctor Dave. (It didn't help that her replacement, Martha, was so comparatively uninteresting.) But now it feels crippling to imagine losing either Amy or Rory. Let alone both, as suggested in the elegiac coda. What we have here is a programme that's always worked on the mind. But now it works on the heart, too: not manipulatively, not in a tear-jerky way as the appalling last act of *The End of Time* tried so unsuccessfully to do; but by honesty. By being, if we can say this about a group of time-travellers, *realistic*.

Yes, after the events of the early part of *The Eleventh Hour*, Amy would grow up a little bit crazy; and merely meeting the Doctor again twelve years later wouldn't in itself fix that. Yes, Rory would consistently feel threatened by having the Doctor around, however much the Doctor didn't intend it. And, yes, the kind of person who could cope with slightly-crazy Amy and her Dream Doctor would indeed be someone much like Rory: thoughtful, consistent; dependable, but not in a doormat kind of way. He's quietly made himself one of the more likeable and admirable characters in television.

And I still can't shake the feeling that he is "The best man I ever knew", that River Song is going to have been imprisoned for killing.

Much has been written, and rightly so, about how, since 2006 or so, the programme has increasingly fetishised the Doctor himself. When in the Series 1 finale, *The Parting of the Ways*, he referred to himself as The Oncoming Storm, it was a shock because the Doctor we knew simply didn't think of himself that way. It was a perfect dramatic moment because the Doctor himself was in shock at the realisation that he was facing Daleks – just as he had been in the brilliant earlier episode *Dalek*, in which he also acted out of character (but in a way perfectly in keeping with the story). The Daleks' presence invoked that side of him and showed us a glimpse of a Doctor we'd not known.

But with a worrying frequency, that kind of showboating, that do-you-know-who-I-am vibe, started becoming the norm. Russell T. Davies did it all the time: the Doctor solved problems by being The Doctor; and Moffat also fell into that trap a couple of times, notably when he faced down the Vashta Nerada in *Silence in the Library*. The Doctor had become not just a traveller or a problem solver, but a warrior. And he seemed pretty pleased about it.

So it's been a particular pleasure over the last dozen or so episodes to watch Moffat and the other writers consistently cutting away this action-heroey aspect of the Doctor. It's been done subtly enough, and with enough variation, that it's not hitting us over the head. But it's addressing the issue not just by turning its back on the way the Doctor had been developing, but by actively subverting it.

— In *The Pandorica Opens*, the Doctor grandstands at Stonehenge, and is allowed to think he's frightened all the bad guys away with his *I! Am! The! Doctor!* shtick. But that's shown to be a ruse by enemies who have grown as used to this as we have.

— At the end of the same episode, all his ideas of himself are inverted when it transpires that he is "a goblin, or a trickster or a warrior. A nameless, terrible thing, soaked in the blood of a billion galaxies. The most feared being in all the cosmos."

— In a more mundane way, one of the best elements of *Curse of the Black Spot* is the way the Doctor makes a whole sequence of completely wrong guesses about what's going on (and is scientist enough to abandon each one in turn).

— In the finale to the first half of this series, *A Good Man Goes to War*, the Doctor is shocked to find that whole cultures identify him as a warrior rather than a healer or a teacher.

— In *The Girl Who Waited*, 36-years-older Amy hasn't just lost her faith in the Doctor who couldn't save her, but actively hates him.

— And now in *The God Complex*, not only can he not save Amy, but his inability to do so, and her recognition of that, is exactly what does save her.

Oh, this is clever stuff. The companion has traditionally been the viewpoint character in Doctor Who, the person that we identify with. And so, just as we'd been drawn into the revised Doctor (the goblin, the warrior, the Man Who Thinks He's It) so Amy was drawn into the same uncritical, close-to-worship perspective. And now, as she is able to step out of that illusion, so we follow her. She sees now that that's never what the Doctor really was; and so do we. It was how some other people saw him (notably the Daleks), and from time to time he was as seduced by that notion as any of us might have been. But it was never true.

Killer or coward? Coward, every time.

But those aren't the only choices, are they? Killer, Coward or Mad Man With A Box would be a fairer multiple choice question. But it's a mad man who expects the most of people, who retains a near-miraculous capacity for thinking the best of them despite having been disappointed thousands of times (and once more in *The God Complex*). He's a mad man with a box who knows how to think. And observe, and draw conclusions. And how to rethink when they're proved wrong. And to help others to do all those things.

In the end, Doctor Who – at least since 2010 – is a fantastically optimistic programme, because it shows us someone who we can realistically expect to become. We can't be The Oncoming Storm, the goblin, the trickster. But we can think, observe, rethink, expect the best of others and ourselves, forgive when people fall short, help them to try again. Those, really, are the qualities that distinguish the Doctor. And they are what I want to be, too. And I can.

So we approach the end of the series with a recalibrated perspective on the Doctor. And it seems that we approach it without Amy and Rory (though we know from extra-textual sources that they will be back for Series 7).

Tonight it's *Closing Time*, and I am a bit worried by that. I always avoid watching the previews, so that I know as little as possible about what I'm going to see, but I've not been able to avoid finding out that *Closing Time* is a sequel to *The Lodger*. I loved that episode, but in part because it was so very self-contained, a sort of holiday from the main story; and because it wrapped up its whole rom-com subplot so neatly. I don't see how a sequel can really work, and I especially struggle to see how it can tie in to the arc, which it pretty much has to with only two episodes left.

We shall see.

Thoughts in 2013

Sheesh, I really went on about the idea that River was going to kill Rory, didn't I? Just couldn't let it drop. And of course I was totally wrong.

It's nice to see that, so very close to the end of the series, I was still so very positive. I do still think that *The God Complex* is one of the very best New Who episodes, and stands up very well to multiple viewings. Given that I'd also been so positive about the previous stand-alone, *The Girl Who Waited*, and that the mid-series two-parter had been such a wild ride, I suppose it makes sense that I approached the conclusion with such optimism.

Episode 6.12. *Closing Time*

[Posted on September 27, 2011]

At the end of my *God Complex* review, I worried about *Closing Time*: "I don't see how a sequel can really work, and I especially struggle to see how it can tie in to the arc."

Well, I needn't have worried.

Gareth Roberts wisely avoided re-treading *The Lodger*'s Craig-and-Sophie romantic plot, by skipping straight to the part where they've been happily together for a while and have a baby. And I think it's fair to say that the baby was the star of the show.

I don't have a lot to say about *Closing Time* beyond that it was very, very funny. Not very scary (although with one truly horrific moment), not very suspenseful, not at all emotionally complex (again apart from one moment, Amy and Rory glimpsed distantly) and not remotely timey-wimey. Just very funny, with a near-constant stream of laugh-out-loud moments, and just enough plot to hang the set-pieces on.

Is that enough? Well, it was enough for Friends to run for ten seasons, and Frasier for eleven – both shows that I thoroughly enjoyed, though without ever truly loving the way I do Doctor Who and Buffy and Veronica Mars. If that was the only thing Doctor Who ever did, it would be a much lesser show than it is; but if it never had laugh-out-loud funny episodes it would also be the poorer for it. *Closing Time* is dessert. A meal without it is still a meal, but the very best meals include it.

In a move that should please those who prefer Doctor Who as an episodic smörgåsbord, the "arc" material was kept to a minimum: a brief interlude with River and a few moments in which the Doctor prepared, both physically and emotionally, for the forthcoming events of *The Impossible Astronaut*. So the last episode of this series, *The Wedding of River Song*, will have to carry all the weight of all the unresolved questions, including a few that go back to the end of last series.

My youngest son had misunderstood the chronology and thought that *Closing Time* itself was the final episode. Actually, wouldn't that have been great? That final scene of the be-Stetsonned Doctor stepping grim-faced into the TARDIS, off to meet his doom, with no hope (that we can see) of escape. That would have been a tough way to end.

What do we know about the Lake Silencio incident?

[October 1, 2011]

So tomorrow night sees the final episode in Series 6. We know from the end of *Closing Time* that the Doctor is off to Lake Silencio to enact the events of *The Impossible Astronaut*. He even has his Stetson. He has the TARDIS-blue envelopes in which he is going to send the invitations to Amy and Rory, River, Canton Everett Delaware III and his two-hundred-year younger self.

We know, from having seen *TIA* before the Doctor has, how things are going to happen. So let's review what we know, and see if we can put it all together into a credible hypothesis. Having seen episodes 2–12, I am now going to go back and watch the first part of episode 1, *The Impossible Astronaut*, again, and note the relevant clues. Off we go.

—

@1:38 Amy: "He said he'd be in touch." / Rory: "Two months ago." / Amy: "Two months is nothing, he's up to something, I know he is." This exchange suggests that from Amy and Rory's perspective, *The Impossible Astronaut* takes place after the Doctor drops them off at their house at the end of *The God Complex*. But I don't think that can be right, as we have followed Amy and Rory's timeline pretty constantly through the series. They were travelling with the Doctor right up to the time of the drop-off, so I think this must be a red herring. (Or just a mistake.)

@3:13 just after "I wear a Stetson now; Stetsons are cool." River shoots the hat right off the Doctor's head. We can't tell exactly how far away she was, but far enough that the others didn't notice her approaching. What does this tell us? River is a good shot; so good that she's confident enough to shoot the hat off the man she loves without worrying about hitting him. This will be important later.

@3:50 "I've been running. Faster than I've ever run. And I've been running my whole life. Now it's time for me to stop. And tonight I'm going to need you all with me." The Doctor's line, and the downbeat delivery, are very much of a piece with the latter parts of *Closing Time*. Likewise @5:54 "Human beings. I thought I'd never get done saving you."

@5:22 Amy sees a Silent, and of course immediately forgets about it. The presence of a Silent at the scene of the Doctor's death indicates their involvement (or it's a very odd coincidence). Of course we know that the Silence are associated with Madame Kovarian, because there are two of them with her at the end of *Closing Time* when the newly Ph.D'd River is put into the space-suit.

[Which reminds me: all the time we've known River, she's been *Doctor* River Song, which means that all those adventures happened *after* the sequence in which she was put in the suit and left in the lake. In particular, I think we can conclude that the River at the picnic is from later in her own timeline than the River in the lake.]

@6:00 Canton Everett Delaware III turns up, and the Doctor acknowledges him. He's obviously expecting him. No-one talks to him at this point. He's arrived just in time to see …

@6:20 The astronaut standing in the lake. Doctor: "You all need to stay back. Whatever happens now you do not interfere. Clear?" He's not surprised to see the astronaut. Why not? He knows when and where he is scheduled to die from the screen in *Let's Kill Hitler*, but I don't remember that saying anything about how. Has he been finding out more?

Why is the astronaut in the lake? Of all the ways that Madame Kovarian and the Silence could arrange to have the Doctor killed, why this bizarre way? I have no ideas on this. I think by now we pretty much have to assume that it is younger River in the suit (although at this point in Series 5 we all assumed it was the Doctor in the Pandorica, and look how that turned out.)

@6:50 a decidedly careworn Doctor speaks to the astronaut. "Hello. It's OK, I know it's you. Well then …" They continue to speak for another fifteen seconds but we don't hear the rest.

@7:15 the astronaut shoots the Doctor. Amy runs towards him. River restrains her: "Amy, stay back. We have to stay back." She gives the impression of having more idea of what is happening than the other two.

@7:20 the astronaut shoots the Doctor again. He starts to regenerate, but @7:50 the astronaut shoots a third time, mid-regeneration, interrupting the process. The others run towards the Doctor.

@8:10 River shoots at the astronaut. (As she stands up to do so, she looks resigned more than sad or angry.) She fires five shots, all from pretty close range, and misses every time. She pulls the trigger a sixth time but there is no shot – presumably because she used a bullet earlier shooting the Doctor's Stetson off. Why does River miss? We have already seen that she is an excellent shot, able to safely shoot the Doctor's hat off from similar range, yet she fails to hit a much larger target even once from a much shorter range. My best guess? The Doctor replaced her bullets with blanks. (After all, we've seen him pull similar tricks on immediately-post-regeneration Assassin River in *Let's Kill Hitler*.)

@8:22 River says "Of course not." This could be construed as "of course there isn't a sixth bullet" but it's much more reasonable to read it as "of course I missed". Does that mean she knows it's her in the suit, and of course she wasn't killed otherwise she wouldn't be there now?

@8:33 River says "Whatever that was, it killed him in the middle of his regeneration cycle." The "whatever that was" is strange if she knows it's her.

@8:45 we have the escape routes cut off. Amy: "Maybe he's clone or a duplicate or something". But her thoughts are immediately shown to be incorrect by Canton's first words: "I believe I can save you some time. That most certainly is the Doctor. And he is most certainly dead. He said you'd need this." (A can of petrol for burning the body.)

@10:01 they cremate the Doctor's body. More ensuring that we know there is no way back. It was the real Doctor, he is dead, and his body is destroyed.

@12:30 "This is cold. Even by your standards this is cold." River was not expecting to see the younger Doctor. However much she knew in advance of these events, she didn't know this part.

—

What does all this mean? The key questions are:

— Who is in the space-suit? Let's assume it's River, from the part of her timeline when she's just obtained her doctorate.

— Does present-day River remember the events now happening from her earlier perspective in the suit? The evidence is equivocal.

— Why does present-day River miss the astronaut with all five of her close-range shots?

— Why does the Doctor go willingly to his death?

— What are the Doctor and the astronaut talking about for those fifteen seconds?

And most important of all ...

— How can the Doctor be saved when we know (A) that it is really him, not a clone or a duplicate; (B) that he really is dead, with no chance to regenerate; (C) that his body has been burned?

And, not obviously related, but worth throwing in:

What is the "first question" which, when asked, will (the Silence believe) cause the universe to end? And how is it relevant to Kovarian's anti-Doctor crusade? Does she believe that he is going to ask that question, should he survive?

Well, I'd hoped that laying all the evidence out here would guide me to a flash of insight, but I'm afraid it's not happened. I am just as mystified as when I started.

Thoughts in 2013

Back when I posted the blog entry, the very first commenter, Oliver Townshend, wrote:

"Well we don't actually know if it is the Doctor's body, despite what Canton says. After all he could have been lied to by the Doctor (Rule 1). So it could be a ganger. And you'd want to burn a ganger's body to disguise that fact wouldn't you?"

And I, so young and naïve, replied:

"It's true that the Doctor could have lied to Canton about it really being him. But I don't think so: I think that that would constitute the programme itself lying to the audience, which is Just Not On. So I don't believe it was a ganger, and I don't believe it was a Teselecta. Moffat has to play by the rule that he himself has laid down."

And in a later comment on the same thread, I reiterated:

"I just don't see that it would be fair for the Grand Moff to give us a Ganger Doctor when we were told so explicitly back in *The Impossible Astronaut* that "That most certainly is the Doctor. And he is most certainly dead"."

What a fool I was.

Episode 6.13. *The Wedding of River Song*

[Posted on October 6, 2011]

And so we come to the end of Doctor Who series 6. So many questions to answer, so much ground to cover, so many ideas to tie together. Were they answered? Was it covered? Were they integrated? Will this so-called review consist entirely of questions?

You could characterise Moffat's work as Doctor Who show-runner as a constant surfing on the very edge of the possible. It's beyond question that he's given us a much denser, faster-moving Who than ever before; and – most important – a Who that is richer in *ideas*. The main arc of Series 6 has included an at-times bewildering array of concepts, including more time-travel paradoxes than you can shake a stick at. There are writers who you feel safe with – you know what you're going to get from a West Wing or Frasier episode – and then there are the writers who might do *anything*. Joss Whedon is one; Moffat is another.

When Moffat's ideas work (which is more often than not), they fly. Up to the start of this series, it's been unquestionable that half a dozen or more of the best ten New Who stories have been his. (*The Empty Child/The Doctor Dances*; *The Girl in the Fireplace*; *Blink*; *Silence in the Library/Forest of the Dead*; *The Time of Angels/Flesh and Stone*; *The Pandorica Opens/The Big Bang*; *A Christmas Carol*. Candidates by other writers: Robert Shearman's *Dalek*, Paul Cornell's *Father's Day*, Russell T. Davies' *Bad Wolf/The Parting of the Ways*, Cornell's *Human Nature/The Family of Blood*; Davies' *Midnight*; Gareth Roberts' *The Lodger*. Just so you know).

But a strange thing has happened as I've watched the four pre-*Wedding* Moffat episodes this year. After each of *The Impossible Astronaut*, *Day of the Moon*, *A Good Man Goes to War* and *Let's Kill Hitler*, I've found myself feeling only guardedly positive. Positive, yes; I had a lot of good things to say about all of those episodes. And yet they posed so many questions, and answered so few, that I found myself always reserving judgement – thinking "well, we'll know how good it was when we've seen the next one". Delayed gratification is all very well, but it seems to have reached a point where no one episode makes sense alone – not just because you need to know what came before, but also what is going to come after, before you can form a coherent view of its events.

There have been times when I've wondered whether it's getting to be too much work; but then the episodes in question have been so fascinating, and so funny, and so dramatic, that it's been easy to look straight past the complexities – at least in the short term – and just enjoy the ride. But the problem with that approach is that the episodes are writing cheques that the series finale needs to be able to cash. It's a tall order.

And the end of Series 5, I felt that *The Big Bang* absolutely pulled it off – it answered most of the questions, and those that it left unanswered had the feel of next-series teasers rather than overlooked details. Better still, it included very clever moments like the explanation of why the Doctor got his jacket back in the middle of *Flesh and Stone* – a true Mind Blown moment. But it's interesting to think about how Moffat did that. When you're learning to ski, one of the hardest lessons to absorb is that you need to point your skis downhill because that gives you much more control than staying side-on and skiing across the hill. Full Speed Ahead And Damn The Horses turns out to be the best way to ski, and that's the approach that the Grand Moff took in *The Big Bang* – starting out not by explaining the mysteries accumulated in previous episodes, but by piling on *more* mysteries. Most notably, what the heck was Amy doing inside the Pandorica rather than the Doctor? That was maybe the single most startling What The Heck?! moment of TV I've ever seen.

So *The Big Bang* worked, absolutely.

But then in *A Good Man Goes to War*, Moffat pulled the same point-the-skis-downhill manoeuvre by introducing a whole nother bunch of concepts – the Future Church now opposed to the Doctor instead of allied with him, the Headless Monks, the Sontaran nurse, the Silurian detective, The Pirate That No-One Really Wanted To See Again, and much, much more. Again, it worked; but again, largely on sheer exuberance. And, unlike *The Big Bang*, it left just as many open questions behind it as it resolved. So it was satisfying as a mid-series semi-finale, if you will, but wouldn't have done as the series finale.

Which finally brings us to *The Wedding*. Just as a reminder (from the last post), we wanted to know 1. why the Doctor had to die; 2. why River had to be the one to do it; 3. why she had to do it in the form of an Impossible Astronaut; 4. why there was a Silent there; 5. why Present-Day River missed Old River with five shots from point-blank range; 6. why she said "of course not" after missing; 7. what the Doctor and the Astronaut said to each other; 8. how the Doctor could avoid death when Canton told us "That most certainly is the Doctor. And he is most certainly dead"; and 9. what is the "first question" that the Silence believe must never be asked.

Well. We got answers to #1 (it's a fixed point in time), #7 (we heard the conversation this time), #8 (it turns out it was a duplicate, and Canton was lying or mistaken), and #9. No joy with the other five. And these don't seem to be the kinds of questions that will roll over into the next series. It looks to me like they've just been dropped on the floor.

And this is a tragedy not only because it makes *Wedding* inadequate but because it also rewrites the earlier episodes and makes them less than they were. There's no question that the astronaut, the conversation by the lake, and the death of the Doctor were iconic images and memorable moments. But what do they mean?, we all asked ourselves at the time. Turns out, they mean nothing. It might just as well have been Time-Grabbed Rory on a hang-glider, with the Lead Piping, in the Conservatory. River's missed shots and "of course not" were fascinating. Now they appear to have been merely random.

So if I seem very negative about *Wedding*, I think that is the main reason: because its failure echoes back in time and lessens earlier episodes (a suitably timey-wimey phenomenon in itself). It wasn't just a lesser episode, it made the whole series a lesser series.

It saddens me because I thought Moffat had A Plan that would tie it all together and make it all make sense. One of the great things about *The Empty Child/The Doctor Dances*, Moff's first New Who story, was that it all made perfect sense in story-internal terms. The strange and disturbing behaviour and abilities of the eponymous child really did follow reasonably from their cause; and it was a cause we were given all the necessary clues to guess if we were clever enough. I would have said that tight, coherent plotting was one of Moffat's greatest strengths – it's certainly the main reason I was so delighted when I heard that he was to be Russell T. Davies' successor.

But the resolutions to this series just felt … careless. To pick one example, we were told very clearly back in *Let's Kill Hitler* (by the Teselecta robot) that "The Silence is not a species; it is a religious order or movement. Their core belief is that silence will fall when the question is asked." Yet now it seems it's fine to *ask* the question – the problem comes if it's *answered*. There seems to be no reason for the change. As far as I can see, it's just bad continuity.

So there's all this going on – more new concepts (time has stopped, the Doctor is for some reason a sort of court-jester/prisoner, Amy and Rory are "alternative"), important ideas from earlier dropped on the ground, and no resolution that makes sense. (The Silence's plan to kill the Doctor is incredibly convoluted, long-winded and error-prone even by the standards of Doctor Who villains.)

All of this I could possibly forgive if *Wedding* had the flamboyance, the effervescence, the sheer *joie de vivre* of Moffat's better episodes – including some from this series, but most especially *The Big Bang*. But where that episode sparked with energy and made me laugh out loud over and over again, *The Wedding of River Song* felt laboured by comparison. Unusually for a Who episode, I can't recall a single moment that put me in danger of falling out of my chair at the sheer Whoness of it all.

So we reach the end of this series of reviews on a very unsatisfactory note. I didn't intend to write anywhere near so negatively about *The Wedding of River Song* as I have done, but I've found as I'm writing that my frustrations with it have grown clearer and clearer, with no corresponding growth in affection.

A real shame. I thought early in this series that it was shaping to be the best I've ever seen. But in the end, it's less than Series 5, and possibly also less than Series 1 (though still better than 2, 3 or 4, sorry David!)

Next up will be the Christmas special – a presumably stand-alone story in which I hope we will see that Moffat has not misplaced his mojo. For the next series, I now have to sadly join the ranks of those who want to see the arc de-emphasised and a return to more of an anthology show. If this series' arc had been made to work it would have pushed Doctor Who to a whole new level. But, uh, it wasn't and it didn't.

More thoughts on *The Wedding of River Song*

[Posted on October 7, 2011]

24 hours on from writing my review of *The Wedding of River Song*, I'm still a bit shocked at how negative it turned out. And I still don't really understand why I liked it so very much less than, say, *The Big Bang*. But I did have two more thoughts I wanted to share; plus a lot of interesting points have been made in the comments, some of them deserving a public response.

How did the Doctor cheat death?

In one sense, I have no problem at all about this. We've been told repeatedly that the events at Lake Silencio are one of those Fixed Points In Time that David Tennant pulled out of thin air in *The Fires of Pompeii*, and so that those events have to happen. But, as Douglas Adams pointed out in one of the very brief prefaces to *Mostly Harmless*: whatever happens, happens. The events at Lake Silencio are whatever happened, and we now know that the fixed point was *never* that the Doctor had to die, but that the Teselecta robot had to be shot and burned. By arranging for the Teselecta to stand in for his 1100-year-old self, the Doctor had already solved the problem of his own death before the end of *The Impossible Astronaut*. It was never him.

So why did the Doctor not just tell everyone that? Because the Silence wanted him dead, and the only way to bring their sequence of plots to an end was by letting them believe they had succeeded. (Remember, there was a Silent at the lake, witnessing the events.) For this to work, Amy and Rory, and River and for that matter Canton, had to absolutely believe that they were seeing what they thought they were seeing.

That would have been fine, if emotionally tough on the Doctor's friends. But Old River badgered it all up with her unwanted compassion. By refusing to go through with her part in the pre-ordained Fixed Point events, by discharging her weapon harmlessly instead of shooting Teselecta Doctor, River created the paradox that caused time to collapse on itself. The purpose of the rest of the episode was to get to the point where River could be persuaded to do her job. And it's for that reason that the Doctor presumably initiated the very hurried wedding.

All of which would have been fine – rather clever, in fact – were it not for Canton Everett Delaware III turning up with his can of petrol and telling us these words: "I believe I can save you some time. That most certainly is the Doctor. And he is most certainly dead." Which was not true.

Note: telling *us* these words. You can easily come up with the in-story dramatic explanation for the lie: the Doctor lied to Canton, which is after all Rule Number One, "The Doctor lies". But, dammit *no*, Moffat, it won't do. The way that scene was set up, Canton's words were not just spoken to Amy-Rory-and-River, they were spoken directly to the audience. They were the words of the Grand Moff himself, raising the stakes and telling us that this wasn't going to be easy. The Doctor we were looking at was not "a clone or a duplicate or something", as Amy had it. We had Moffat's word. But it wasn't true.

You know what? Cut that line of Canton's, and the whole episode would work much, much better.

The River/Doctor relationship

I hadn't noticed it until my wife pointed it out, but the River/Doctor relationship is strangely passionless. We don't at any point have the sense that these are two people in love, beyond River's generic the-Doctor-is-the-most-wonderful-man-in-the-universe love, which everyone has. And there is certainly nothing passionate in his attitude to her. In fact, the whole relationship is based on nothing more intimate than very stylised flirting, not wholly dissimilar to what you might find in a Jane Austen novel.

So when the wedding comes, it lacks emotional punch, and the kiss doesn't carry any weight. Yet when Ross and Rachel got together on Friends, or Niles and Daphne in Frasier, or indeed Veronica and [SPOILER REDACTED] in Veronica Mars, there was a tension, an intensity that was wholly lacking between the Doctor and River. (Come to that, that intensity *was* present between the Doctor and Rose, though the nature of that relationship was much less straightforward and hugely more interesting.)

So what is going on here?

Well, it could be that Smith and Kingston are just not selling it. It's a possibility: I think Smith is a sensational Doctor, but he's strong in all the traditionally asexual aspects of the Doctor's persona – curiosity, intelligence, compassion, volatility – and not necessarily as a romantic lead. And I think Alex Kingston's performances as River Song have been uniformly horrible: mannered, arch, perpetually smirking. Mocking us. Like the Gimli parody in the Jackson *Lord of the Rings* films. So her inability to convince as someone in love is not a surprise.

But I'd like to think it's part of a broader plan. That by design, the Doctor is not really into the relationship, and that he's going along with it essentially because he needs to in order for his plan to work. Hence (going back to my earlier point) he initiates the wedding basically in order to persuade River that, yes, he knows he's loved, and can he now please go back to getting shot?

But the wedding fails to persuade River, maybe because she subconsciously knows his heart is not in it. Which is why he reveals to her that his body is in fact the Teselecta. And that revelation is the crack in the Doctor's otherwise perfect plan for disappearing without trace. Because River knows he's alive, and she tells Amy, and they tell Rory, and … At some point, it's going to get back to the Silence, isn't it?

Ambition

At the beginning of Series 6, I was very enthusiastic about the Big

Arc: "it's better to err on the side of asking too much of an audience than too little. I like it that Doctor Who is throwing so very much at the wall and seeing what sticks, and I love it that it trusts us enough to make sense of it all." I suppose my sadness with *Wedding* is that this series was set up to be so much more than any of the earlier ones, but didn't follow through. One response to that is to think they shouldn't be so ambitious next time; another is to say they should be *more* ambitious, try for the same level of complexity but invest more effort into coherence and co-ordination, so that in the end it all makes complete sense.

Eight years ago, in his review of the Ang Lee *Hulk* movie, Andrew Rilstone wrote something that has stayed with me: "The whole thing doesn't quite work, but it's the sort of failure one would like to see rather more of." That's pretty much how I feel about Series 6. Its failing comes about by trying to achieve too much and not quite managing; that's easy to forgive.

Series 6 summary and retrospective

The Silence's plan

The Silence believe that silence will fall when the Question is answered (*not* when it's asked, as we were originally told back in *Let's Kill Hitler*). Despite their rather confusingly chosen name, they (the Silence) believe it would be a bad thing for it (the silence) to fall. They want to prevent that from happening.

The Question is "Doctor Who?", and now that all the other Time Lords are dead, the Doctor himself is the only person who can answer that question. So the Silence reason that the safest thing to do is kill the Doctor so that he can never answer it.

The best, simplest, most efficient and straightforward way the Silence can think of to kill the Doctor is to wait for his companion to become pregnant, kidnap her, replacing her with a Flesh avatar, steal her baby daughter, train that daughter to become an assassin, imprison her in a space-suit, put the space-suit in a lake, and have it walk out of the lake and shoot the Doctor. It's almost toooo easy.

The tragedy of Series 6 is that actually, now I've had a couple more years to think about it, I find myself wondering whether in fact it *does* work – but Moffat never bothered to explain it to us. Here's my best attempt at laying out all the key events, from (more or less) the timeline of the Silence.

What actually happened and why

The Doctor is very hard to kill, in part because his mastery of timey-wimey means that even if he is killed (as for example in *Turn Left*) he pops up again on an alternative timeline.

So to kill the Doctor permanently and properly, the Silence need to make that death a Fixed Point – which Doctor Who mythology tells us can't be changed once it's happened.

Dorium tells us in *The Wedding of River Song* that Lake Silencio is "a still point in time. Makes it easier to create a fixed point." So the Silence plan that this is where the Doctor will be killed.

But merely killing the Doctor at a still point won't be enough to make a fixed point. To do that, they need the killing to be done by another time-saturated being. A Time Lord would be ideal, but they are all gone. So they plan to make a new time-being who they can use.

They can't make another actual Time Lord, but they can forge their assassin from someone with a "time head", as Amy memorably puts it in *The Impossible Astronaut*. As soon as Melody is conceived on board the TARDIS, saturated with time energy, the Silence kidnap Amy (*Day of the Moon*) and make the substitution. They take Real Amy to Demon's Run, and replace her with a Flesh avatar that she is unwittingly controlling in real time from light years away.

Real Amy's pregnancy continues as she lies unconscious at Demon's Run, while the Flesh avatar travels with the Doctor through episodes 3–6. The Doctor dissolves the avatar (end of *The Almost People*) and Real Amy wakes up in time to give birth to Melody.

Melody is herself replaced by a Flesh avatar, and Madame Kovarian escapes with Real Melody (*A Good Man Goes to War*). She's brought up on Earth, in the orphanage that Amy visits in *Day of the Moon* – hence the photograph that Amy sees there. She's trained to kill the Doctor.

Somehow – this isn't clear – young Melody finds herself in the backstreets of New York, and regenerates (closing scene of *Day of the Moon*).

Somehow – this *also* isn't clear – the regenerated Melody, now known as Mels, finds her way at a young apparent age to Leadworth, where she is Amy's school-friend (flashbacks in *Let's Kill Hitler*). Perhaps she went to Leadworth in the hope of finding her quarry there. (Timey-wimey bonus: Amy names her daughter Melody after her school-friend, who as it turns out *was* her daughter.)

Some years later the Doctor turns up and Mels joins him, at gunpoint, in the TARDIS (*Let's Kill Hitler*). She regenerates into River and tries to kill the Doctor, but her programming is not strong enough and her heart isn't in it. Instead, she uses up all her own remaining regenerations to *save* the Doctor rather than killing him.

The Silence realise that River will not willingly fulfil her role. She goes off to (why not?) study archaeology, but on the day she gains her doctorate Kovarian and the Silence return and put her into the spacesuit (the end of *Closing Time*), which is intended to *force* her to do her job.

In that suit, she emerges from Lake Silencio at the appointed time. But, thinking that the Doctor by the lake is the real Doctor, she resists both her programming and suit, and does not do as the Silence intended, instead discharging her weapon harmlessly (*The Wedding of River Song*). The Doctor is not killed, the fixed point is violated, and time collapses on itself (the start of *Wedding*).

The Doctor tries to persuade River to redo the killing, properly this time, because it's the only way to repair time. To this end, he submits to the wedding (not particularly enthusiastically to my eyes). His plan is that she will then *to the best of her knowledge* kill him, fixing time – though *he* knows and no-one else does that it's the Teselecta that will be shot and burned.

But because the wedding turns out to be not enough to persuade River, the Doctor reveals his secret. Knowing this, River goes through with what she now knows to be a staged fake killing (*The Impossible Astronaut*) – and *this* killing, rather than the Doctor's actual death, is the fixed point. (Actually, it always was, but no-one knew it.)

Subsequently, River's older self returns to *The Impossible Astronaut*, this time as an observer. She *appears* not to understand what's happening at that point – but that's because she's playing dumb to avoid giving the game away to Amy and Rory.

But because River knows that the Doctor survived, and can't keep a secret, she eventually does tell Amy and Rory (the very end of *Wedding*).

So the Doctor's secrecy plan is compromised. That doesn't seem to have had any consequences yet, but who knows what might be planned for Series 8? The Silence have stopped coming after the Doctor only because they believe their plan has worked, and that he was killed at the Lake Silencio fixed point. If they find out they were mistaken, they will presumably come for him again.

So did it work?

Well, yes.

But no.

All of these suggested solutions are perfectly good speculation, and just the kind of thing that I enjoyed thinking about as the series progressed. The problem is that now it's over we're still speculating. A finale has a duty to *show* us the solutions we've been grappling for throughout. And it Just. Didn't. Do it. At this stage we shouldn't be speculating any longer about why it was River, In The Lake, With The Space-suit. We should be saying "Oh, so *that's* why!" and telling each other how impressed we are by how it all tied together – like we did with the Doctor's jacket in *Flesh and Stone*.

I would *love* to sit down with Moffat for half an hour over a beer. I'd want him to tell me whether my version of events above is correct, and fill in the details – like how Melody found herself on the streets of New York. But more importantly, I'd want him to tell me why Series 6 never explained itself. Why he brought it so achingly close to be being the best series of anything ever, but didn't quite bother to join up the dots.

Because it was so close.

Christmas 2011: *The Doctor, the Widow and the Wardrobe*

[May 17, 2012]

Unfortunately, this is going to be a very tedious excuse for a review, because once again, I'm going to be overwhelmingly positive. I was very disappointed by the final episode of Series 6, and remarked that "Next up will be the Christmas special – a presumably stand-alone story in which I hope we will see that Moffat has not misplaced his mojo". And indeed we did.

I remember, on first seeing *DW&W*, thinking that the beginning and end were outstanding but the middle was lacking. On watching it again, I kept waiting for the beginning to conclude – for the outstanding bit to come to an end – but it just kept surprising and delighting me. That said, the first twenty minutes or so, up until they go through the box into Narnia, really were a catalogue of all that is sensational about Who.

It's not just the individual qualities. It's the juxtapositions. The crash-bang-wallop opening is followed by the gentle humour of the Doctor's first hapless encounter with Madge. More startling, the Doctor's goofy exposition of the modifications he's made to the house runs into the brick wall of Madge's repressed sadness at the loss of her husband and her inability to tell the children; and then that's capped by a piece of honest-to-goodness wisdom from the Doctor:

"Every time you see them happy you remember how sad they're going to be. And it breaks your heart. Because what's the point in them being happy now if they're going to be sad later. The answer is, of course, because they are going to be sad later."

Stated baldly, it sounds like a crude collision. In fact, it's anything but. Sympathetic direction lends the progression a sense of inevitability, but as so often its Matt Smith's luminous performance that really sells it. Like Tom Baker he is believable as a childlike figure, darting delightedly from one minor excitement to the next: "A window disguised as a mirror, and a mirror disguised as a window!". But very much unlike Tom, bless him, Smith also convinces as the ancient wanderer who has seen too much, and who speaks to Madge from the depths of a genuine and heartfelt compassion. He is surely the Doctorest Doctor we've ever had.

Following on from that delicious character-based opening salvo, the actual story, once it gets started, has an almost impossible standard to live up to. And sure enough it does fall away a little, a very little, in the middle. The business with the ents is fine, and makes a perfectly good rationale for what follows, but honestly isn't particularly inspired. Yet even here, we repeatedly get glimpses of the Doctor's endlessly exasperating yet kind nature:

Lily: I don't understand. Is this place real? Or is it fairyland?

Doctor: Fairyland? Oh grow up, Lily!

[A beat]

Doctor: Fairyland looks completely different.

And then the conclusion – Madge has to tell the children that their father is dead; and then, he's not. Is it a cheap Happy Ending? Not for me, but then I have three children so I am a sucker for family stuff. It's too easy for me to imagine what it would do to Fiona and the boys if anything happened to me; bringing Daddy back at the end *DW&W* was very powerful for me. And it made enough narrative sense for me to be able to swallow it.

So all of this leaves me wondering whether I've completely misinterpreted Moffat. Because he is now the show-runner, we've been assuming he's all about the series-long arc – and to be fair, he did that brilliantly in Series 5. But if I am not being too harsh in saying that he muffed it in Series 6, that still leaves him as the master of the one-off. I'm on record as saying that the previous Christmas special, *A Christmas Carol*, is one of my very favourite Who episodes; now *DW&W* joins it. And come to think of it, *The Girl in the Fireplace* and *Blink* were also very much one-offs. And although *The Empty Child/The Doctor Dances* was a two-parter, it stood alone within Series 1. Apart from introducing Captain Jack (thanks a lot, Steve!), it could have come anywhere in the Series 1 chronology.

So my new theory is: Moffat is the master of the self-contained story. Which I guess means that the way the Series 5 arc turned out was just luck.

Just kidding, of course. That wasn't luck, it was genius. The challenge for Moffat now is how much to dial back the Crazy from its Series 6 level, so that he can make something as close as possible to that level of ambition and flamboyance while retaining a hard, coherent narrative core.

Series 6

Series 6 had been broadcast in two blocks – one in spring and one in autumn, with summer breaking apart the two halves of the *Good Man Goes to War/Let's Kill Hitler* two-parter. That structure worked pretty well, leaving us plenty of time to work up an appetite for the second half of the series and to speculate about all the mysteries the first half had set up. Series 7 took this mid-series break approach even further, broadcasting the two blocks in different years. As a result, it could hardly help but be approached as two more-or-less separate very short series.

This series of two halves faced three challenges – one for each half, and one for the series as a whole: saying goodbye to Amy and Rory; introducing a new companion; and bringing the Doctor back down to earth after his realisation at the end of Series 6 that he'd become too big.

Episode 7.1. *Asylum of the Daleks*

Aaand we're back! Hit the ground running: the Doctor inside the eyestalk of a giant Dalek statue, a woman pleading for help. And straight away he's thinking. You can hear it in every word he speaks. This episode is going to demand a lot of suspension of disbelief, but Smith is on top of his very considerable form, and holds it all together. The clarity of his enunciation, the care in his choice of words – it all speaks of a Doctor not quite sure of his own place in the universe, but – as always – impishly, imprudently curious. I can't help myself: I'm drawn straight back in.

And speaking of quality of acting: Amy's half-choked-off "Rory" as he leaves her dressing room is perfectly judged. Amy's and Rory's story in this episode is very rushed and not really believable; but if it fails, it's certainly not due to any lack of commitment on Karen Gillan's part, nor Arthur Darvill's. I don't believe Doctor Who has *ever* had such a trio of extraordinary actors, able to sell the moment even in the midst of the most unlikely and distracting situations.

From the titles, we cut to our first look at Clara. On watching this episode for the second time, the clues are all there right from the start. The circular door that she boards up looks how the inside of a Dalek's eye-stalk would look; so does her circular screen. The boards, of course, would never suffice to keep Daleks out. She throws away not just the soufflé but the dish that it's in – something you would never do. Everything about Clara is too bright, too breezy, too artificial. And yet the ending, when it came, took me completely by surprise. *Asylum* is an episode well worth watching twice, so that you can catch the tone clues that all is not as it seems in Clara-land.

The heart of the story is a neat reversal – a sort of counterpart to Series 5's *Victory of the Daleks*, where the World War II allies recruited them. This time around they recruit the Doctor. Why don't they just exterminate him? They explain:

Dalek Prime Minister: Does it surprise you to know that Daleks have a concept of beauty?

Doctor: I thought you'd run out of ways to make me sick. But hello again. You think hatred is beautiful?

Dalek PM: Perhaps that is why we have never been able to kill you.

It's been a recurring theme since the 2005's Series 1 that the Dalek's view of the Doctor doesn't match his own view of himself. He doesn't like being called the Predator of the Daleks. But on the "perhaps that's why" line, Smith doesn't react extravagantly. He holds his face stiff; stiff even. Doubt is creeping into his mind. A fear that there is justice in the Dalek's comment. It's quiet moments like these that lift *Asylum* above a mere romp and lend it real weight.

With that said, it *is* a romp, most of the time:

Doctor: You're going to fire me at a planet? That's your plan? I get fired at a planet and expected to fix it?

Rory: In fairness that is slightly your M.O.

Doctor: Don't be fair to the Daleks when they're firing me at a planet!

Which of course brings me to Rory. One thing I've not really brought out in the Series 5 and 6 reviews is my growing affection for Rory, and his commendable good sense. With Amy so flighty and the Doctor so Doctorish, it's often Rory who provides the solid ground for the rest of the characters to orbit. But to reduce him to this would be a disservice: there's a real insight in his character, a pragmatism alongside the self-sacrifice (as when he tries to give Amy his anti-nanocloud bracelet) and a sly wit. Although I said earlier that Donna may still be my favourite of the new-series companions, the Amy-and-Rory combo beats her hands down.

Which is why it's such a dirty trick that *Asylum* begins with them broken up and divorcing. I can see what Moffat was trying to do here. Amy and Rory's story was told by the end Series 6, yet he wanted to keep them around because he presumably liked them as much I did. But just to bring them back in with "and then they started travelling with the Doctor again" – especially after the elegiac coda of *The Doctor, the Widow and the Wardrobe* – would have felt terribly lame. Moffat wants conflict, and I won't blame him for that. But to dump us in the middle of the divorce and the put it all back together again in half an hour is not just rushed, it's frenzied.

Still, there are moment even in this subplot that work superbly. I mentioned Amy's half-hearted call to Rory as he walks out of her dressing-room near the start. When Amy is the first of the three principals to awaken after they land on the asylum planet, it's notable that she calls out "Rory! Doctor!" in that order. And then there's Amy's dismissive delivery of her non-explanation to the Doctor: "Oh, stuff! We split up, what can you do?" It rings false: we know it, the Doctor knows it and Amy knows it.

The subtlety of all this is astonishing, especially in the context of an episode whose USP is the presence of every Dalek design from the series' history. This is the kind of thing I think of whenever I hear people claim that the classic series was better than the revived version. It's a claim that doesn't bear up under the slightest examination: every single actor in pre-1989 Doctor Who is munching the scenery. Even in universally lauded stories like *Genesis of the Daleks* or *The Talons of Weng-Chiang*, the actual acting is dreadful: arch, mannered, declaimed, more suited to a Regency-era costume drama than to the kind of story Doctor Who tells. We've come a long way since then.

And then we have the high-point of the episode – the big reveal at the end, which I have to admit brought actual tears to my eyes even the second time I watched it: the Doctor's discovery that Clara is a Dalek, and her own gradual acceptance of the truth. It takes a lot to sell an idea like that, and it's to the episode's credit that it carries you along with it, right into the long, long moment when the Doctor stares at her – for once in his life, lost for words.

The word "appalling" gets over-used a lot now. It's taken to mean "not very good", so that for example a sub-par episode of *Buffy* might get described as appalling. This episode reminds us what the word means. What they did to Clara appals. It's literally inhuman. *Asylum of the Daleks* gives it its full value.

So I didn't expect to say this, but it comes out as one of my very favourite episodes.

And a special bonus: "You're a tricycle with a roof." How can you not love that?

In praise of Rory (consisting mostly of a digression about how terrible Torchwood is)

I've written a lot about superlative performances from Matt Smith, and quite a bit about Karen Gillan. I wonder if my affection for Rory has got a bit lost in all of that. His role is obviously less flashy than the Doctor's, or indeed Amy's, so he doesn't get to shine in such an obvious way. Yet he's established himself as one of the most likeable characters in all of television, not just in Doctor Who.

I only recently realised why this is. He's one of only two adults in the whole Doctor Who universe. (Sarah-Jane is the other.) The Doctor himself of course is childlike, and we love him for it ("There's no point in being grown up if you can't be childish sometimes"). It's part of his character. But the main companions share the Doctor's tendency to rush off into situations they don't understand, assuming they can figure out the details later. Only Rory seems aware of what's really happening, of what the stakes are, and of what his decisions might imply.

Elsewhere in the Doctor Who universe, we have The Dreadful Torchwood. This of course was the other spin-off, aimed in the opposite direction from The Sarah Jane Adventures. Instead of aiming for the kids among Who's fans, it would aim at the adults. It would be an adult programme dealing with more serious and darker themes, in a deeper and more mature way than the parent programme could do.

That is a description of a truly awesome TV programme.

Unfortunately, Torchwood isn't it.

It turned out that Russell T. Davies' idea of "adult" meant that the characters would say bad words; his idea of "more serious themes" meant that there would be a lot of snogging and shagging; and his idea of "mature" was that Every. Single. Character would be sexually incontinent, and constitutionally incapable of honesty or faithfulness or the slightest emotional maturity.

I don't know whether you picked this up, but what I just wrote included the observation that the notion of "maturity" as expressed in Torchwood actively excludes any actual emotional maturity – the ability to deal with problems rationally, for example, or to handle conflicts without throwing a tantrum, or to reconcile opposing points of view without melting down. In Torchwoodland, these abilities are not "mature". They can't be, since they don't involve Swearing, Snogging and Shagging, the Three S's that every Torchwood episode has to include. Throw in Selfishness, or rather Self-obsession, and you have Four S's.

So this was the first two series of Torchwood – a programme that was as mature as a thirteen- or maybe fourteen-year-old boy, a programme that left me truly worried that anyone could attain an adult age while still being quite so shallow and, well, childish.

I am not using the word "childish" here merely as an insult, but a dispassionate description. In every important respect, the Torchwood characters behave like children:

— When they see something they want, they take it without thinking about the consequences; when they think of something they want to do, they do it without thinking about the consequences.

— When things don't go their way, they get angry rather than finding ways to cope with the disappointment or work towards a solution.

— When people disagree, they shout at each other rather than making any effort at rationally picking apart the point of disagreement.

— When a mysterious artefact is found, someone *always* plays with it, not bothering to figure out what it is or what it does or what the consequences might be.

I am the father of three sons (ages 15, 13 and 11), and these are *exactly* the behaviour patterns that Fiona and I have spent the last decade and a half helping them to outgrow. They are, for that matter, the behaviour patterns that nursery-school teachers work to help four-

and five-year-olds to outgrow. I can only assume that the nursery schools in Fictional Cardiff twenty years ago were really, really bad.

What makes Torchwood even worse is that the characters, as well as behaving like children, live in a child's world where they are insulated from all the consequences of their bad choices. However abjectly they fail to act like even adequately competent or decent human beings, let alone the front line in our battle against the Alien Menace, nothing bad happens to them. Again and again in Torchwood, people get shot. Shot with, you know, guns, which kill people. And again and again, they shrug it off – often sprinting merrily around a matter of moments after being shot. It's paintball with special effects. When someone finally does have the decency to be fatally shot in the middle of Series 2, it takes that person seven episodes to finally, decently, die.

All of this is exemplified particularly well in the last episode of Series 1, the absolutely abject *End of Days*. This is the episode, you will recall, in which most of the characters decide it would be a good idea to open the rift that will tear the universe apart, because it might – for example – let Owen see a woman again who he once fancied. Needless to say, everyone shouts at everyone else; after a while, to my cry of "Yes, finally!", Ianto shoots Owen. But, sure enough, something as trifling as being shot is not going to slow Owen down and he opens the rift anyway. *Of course* he does. Owen is *always* getting shot and walking away. You know how some people, whenever they're at a party, will do a favourite bit of coin magic? Owen is like that, but his trick is to get shot with no ill effects. So of course the rift opens, and out comes – I swear this is true – a Giant Monster, straight out of a 1970s Japanese Monster Movie, only with less convincing special effects. And it has a superpower, which is that everyone who sees it dies. Except that Captain Jack doesn't, because he rolled 18 for Constitution, and can't be permanently killed – a Special Power that comes in handy surprisingly often. (You know what Chekhov said: if there's an Invulnerability Superpower hanging on the wall in Act 1, then Captain Jack has to be killed over and over again in Act 3.) So, needless to say, this causes Godzilla to vanish in a puff of logic and all is well. I seem to recall that

Owen has mild chest pains for a couple of days.

Ugh. You know, it hurt me to type that synopsis of *End of Days*. It gave me a brain-hurt. I had hoped never to think of that episode again.

And by the way: Captain Jack is the Worst. Hero. Ever. Of all the Doctor Who characters to build a spin-off on, they picked the one who is absolutely incapable of any dramatic tension, due to that little can't-be-killed thing. And John Barrowman can't act. He just can't do it. He always looks like he's in pantomime. I keep expecting him to shout "Oh no it isn't!" or "He's behind you!" The greater the emotion of the moment, the more obviously he's not up to conveying it – he hams, he gurns, he bulges his eyeballs, but the one thing he doesn't do is act. I will admit that he is pretty; a lot like Matt LeBlanc, in fact. Like LeBlanc, he doesn't act; in part because, like Joey from Friends, his character is fundamentally shallow.

In fact, spinning Torchwood off from Doctor Who and building it around Barrowman's Captain Jack is about as dumb as spinning off a sitcom from Friends and building it around LeBlanc's Joey Tribbiani.

Har. See what I did there?

So these are some of the reasons that watching the first two series of Torchwood was a punishment. (To be fair, the self-contained Series 3, *Children of Earth*, was rather different and much better.) I would cross the street to avoid having to meet any of the Torchwood principals.

Against that backdrop, Rory is a breath of fresh air. He feels like a real person, somehow parachuted into the middle of all the insanity. (Yes, he was plastic for a couple of thousand years, but I think we can overlook that.) He's the grown-up. One area where Buffy scores over Who is the relentlessness with which characters' actions have consequences. In that respect, Buffy feels much more like real life than Doctor Who does. Rory would be at home in that world; Amy would be completely lost.

I'd buy Rory a pint.

Episode 7.2. *Dinosaurs on a Spaceship*

I have a complicated relationship with this episode. I love dinosaurs – I'm a dinosaur palaeontologist in my spare time – and I love spaceships. I love dinosaurs *on* spaceships. But I didn't love *Dinosaurs on a Spaceship*, at least not the first time I watched it. I felt the episode was lazy, that having made its brilliant titular statement, it just sat back and expected everything would be OK. It felt like high concept as a substitute for, rather than driver of, plot.

Mind you, I watched it on my own, on the laptop, late at night when I was tired after a very demanding day at a conference, so I really wasn't seeing it under the best circumstances. So a few months later I watched it again, with the boys this time, and enjoyed it a lot more. It didn't seem quite so thin, and I picked up on more of the individual moments: things like the Doctor's disappointed delivery of the line "I liked you before you said missiles", and Rory's undemonstrative but very apparent distaste when the Doctor unthinkingly kisses him for having a good idea.

Then I watched it a third time before writing this review, and now I really don't know what I think any more. It's certainly disjointed, and the cast really doesn't start to make sense. Queen Nefertiti was a complete non-event: there was no reason at all for her to be there, and once there she didn't achieve anything. Same goes for the explorer guy whose name I couldn't even remember (which is telling in itself; he's John Riddell). Hands-down winner in the Guest Cast Stakes was most certainly Arthur Weasley as Rory's dad Brian, in a role that expressed perfectly appropriate bafflement with just enough bashful heroism to balance it out. I'd be happy to see more of him. But overall the sense is that Chibnall just threw together a more or less random bagful of characters and hoped something would happen to make them work.

It didn't.

This kind of thing was a much more frequent problem during Russell T. Davies' reign. His account of his time as showrunner, *The Writer's Tale*, is in equal parts fascinating and infuriating. We already quoted his words on *The Fires of Pompeii*, from page 177 – "keeping lots of things in the air, making them look pretty, hoping that they won't crash." But merely putting a lot of Stuff in a place together doesn't in itself get you anything. It doesn't give you character, or a plot, or relationship. And that's as true in *Dinosaurs on a Spaceship* as it was in *The Fires of Pompeii*.

In particular, the attempt to develop sexual tension between Nefertiti and Riddell doesn't come off at all. They can trash-talk at each other all they want; they can raise their eyebrows and purse their lips and exchange meaningful glances. But there's no spark there, no hint of anything that could lead to any kind of relationship. (As indeed there could hardly be between an Egyptian queen from 3350 years ago and a British hunter from the early 1900s, who will not even be able to understand a word of each other's language once they're out of the TARDIS's translation field.)

And while I'm on the subject, I have to say I am not at all keen on the continuing sexualisation of the Doctor himself, this time seen in the prelude with Nefertiti. My problem with it is that by adding this aspect to the Doctor's character, it subtracts from the distinctiveness of that character. More is less. By taking on elements of other hero characters, he becomes more like every other hero. But we already *have* every other hero: the whole point of the Doctor is that he's *not* the same. Just as his solutions are based on thought and insight and compassion rather than violence, so his relationships are based on companionship and fraternity rather than romantic/sexual attraction. The more you erode that, the less you have.

Shall I complain about *Dinosaurs on a Spaceship* some more? Yes, I shall. Regarding the Mitchell and Webb robots, surely the first requirement of comic-relief characters is that they should be comic? I assume the humour was supposed to derive from the robots having such petty personalities, like young children. But that kind of writing needs a light touch that Chibnall lacks. P. G. Wodehouse might have made it work. Douglas Adams almost certainly would. But Chibnall is no

Wodehouse or Adams.

Oh, and one more complaint, if you'll indulge me: a pet hate. When Brian has been slightly shot by a robot, Rory administers a painkiller. "This won't hurt", he says. "Ow!", exclaims Brian as the needle goes on. And Rory says: "I lied". Really, Rory? *Really?* Et tu, Rory? That joke was very slightly funny when I first heard it (maybe in *Die Hard?*). It was already a travesty by the time Gollum recycled it as "Smeagol lied" in *Return of the King*. To hear it from Rory is ... it's like a betrayal – especially after everything I said about Rory The Grown-Up last time. It's inappropriate to his character. It's like that Big Train sketch, where Florence Nightingale has to be dragged effing and blinding from the room.

And yet, and yet ...

There we were at the end, watching Brian with his cup of tea and box of sandwiches, sitting in the TARDIS doorway, looking down at the Earth. A moment encapsulating both wonder and contentment. There's more magic in those ten seconds than in the rest of the episode put together. I can't not love that.

Episode 7.3. *A Town Called Mercy*

A Town Called Mercy is one of those episodes that reaches towards greatness – which I applaud – but doesn't get there. Some episodes (*The Waters of Mars*, *Victory of the Daleks*, *The Impossible Astronaut*) come close but just fall short. In the case of *A Town Called Mercy*, the flaws are more fundamental, and despite some delightful moments, the whole things is pretty unsatisfying.

The episode is built around two things: the Wild West setting, and the moral dilemma of what to do with Kahler-Jex. To my mind, the first element works triumphantly. No doubt historians could pick a hundred holes in what is admittedly more of a Wild West theme-park town than anything very realistic. But it feels coherent enough to work as a setting for a story. It sets up some classic Doctorish moments ("Tea. But the strong stuff. Leave the bag in"). Maybe best of all, it looks gorgeous. Like *Vampires in Venice* and *Vincent and the Doctor*, it's a feast for the eyes. Against these bright blue skies and broad desert vistas, the visuals of last week's spaceship-bound dinosaur romp seem not just claustrophobic, as was surely intended, but unimaginative – something that Doctor Who can never afford to be.

Many of the best moments are wordless. Having been thrown outside the town's perimeter, the Doctor picks himself up, makes a move to step back inside, and sees the townspeople draw their guns as one. His half-disappointed half-resigned "Ooohh" is yet another example of Matt Smith's pitch-perfection. Shortly afterwards, having been rescued by Marshall Isaac, he looks absurdly pleased with himself, as though he's done something terribly clever and expects the townspeople to acknowledge it. More seriously, later in the show as he watches Jex's videos of the experiments he's performed, Smith's impassive expression is more powerful than any amount of howling rage would be.

It's not just the Doctor, either. Amy and Rory's shared silent moment when the Doctor says he's going to get past the Gunslinger "with a little sleight of hand" is priceless. Likewise the preacher's gently despairing shake of the head as the Doctor rides his horse away on the line "He's called Susan, and he wants you to respect his life choices". I admire the way these moment are generously thrown away rather that built up into big comedy moments. There's a genuineness and spontaneity about them that makes them feel like expressions of character rather than comedy for its own sake.

All of this made me wonder who the director was, since he'd done such a good job in this area. It turns out to be Saul Metzstein, who I'd not heard of before. He had also directed *Dinosaurs on a Spaceship*, which I thought was much weaker in this respect. Perhaps much of this comes down to the acting. *Dinosaurs* was handicapped by the watch-me-acting performances of Riann Steele as Nefertiti and Rupert Graves as Riddell, whereas *Mercy* runs mostly on the assured work of the three core characters. Metzstein would go on to direct the Christmas special and two episodes in the second half of Series 7, which we'll get to in due course.

But no amount of fine individual moments can save *A Town Called Mercy* from the fundamental problems of the moral dilemma at its heart. It's set up cleanly enough: Jex is, unambiguously, a war criminal. The Gunslinger has a legitimate desire not only for revenge but for justice. The question is whether the Doctor should hand Jex over to be executed, or protect him.

In many respects it's a classic Doctor Who arrangement, not all that dissimilar to the much-praised (but not actually all that good) "Do I have the right?" sequence in *Genesis of the Daleks*. What makes *Mercy* more interesting than *Genesis* is the Doctor's identification with the condemned criminal. Initially this aspect is handled with a very light touch. "War is another world", says Jex. "You cannot apply the politics of peace to what I did. To what any of us did." The Doctor walks quietly away from the table during this speech, and has no further contribution to make to the conversation. Any intelligent viewer will make the connection. But sadly the episode doesn't trust us to get it, so Jex hammers the issue home: "Looking at you, Doctor, is like looking to a mirror. Almost. There's rage there, like me. Guilt, like me. Solitude."

Yes, yes. We get it.

That loss of trust in the audience is troubling, but not fatal. What really kills the episode is that it just doesn't seem to know what to *do* with the moral dilemma. It lays the pieces out on the board, but doesn't know what moves to make. After discovering his crimes, the Doctor decides to hand Jex over. Why? We don't know, he just does. Amy grabs a gun to prevent him, and isn't overpowered by the townspeople. Why not? We don't know, she just isn't. The Doctor changes his mind and decides to save Jex. Why? We don't know, he just does. And then comes the worst moment in the whole episode: as Jex hesitates and the Gunslinger approaches, Marshall Isaac flings him aside and is himself killed, by the Gunslinger.

As a piece of plotting, this is an appalling misstep, because it means that at best the Doctor's change of heart has meant that one man has died instead of another – and for that matter, a good man has died instead of a bad one. Worse, at the end of the episode, Jex will deliberately kill himself, in a rather vague stab at atonement. So the upshot of this is that all Amy's intervention achieved was to ensure that Isaac and Jex *both* died instead of just Jex. Simplifying the equation, Amy killed Isaac. Not deliberately, but that will be scant consolation to his wife and children.

We can only draw the conclusion that the town of Mercy would be better off if the Doctor and his friends had never come. Isaac would have kept Jex in jail until the Gunslinger gave his ultimatum. At that point, they would have reluctantly handed him over, he would have died (just as he does anyway) and Isaac would have lived.

This kind of thing bothers me intensely – especially when, as here, it's presented as a happy ending. The story as it stands could still have worked had the Doctor recognised that his interference had been a net negative; had there been some soul-searching and introspection. But there's no hint of this.

So we're left with an episode that raises profound moral questions, but has no idea what the answers are. By moving the pieces around the board fast enough it hopes to bamboozle us into not noticing. I sort of wish it had worked.

Episode 7.4. *The Power of Three*

Just like its immediate predecessor, The *Power of Three* aims at something unique and significant, but falls badly short. And like *Vincent and Doctor*, that failure comes about not so much through actual mistakes as through failure of nerve. *Vincent* is an episode that splits fannish opinion more or less cleanly into lovers and haters, with not much in between. But among those who love it, there's almost unanimous perplexity over what the invisible turkey was doing in there. It wasn't necessary, and in the end all it did was take the focus away from the much more interesting story that was being told about Amy's coming to terms with losing not just Rory but even her memory of him, and about Van Gogh's unique perception that could see that process taking place. That core thread, plus Vincent's complex mental state, plus the gorgeous visuals, should have been easily enough to carry that episode with no need for invisible poultry. But someone felt that a monster was necessary; and so a monster we got.

The failure of nerve that besets *The Power of Three* is different. There is an alien threat, as indeed there needs to be: the threat is central to the episode. The problem is that the resolution of the threat is muffed so badly that it casts the rest of the episode retrospectively into a bad light. The last fifteen minutes makes no sense at all, even by *Doctor Who* standards, and that incoherence rewrites the first half-hour into absurdity.

Which is a shame, because those first thirty minutes are a lovely little chamber piece. Amy and Rory's ambivalence over how strongly to commit to their Doctor-free normal life is a real issue, and one that is explored with a light touch that's a welcome surprise coming from the pen of Chris Chibnall, not an author generally noted for subtlety. The Doctor's initial bafflement at this, and gradual creeping understanding, is nicely realised. His attempts to join them in their normal life are played for laughs, successfully. And the backdrop mystery of the black cubes is handled very realistically.

The mystery of the cubes' sudden appearance may owe something to Nicholas Fisk's juvenile novel *Trillions*, but that's not something that worries me too deeply. Doctor Who has a long and honourable tradition of reworking ideas from many different sources. In Fisk's novels, the eponymous Trillions are tiny geometrical shapes which fall from the sky like snow rather than simply appearing overnight while, conveniently, no-one is watching. That is an aspect of *The Power of Three* that really stretches credulity, even by Doctor Who standards. One aspect of the cube mystery is how they appeared: can we really believe that not one of the seven billion people on the planet saw one arrive? Or, even more unlikely, that none of the millions of always-on surveillance cameras in Britain caught an appearance?

But skipping lightly over that problem, the world's reaction to the cubes is frighteningly believable: the initial burst of panic, fading to mute, uncomprehending acceptance, and eventually the absorption and even welcome of the cubes into everyday life – their use as paperweights, door-stops and menu-card holders. If anyone doubts that this is exactly how public reaction would play out in life, we need only think about those surveillance cameras we just mentioned. Somehow, while we were all looking the other way, the UK – our pleasant little nation – became the most surveilled country in the world, as measured by number of CCTV cameras per person. Yet there has been no outcry over their slow invasion, and now we take it for granted that every car-park, every playground, every shopping centre, will be infested with cameras.

It gets worse. Thanks to the whistle-blower Edward Snowden, we now know that the NSA (National Security Agency) in America and GCHQ in Britain routinely listen in on our phone-calls, keep permanent records of who calls who when and from where, and track our emails similarly. We don't yet know how much Internet encryption they have cracked or subverted, and how much more of our private lives may not be private. This appalling police-statism generated something of a public response when the first revelations were made public, but with distressing predictability, the reaction seems to have been less with each increasingly outrageous revelation. It seems that whether we face domestic spying or little black cubes, we are quick to lapse into passivity. We're ripe for the plucking.

In Doctor Who, of course, we have the Doctor to save us from our slow invasion. In real life, we're not so lucky.

So. The cubes are a fascinating rhetorical device with limitless potential for satirical comment as well as a promising hard-SF proposition. Given the premise, the story could go in many different directions, all fascinating.

Oh dear.

I'm cool with the domestic comedy angle. It was genuinely funny, and also rather touching. But the sci-fi aspects were utterly bungled. Credibility was again stretched by the idea that *no-one* on the Earth had made a serious attempt to cut a cube open; and maybe even more by the Doctor's not doing so. Brian's dedication to watching his cube was funny, but made no sense given all the Doctor's technology. But far, far, far worse than these missteps was the plainly apparent fact that Chris Chibnall had no more idea what was in the cubes than we did. All that set-up, and no pay-off. It just doesn't do to show one of them firing lasers, one taking blood samples and one playing The Birdie Song. All that tells us is that a writer who couldn't think of anything hoped to bluff his way through by giving us *every*thing instead.

The hexagonal-mouthed drones made no sense at all, and were connected with nothing at all. The little girl whose eyes changed colour made no sense at all and was connected with nothing at all. The bad guy with the skin condition on the spaceship made no sense at all and was connected with nothing at all. Having explained his plan to the Doctor, he then obligingly retired, playing no further role, and left the Doctor to reprogram the cubes. Cubes which had suddenly started giving people heart-attacks after first having waited for a year. *Why* did they wait? No reason. No reason at all. Why did the Doctor leave all those sleeping patients on the bad guy's ship to be blown up? No reason.

I criticised *Dinosaurs on a Spaceship* for thinking it was enough to take dinosaurs and spaceships and ram them together at high speed in the Large Idea Collider. But at least it took the trouble to ram them together. There was a reason for the dinosaurs to be *on* the spaceship. *The Power of Three* doesn't even do that. It's half an hour of cubes, then five minutes of hexagonal-mouthed drones, then five minutes of Skin-Complaint Guy, then five minutes of the Doctor making everything nice. Sheesh.

And the reason I'm so upset about this is because the first half-hour was one of the best the show has produced. Not only funny, not only politically astute (unless I'm reading too much in), and not only emotionally touching – but truly fascinating. It was the first half-hour of a truly great episode. But *The Power of Three* wasn't it. It's the worst dropped ball in the whole of the revived series.

Finally: the title *The Power of Three* is altogether meaningless, isn't it? If anything, *The Power of Seven* would have made more sense, given the significance of that number to the Big Bad. The final scene suggests we're meant to read it as referring to the power of the Doctor/Amy/Rory combination, but in fact the resolution to the story doesn't involve any meaningful input from the latter two at all: it's all down to the Doctor. So *The Power of One* would have been an option, but they really should have called it *The Slow Invasion*.

Episode 7.5. *The Angels Take Manhattan*

And so we come to Rory and Amy's exit. I found it astonishing that towards the end of Series 6, several commenters on my blog were saying they were ready for the Ponds to leave. To me, they remain by some distance the most fully realised, and likeable, of all the Doctor's companions, and on that basis I'd have been happy for them to continue indefinitely.

On the other hand, I did have some sympathy with the perspective that their arc had been completed – that when the Doctor dropped them off at their new house at the end of *The God Complex*, they'd successfully made the transition away from being Doctor Groupies into Real Life. In that light, the Doctor's visit to their comfortable domesticity at the end of *The Doctor, The Widow and the Wardrobe* made perfect sense as a bookend to the Amy-and-Rory story: no longer were they joining in with the Doctor's adventure; he was joining in with theirs. So there's a real case to be made that that should have been their last appearance.

On the other hand, while that approach would have had more structural integrity, it would have robbed us of these last few episodes with the Ponds. And however harsh I might have been on *Dinosaurs on a Spaceship* and *The Power of Three*, I really wouldn't have wanted that. (Not to give the game away in advance, but that opinion has if anything been strengthened by the subsequent episodes with Clara, a character that has not engaged me in anything like the way the Ponds did.)

Still, having passed on the option to bow out cleanly on the elegiac coda to the Christmas episode, Moffat had taken on the heavy responsibility of giving the Ponds another and different goodbye – one worthy of them. He'd already left them in comfortable suburbia once; doing the same thing again was not going to get the job done. He had to come up with something radically different.

As so often with Moffat's recent episodes – and in flagrant contrast to his nearly packaged early stories – there seemed to be a lot of loose ends. Places where something happened that was cool, but didn't tie in strongly with the rest of the story. Rory was captured, along with River, by the henchmen of the gang boss Mr. Grayle – but why? They had no use for him, and just shoved him in the cellar. Come to that, why did Rory find himself in 1938 with River at all? Was he touched by an Angel without knowing it? We've never seen that happen before. The bit where River broke her own wrist to escape from the Angel's grasp was cool, but didn't follow from anything and didn't lead to anything.

But this was one occasion where I didn't care too much about such oversights. *The Angels Take Manhattan* worked, and worked well, for three important reasons.

First, the time-travel paradoxes, and especially Melody Malone's novel, were very well handled. By treating that novel initially in a knockabout way, playing it for laughs, Moffat cleverly worked in a real sense of the uncanny as its significance became more apparent. If at times in Series 6, we've felt rather clubbed over the head by Moffat's time-travel paradoxes, this time we felt drawn along a path, discovering the way as we went.

Second, the emotional pitch was superbly judged. It would have been so easy to overplay – I cringe internally when I imagine how Tom Baker would have gurned his way through some of the *Angels* scenes, and the RADA-approved anguished faces he would have pulled. The simple fact is that we live in an age of much, much better acting than thirty years ago. The stock "fear", "anger", "shock" and "sadness" faces of 1980s television are a bit of an embarrassment when we see them now, and the strongest reason why old Doctor Who episodes seem dated – a much worse problem than the cheap props and unconvincing sets. Matt Smith has consistently underplayed throughout his tenure, to very good effect – witness, for example, his response to Cleaves killing the ganger in *The Rebel Flesh*. Because he's nearly always been very composed in his emotional responses, it's all the more affecting when the mask does slip, as it does several times in *Angels*. There are similarly well-modulated performances from Amy and particularly from Rory, as he assimilates the news that he is predestined to live out his life in the Angels' battery farm.

Best of all, the episode turns, not once but twice, on choice. It's a theme that emerges repeatedly, not least in the Doctor's repeated insistence that once you know your future you can't change it. It's to the unflappable Rory's credit that, knowing this, he nevertheless damned well *does* change the future, when he and Amy choose to jump off the roof. You can argue about how much sense that does or doesn't make, but as a summary of Rory's character it's spot on. He understands the situation; he makes a decision.

And if Rory's choice is rather beset with Yes But How Would That Work?, Amy's choice at the end of the episode is clearer and starker. I admire how the ending harks right back to the Series 5 episode *Amy's Choice*. Back then, although the choice was presented as between two different worlds, it was always really between the Doctor and Rory. Now, at the very end of Amy's time, the same choice is presented; and she makes the same decision, but this time without hesitation. In the middle of a series about monsters and aliens and time-travel, the emotional core has been Amy's and Rory's relationship, and it's striking that when it comes down to the final moments, that relationship is the *clear* winner. Staying with the Doctor isn't even an option for her. It's not on the Things To Consider agenda. She's going with Rory, end of. Could it be that some of the Doctor's evident anguish is not so much at the thought of losing Amy, but more his realisation of his own dispensability? He's been used to being the centre of the universe, especially his companions' universes. But Amy's grown up. Must be hard for him to take.

So I love the ending, despite all the obvious objections. ("Yes, but why don't they take the TARDIS to 1930s Boston, get a train to New York and rescue Rory?") It hinges on Amy having – well, I was going to say that she'd out-grown the Doctor, but that's not exactly right. She still loves the Doctor and hates to lose him. But she loves someone else more, and that's as it should be.

The worst flaw is that we never see Amy and Rory in their 1930s New York life, so we're not given a lot to go on beyond Amy's afterword in the Melody Malone book. I for one could have used a swift montage of their growing old together.

That flaw is somewhat addressed by *P.S. What Happened to Brian and the Ponds?*, a scene that was written (by Chris Chibnall, but let's not hold that against it) but never filmed, apparently due to time constraints. It did eventually get put together as an animated storyboard with dialogue. It's easy to find on the Web and well worth tracking down, providing some sort of closure for Brian. It shows Amy and Rory's adopted son Anthony delivering a letter from them to Brian, about a week after he'd last seen them. Even as a storyboard, it's touching – in part due to Mark Williams' typically understated performance.

In the end, despite the logical gaps, I'm really happy with *The Angels Take Manhattan* as Amy and Rory's swan-song. Their exit is worthy of them.

Christmas 2012: *The Snowmen*

The numbering gets complicated here. The 2012 and 2013 episodes are, together, considered to constitute a single series, even though the last of the 2012 batch, *The Angels Take Manhattan*, felt so much like a series closer. Since this is the first time a single series has spanned multiple years, the Christmas special is uniquely part of the ongoing story rather than a complete standalone. Wikipedia seems to consider the first of the next batch of episodes to be number 6 (so that the 2013 half-series runs from 6 to 13), and *The Snowmen* is rather inelegantly designated as episode x2 (with the previous Christmas special being episode x).

During the Russell T. Davies era, after the first Christmas special (*The Christmas Invasion*, David Tennant's debut), I learned to have low expectations at Christmas. The remaining specials (*The Runaway Bride*, *The Voyage of the Damned*, *The Next Doctor*, *The End of Time* parts 1 and 2) were all pretty weak by the general standards of the series. They're more than usually stupid episodes, suffering from a severe case of Davies' Disease, i.e. the tendency to just not care whether it makes sense or not.

So it was a delightful surprise when Moffat's first Christmas special, A *Christmas Carol*, turned out to be one of my very favourites. And the best parts of *The Doctor, The Widow and the Wardrobe* arguably surpassed even that (though the story as a whole didn't work quite so well). As a result, I came into *The Snowmen* with some actual expectations. Did it meet them?

It did, mostly. Part of what's so good about Matt Smith's portrayal is that he continues to surprise. You can't always predict how he's going to react to a given situation or person, but (with very few exceptions) whatever he does do proves completely consistent with his character. This time, post-Manhattan, he starts out misanthropic and self-absorbed, but is quickly drawn into Clara's problem by a quintessentially Doctorish mixture of curiosity and compassion.

While I am not particularly interested in Madame Vastra and Jenny Flint, I was delighted to see the return of Strax, the Sontaran Nurse from *A Good Man Goes to War*, a character of rich comic potential. I'm reminded of Marvin the paranoid android from *The Hitch-Hiker's Guide to the Galaxy*. He was originally intended to be a one-shot character because he is essentially built on a single joke; but Douglas Adams kept finding things for him to do, and because of the excellent writing the character became established as eventually one of the most loved in the series. In the same way, the single note of the Sontaran nurse joke seems to have legs. We laughed a lot at Strax.

But of course much more important is the new companion, Clara Oswin Oswald, played by Jenna-Louise Coleman. For now the signs are good but the jury's not yet in. At times her delivery was rather too mannered, in (I hate to say) a rather River Songish way. But then that might be because she was portraying a governess, which is intrinsically a rather mannered role. We'll see how she gets on when she's able to settle down and start being herself.

What I loved about her character was how fiercely but casually intelligent she is. The Doctor often works well when bouncing off a character who is his equal, but previous attempts to provide him with one have not always come out well. Back in the day, Romana was meant to be cleverer than Tom Baker's Doctor, but we were told this rather than showed it, and never quite swallowed it. More recently, Martha was meant to be a counterbalance to Rose, someone capable of a more equal relationship with the Doctor, but in the end her character wasn't interesting enough and Freema Agyeman wasn't enough of an actor to pull it off. Then of course there is River Song, but in her case being a step ahead of the Doctor manifested in a collection of quirks, tics and catch-phrases that reminded us of nothing more than a not-very-clever person trying to appear clever.

Against that backdrop, it was refreshing to see Clara's intelligence actually in action rather than merely hearing it described. The whole sequence with the umbrella was a delight – quick, clever and believable.

Better still was the Doctor's palpable enjoyment, and satisfaction in having found someone who could keep up with him and maybe even get a step or two ahead.

And I just loved this image of Clara climbing the invisible spiral staircase up to the TARDIS above London. Shame it was on screen for such a short time.

Finally on positives, fine performances from Richard E. Grant and Ian McKellan as the bad guys. So, negatives? Just two, really.

First, the plot was close to making sense (on Doctor Who's own terms) but didn't quite take the trouble to fill all the cracks. I don't think it would have been much extra work to smooth over the rough patches, but it worries me that Moffat apparently didn't care enough to do so.

Secondly, and this is not really a criticism of the episode per se but of the developing Series 7 as a whole, I don't really have any sense of where it's going. Series 6 had a very strong (if flawed) arc; Series 5 was more episodic, but still felt as though it was heading in a specific direction, with its developing Amy/Rory story and its hints of the Pandorica climax. Up till now, Series 7 has felt like a buffet on a pinball table. I hope that over the next eight weeks it settles into a more coherent through-line.

Anyway, I am really looking forward to *The Bells of Saint John* now!

Episode 7.6. *The Bells of Saint John*

And so we're under way with the second half of Series 7 – which really feels like Series 8, as it's separated by the best part of a year from the first half, and has a new companion replacing the much-loved Amy and Rory.

I don't think the mid-series breaks help at all – they break the flow and momentum, and I find that I don't think of Series 6 as being a unit as I do with Series 5 or indeed Series 1. This time, with the much longer break, the effect is even stronger. And I suspect it has the effect of making Moff feel that the episodes need to be more eventy. Episodes 6 and 7 of Series 5 were the relatively self-contained *Vampires in Venice* and *Amy's Choice*. I don't think there's room for those kinds of "mid-series" episodes in the Split Series format. And the programme is the poorer for it.

Well, anyway.

The Bells of Saint John had rather a nice little prequel, which I saw after the main episode. Andrew Rilstone argues that it shows the Doctor at his best: cosmic loneliness distilled down a gentle, thoughtful moment. I wouldn't go quite that far, but I think the episode proper could probably have used a bit more of that.

Bells faced the classic problem of introducing a new companion while telling an actual story; or it sort of did. But not so much, because we've already met (a version of) the character not once but twice. That should have made things easier for *BOSJ*, but somehow the episode didn't seem to capitalise on this work already done, choosing instead to do an essentially cold intro to the character. More frustratingly, it didn't quite seem to be the same character.

And that's important, because at this point, the character looks like a definite downgrade. In *The Snowmen*, there was a quickness to the governess, a sharpness of mind (particularly in all the business with the umbrella) that sold me on the idea that the Doctor might feel an immediate bond with this person, and even become obsessed with tracking her down through time and space. This time around ... not so much. She came across much more as Generic Spunky Girl Companion, with none of that sense of her being a worthy counterpart to the Doctor.

But who is she? One commenter on the blog suggested that the mystery would be best left unresolved – that answering it would be an anti-climax like the one presented by *The Phantom Menace*'s explanation of The Force as caused by midi-chlorians. I don't buy that, though. The Clara mystery is presented as a mystery; I want it to *be* one. I don't think we can make an analogy with midi-chlorians at all, because they weren't the answer to a mystery. The reason they are so universally derided is because they're the answer to a question no-one was asking. The Force worked perfectly well as an ambiguous do-what-you-want-with-it bit of hand-wavy spirituality/magic. Trying to ground it in science-fictional terms not only introduced all sorts of new problems to do with heredity and suchlike, but was completely unnecessary in the first place. Whereas from *The Snowmen* onwards, Clara has been explicitly pitched to us as a mystery that the Doctor is out to solve.

So in doing that, Moff has made a promise, and he needs to come through on it. And because of Series 6, I am not as confident as I used to be that he will do that.

But enough of Clara. What of the actual story?

It worked for me. I know enough about networking to realise that the premise is nonsense from step one, but then Doctor Who has never stood or fallen on the realism of its premise.

The point of the WiFi monster is that that it's a retargeting of the primal ghost-in-the-machine fear for today. It's certainly becoming a familiar trope in Who: something familiar, even comforting, that becomes the conduit for a threat. We could point to the mobile phones of *Rise of the Cybermen*, the televisions of *The Idiot's Lantern* and the sat-navs of *The Sontaran Stratagem*. For that matter, the Weeping Angels of *Blink* and other episodes, while not everyday objects, are essentially the kind of statuary we're used to seeing in public gardens (at least those of us who are English).

Of course this idea of the familiar made uncanny goes back much further than the series reboot in 2005. The most obvious example from the old series is the Autons – shop-window dummies come to life. But it's really only since Doctor Chris that this theme has become such a recurring part of the show, to the point that now when you think of Doctor Who, you think of the TARDIS, Daleks, and familiar technology gone wrong.

Now to a certain point, I am perfectly cool with this. I certainly have no truck with those who criticised *BOSJ* for resembling *The Idiot's Lantern* because it has screens and *Partners in Crime* because it has a businesswoman. Doctor Who has been running for fifty years, and has racked up 234 stories. It simply isn't possible to keep coming up with stories that don't resemble something in that vast back-file.

More than that: it's right and proper that Doctor Who should do some of its work with the familiar rather than on alien worlds. And if I may be permitted to stretch a point a bit, it's laudable if one of the effects of Who is to make us see the familiar in a new way, perhaps even to look with wonder on marvels that we've grown overly used to. Wireless Internet is magical – I well remember less than a decade ago being astonished and delighted by it. It's good to be reminded of that.

And yet ...

It can all feel a bit consequencesey. Roll the D20: technology of the week comes up WiFi! The Big Bad will be ... (roll another D20) ... The Great Intelligence! Roll a D8 and find that the baddie's collaborator will be: a businesswoman! There's nothing wrong with any of these choices. The problem is that they're not made to work together, and so they feel arbitrary. What is it about the businesswoman that makes her a particularly appropriate conduit for the Great Intelligence? We don't know. Why does it choose to use WiFi rather than 3G? We don't know.

Worst of all, the WiFi doesn't seem to *represent* anything. The premise, that joining an uncanny network can steal your soul, is creepy, but it's not made to *mean* anything. And that seems like a terrible missed opportunity. Because of course the ubiquitous availability of WiFi *does* steal your soul – just slowly and incrementally rather than all at once. That is an issue worth thinking about, and one that Doctor Who is perfectly capable of shedding light onto. (I've resisted having a smartphone for many years because I've feared it would dominate my life. Then I got one for a recent business trip when I knew I'd need to meet up with people at an airport. Within four days, I was constantly checking my email on it – exactly as I'd feared. So I got rid of it when I returned from that trip, and don't intend to replace it.)

And here's another metaphor that was dropped on the ground. The office that operated the soul-stealing operation was staffed by people who had been there for years, in at least one case decades – people who had literally given their lives to their jobs. There again is a pervasive and important issue, and one that the programme could usefully address via metaphor. At its best, Doctor Who has a capacity for insight and even wisdom which can illuminate complex concepts. Right now, it doesn't quite feel like it's trying to do that, just racing through each standalone episode. I'd like to see the programme work a bit harder to draw out the substance of its raw materials.

Part of the problem might be the lack of two-parters recently. Although *The Rebel Flesh/ The Almost People* ultimately muffed its exploration of the human status of the eponymous beings, I look back on it now and think that at least it tried – the two-part format gave it the time and space to stop and breathe and look at its issues. I find myself wondering whether the problem now is a failure of nerve: because the ideas in *BOSJ* were certainly rich enough to sustain a two-parter with no fat. Slow down, Moff! Show us the concepts! Explore the ideas! Leave us to chew them over for a week before you start to resolve the problem.

Anyway – I am complaining more than I should: I thoroughly enjoyed the episode, particularly the (in retrospect obvious) twist when the Doctor confronted Miss Kizlet in her office and turned out to be a replicant. And there was a brief – too brief – moment of real poignancy when her history became apparent.

As is so often the case in recent years, this episode raised questions – potentially important ones. Of course we already have the core mystery of the series: who is Clara, and why does the Doctor keep running into her? To this, we can now add: why was the family's WiFi password based on Clara's previous dying words "Run, you clever boy, and remember"?

And why did Clara's call to technical support get routed to the TARDIS? Her conversation with the Doctor runs thus:

"Where did you get this number?"

"The woman in the shop wrote it down. She said it's the best helpline in the universe."

"What woman? Who was she?"

"I don't know. The woman in the shop."

So who was the woman? We're being invited to assume River Song, I suppose, or perhaps Rose; or maybe Aged Amy, although this story surely takes place too late in Amy's timeline. (She must have been about 20 when we met her, and a decade had passed by the time of *The Angels Take Manhattan*, so she was 30 then. Assuming Rory and she were sent back to 1938 again, that would make her 105 years old by the time of *The Bells of Saint John*.)

In her book of places to go, the "Property of Clara Oswald age 9″" inscription has the age repeatedly crossed out and rewritten to form the sequence 9, 10, 11, 12, 13, 14, 15, 17, 18, 19, 20, 21, 22, 24. What happened to ages 16 and 23? She seems too methodical a girl to have just overlooked them. Do I detect the distinctive aroma of timey-wimey?

The problem is that, after the let-down at the end of series 6, I just don't trust the Moff like I used to – I'm not confident that all the clues necessarily point anywhere. That may be a bit harsh: after all, the spectacular denouement of Series 5 did tie up most of its loose ends, most notably the "wrong" jacket in the garden in *Flesh and Stone*. But somehow I feel that Who has slightly lost my trust and has to win it back again. I could do with one of these mysteries being resolved very soon indeed, so I can relax and believe in the master-plan again.

...

And another thing: who did make the TARDIS explode at the end of Series 5? We never did find that out, did we?

Episode 7.7. *The Rings of Akhaten*

There's lots to like in *The Rings of Akhaten*, starting with the decidedly Star Wars cantina-ish marketplace full of outlandish aliens all getting along perfectly well together. It feels sort of like a place, rather than a set. (My wife and I both spotted the cantina homage immediately, and it's since been confirmed by costume designer Will Gorton.)

But on the other hand ...

I am afraid I am really starting to lose patience with Clara. When we first met her as a human, in *The Snowmen*, her defining quality was her quick intelligence and articulate speech. This time, we get:

"So we're moving ... through actual ... Time. So what's it made of? Time? I mean, if you can just row through it it's got to be made of stuff like jam's made of strawberries, so what's it made of?"

It's incoherent and ignorant, all at once. That is not the Clara that the Doctor was so delighted by. And then this terrible, terrible anti-climax:

"OK. So ... so ... so. So ... I'd like to see, I would like to see, what I would like to see is ... [looong pause; Clara spins on the spot an looks straight at the camera] Something awesome."

The poverty of imagination and intellect is palpable.

So that's a problem with the writing, of course, by debutant Neil Cross. Unfortunately, the acting is no better. Coleman perpetually addresses the camera, preens, mugs, and generally behaves more like a children's TV presenter than an actor. When she cracks a joke, she stops to feel pleased with herself. It's "look at me" acting.

It's taken four episodes for me to reach this conclusion – partly just because I am trying to be charitable but also for another reason. In *Asylum of the Daleks*, Clara wasn't human, so Coleman was playing a character impersonating her own idea of what she's like – a subtle challenge. In *The Snowmen*, she was playing a character who led a double life, and so who we needed to see to be acting. In *The Bells of Saint John*, she spent quite a bit of time being dead, so can be forgiven for not quite feeling her usual self. But this time, there is no excuse: Coleman's job is to play the role of Clara, to play it straight, and to show us a person we can believe in. And we don't.

Am I being harsh by going on so much about Clara's deficiencies of writing and acting (and for that matter direction)? Maybe. But the companion is a hugely important character. Doctor Who is a series in which only two characters recur from week to week, so when one of them is below par that's 50% of the recurring cast. That's bad. When Riley was not particularly compelling in Buffy series 4 and 5, that was unfortunate but not disastrous, because he was one of an ensemble cast of ten (Buffy, Joyce, Willow, Tara, Xander, Anya, Giles, Spike, Dawn). But if Clara's character doesn't pick up soon, it's going to undermine the whole of the rest of the series (and likely the next one, too).

All right, I am done criticising Clara now. Let's move on …

As a morality tale, *Rings* has something going for it. As I noted above, all the different alien species seem to get on fine together. They're in a functioning society, and that is a valuable thing. (It's more than you can say for most purely-human societies in Doctor Who.) But as is so often the case with fictional ideal societies, a dark secret lies beneath the surface. This time, it's that peace is bought at the price of a periodic sacrifice: a young girl, The Queen of Years.

Now this is a fascinating set-up. It parallels Ursula Le Guin's famous short story *The Ones Who Walk Away from Omelas*, in which (to quote Wikipedia) "Everything about Omelas is pleasing, except for the city's one atrocity: the good fortune of Omelas requires that a single unfortunate child be kept in perpetual filth, darkness and misery." (I seem to remember reading something similar as an in-passing part of Neil Gaiman's *American Gods*, but I wouldn't swear to it.) In Doctor Who, the situation is simplified by killing the sacrifice outright, or at least handing her over to the evil god to be killed; in some respects *The Beast Below* more closely parallels the Omelas situation.

Much could be done with this. Sadly, not much is. The situation is rather thrown away because of the crowd's complete non-reaction when the Queen, who we'd been led to believe would merely be required to sing, is taken by the evil god. Is that what the crowd expected? Is it what they wanted? Are the horrified? Are they complicit? If so, do they feel guilty? It's impossible to tell, because they all just go on singing.

Now it would be possible to interpret this charitably, as indicating that the production team wanted to leave the crowd neutral to provide a blank moral canvas that we could project our own attitudes onto. Done well, this could draw us to think more intentionally about our own choices – buying clothes made cheaply in Far-East sweatshops, for example. But in fact the effect was one of moral abdication. The civilisation, and so the programme, just didn't seem to have a stance.

Once the girl is sucked into the Pyramid Of Doom, the Doctor and Clara go off to rescue her on a flying motorbike (a motif appearing for the second consecutive week). Jolly japes ensue with some Tusken Raiders armed with blue light. The Queen is rescued, and so needless to say a vampire breaks out of a fish-tank and a nearby planet turns into a giant pumpkin – I hate it when that happens.

Once the Giant Pumpkin starts making faces, the only way to defeat it is with a leaf, which happily Clara has to hand.

Now all of this sounds much more negative than it really is. Despite my apparent scorn for the plot, I did thoroughly enjoy the episode – not least for its visual loveliness and its powerful use of genuinely beautiful diegetic music. It's always fun to see the places and things, and the Doctor himself remains a delight (though perhaps less so in this episode than in most).

Still, *The Rings of Akhaten* feels like two thirds of a great episode: rich setting, beautiful visuals and sound, fascinating moral dilemma, and … then nothing much. Just some running around and shouting. It feels like the production team did all the groundwork, then went for lunch when they should have been building an actual structure on that foundation.

The more I think about it, the more I think that a lot of my favourite stories post-2005 have been two-parters. Moffat's debut, *The Empty Child/The Doctor Dances*. The genuinely chilling *Impossible Planet/Satan Pit*. RTD's high-point, *Army of Ghosts/Doomsday*. Possibly my favourite story of the entire run, Paul Cornell's masterly *Human Nature/The Family of Blood*. Moff's *Silence in the Library/Forest of the Dead*, which has been diminished by the development of River Song but at the time was sensational. And the first of the 11th Doctor's two-parters, *Time of Angels/Flesh and Stone*.

Interestingly, even when a two-parter doesn't really work, like *The Hungry Earth/Cold Blood*, it has space to include remarkable individual passages. In particular, the scene where the Doctor talks to the Silurian prisoner Alaya is my favourite single scene from any Doctor Who ever.

Of course, two-partness is no guarantee of greatness. The judgement of history has not been kind of *The Aliens of London/World War Three*, and it's not clear that Tom MacRae and Helen Raynor had enough clear ideas of where they wanted to take the Cybermen and Daleks in their respective two-parters. But in general, things are better when the episodes have time to breathe.

The Rings of Akhaten could really have benefitted from that more generous structure. A whole week to luxuriate in the visual and aural feast before things got serious, and then a good solid hunk of time in the second part to explore the moral ramification of the society's choices, for the Doctor's and Clara's responses to be considered and explained, and for the resolution to be worked through properly.

Shame.

The reason Doctor Who is the best thing on TV – a discussion

When I posted the following appreciation of Doctor Who on my blog, Gavin Burrows took exception to my analysis, and we went through some back and forth. With Gavin's kind permission, I'm including his comments (and mine) below the article that provoked them. Read on ...

— **Mike** —

Here's the real reason that Doctor Who is, by a huge margin, the best thing on television. Even a rather forgettable episode like *The Rings of Akhaten* can provoke such different reviews as those of Millennium Dome, Andrew Hickey, Andrew Rilstone and myself.

None of us was blown away ("It definitely wasn't anything like as terrible as the previous episode" – Andrew Hickey) and we all had significant criticisms. But we all found interesting things to discuss about it. And this is the important point: we all somehow landed on different interesting things.

Even when Doctor Who is off its game, it generates discussion like no other programme: not just discussion of the plot-speculation kind ("what is Clara?") but investigations of the nature of drama, of metatextuality, of morality, of the nature of the soul, of whether scientific and moral world-views are in opposition or mutually reinforcing, and so much more.

Much as I love Veronica Mars, The West Wing and Arrested Development, none of them do this. I admire all those shows more than Who, but I don't *love* them as much. No other show throws out so many issues for the unsuspecting viewers to chew on, or catalyses anything like the same breadth of discussion.

Doctor Who, I salute you!

— **Gavin** —

Granted, there's a psychic-paperness to Doctor Who. But it seems to me there's a half-empty as well as a half-full reading of this. Don't we all tend to pitch in because it's essentially *incomplete*? ... made up on the hoof, throwing up some semi-considered concept then chasing to the next one in the whirligig rush of everything. You have to make up how those dots can join across those great gaps, which inevitably results in some quite different pictures getting drawn.

This seems almost certainly true of plot speculation. We can argue about things which happened series ago, and in fact we do. But also, I think, it's true of the world-view stuff as well. Which is okay in itself. If *The Rebel Flesh* didn't come to any great conclusions about the nature of identity, well it was only a Saturday night TV show to start with. But there's got to be some dots, some semblance of a picture, or we might as well all separately dream up TV shows then act surprised when they vary.

And I have to confess I find myself leaning more and more to the butter-side-down view as the show continues …

— Mike —

I'm not sure I buy that at all, Gavin. The world is not at all short of shows that fail to connect their dots. But none of them attracts the kind of critical attention that Doctor Who does. What other popular TV series even attempts to explore issues of humanity and identity as *The Rebel Flesh* did? The only candidate I can think of is Dollhouse (and that hardly qualifies as "popular", sadly).

— Gavin —

I think a lot of us who grew up watching the old show have an emotional investment in it, which kind of pulls our critical faculties along with it. There's also the feeling that those emotional investments vary in themselves, that at a young age we were using the show as a trigger for our imaginations and were being encouraged to do so by elements like the Doctor's mystery. So we're kind of used to making stuff around it.

Plus the new show is always selling itself as not just another adventure story, as something whose dots will connect. (Principally in Moffat's comments, but also within the show – its attitude to itself.)

And lastly it should be said – sometimes it *does*. I just think it's not doing that great a job of it at the moment.

— **Mike** —

I'm not sure you're giving enough credit here. When Who rebooted in 2005, I watched it with curiosity, not devotion. It took an episode or two for me to starting thinking "Hey, this is really good". I wasn't reading it through Baker-coloured glasses, but seeing it for itself.

— **Gavin** —

True enough, I did the same. I was first expecting something much more akin to the TV movie. But I think as soon as I did buy into it, all the old feelings came back. It was like bumping into a childhood friend who had done an equal amount of growing up in parallel time.

Now I feel more-or-less as I did over the later Davies years, like an old friend has turned up out of the blue but now they've been crashing on my sofa for three months and I really wouldn't mind them leaving. Or at least the immediate creative team.

— **Mike** —

I do know what you mean about the later Davies years. By the end of series 4, it seemed apparent that he'd long run out of ideas that he *wanted* to do, and was just making stuff up to keep the wheels turning. (Although: *Midnight*.) I don't yet have that feeling regarding Moffat, and yet ... I can see that it could go that way. *The Wedding of River Song* greatly diminished my respect for Moff, not just because as an episode it was incoherent, but because its failure to properly answer the questions posed by the rest of the series retrospectively rewrote *The Impossible Astronaut* et al. to be less than they were. So as late as *Closing Time* I was prepared for series 6 to be the best of them all; but now it looks much less than series 5.

Where to now, Saint Steven? I'd like to see him take some inspiration from his first few scripts, the ones produced during the RTD era. Looking back at *The Empty Child* now, it feels almost claustrophobic compared with the absurdly wide reach of recent Moffat episodes, and that claustrophobia is used to good effect. With the space afforded by the two-part format, the ideas are fully developed, the plot makes complete sense in its own terms, and the whole has a clarity to it that more recent wham-bam episodes have lacked. I wouldn't want him to try to go back to what he was doing then; but I'd love him just to look squarely at it, recognise the properties that made it great, and let that inform the direction he takes from here on.

The thing is, when RTD stepped down, I was delighted – like most people, I think – that Moff was replacing him. I can't think of anyone on the current writing roster who would similarly excite me. I know Mark Gatiss has been mooted, but honestly his episodes (*The Unquiet Dead*, *The Idiot's Lantern*, *Victory of the Daleks*, *Night Terrors*) have not been the greatest. I think I heard someone say Chris Chibnall was under consideration, which would be a disaster.

Given my personal choice, I'd love to see Paul Cornell do it when Moffat's had enough. He's only written three episodes (*Father's Day* and the *Human Nature/Family of Blood* two-parter) but I loved all three, and I particularly like the more contemplative approach that he takes.

— **Gavin** —

Regarding *The Empty Child*: Yes indeedy. Crazy freaky inexplicable stuff happens. Then it all gets explained. Perhaps Moffat's best instincts were always better employed as a writer, rather than a showrunner.

Given one of the show's main weapons is its ability to reinvent itself, I think I'd most like to see a total reboot. Give someone else a go. Give a whole bunch of someone elses a go, showrunners, writers, central characters, the lot.

— **Mike** —

I don't know, Gavin. I am still hoping that the Moff will pull the rabbit out of the Series 7 hat.

Episode 7.8. *Cold War*

Cold War is an old-school episode. It represents the first base-under-siege story for a long time – arguably since *The Waters of Mars*, which would make it Smith's first, and probably only, base-under-siege story. It's easy to imagine it with Jon Pertwee in the Doctor's role, and Jo Grant running around with him. In itself, that's neither a good nor a bad thing, but it's actually rather refreshing to revert to such an classic template after such a long break.

As always with such stories, there's a cleanness to them that arises from the constraints. We're on a submarine. We know what the backdrop is. Who know who the *dramatis personae* are. We know no-one can get in, and no-one can get out. The pieces are laid out on a well-defined board, and the set of possible moves is also constrained.

The submarine ought to be a superb setting for this kind of story because of its inherent claustrophobia, but somehow *Cold War* didn't seem to capitalise on this. Despite the cascades of water, the sub didn't really feel like a tin can under 600 meters of water. Perhaps it's because we never got any real sense of the internal geography: it felt like a bag of unrelated submarine-themed locations rather than parts of a whole, real place. That's a missed opportunity.

Of course it's always hard to convey a place well in a short story. In Firefly, the ship Serenity feels very real and lived-in – but then it's had the benefit of fourteen 45-minute episodes to develop that sense of solidity. To be fair to *Cold War*, the Nostromo in *Alien* has much the same set-of-disconnected-locations feel, despite the two-hour running time. It just seems to me like this is something worth working harder at. There's an intrinsic power in a sense of place, and that is much more than mere atmosphere. The submarine in *Cold War* may *feel* like a submarine, but it doesn't *convince* as one, and the result is that much of the jeopardy is diffused.

Still, it's hardly fair to over-criticise *Cold War* for this when the failing is so commonplace – see for example the settings of some earlier

Eleventh Doctor episodes: the monastery/factory in *The Rebel Flesh/The Almost People*, and the ark ship in *Dinosaurs on a Spaceship*. (In the world of video-game level design, it's considered a sign of failure if a map has to include teleporters: it shows that the natural geography didn't work well enough to fly without the artificial boost. By this criterion, the ark ship is a complete failure. In *Dinosaurs*, the characters repeatedly simply appear where they need to be by magic – not even an attempt is made to tie the parts of the ship together.)

A more fundamental problem with *Cold War* is that it seems confused about the nature of the Ice Warriors. We're told early on that they live by an uncompromising warrior code; that if you attack one of them, you attack them all; that the planet is forfeit. That is an implacable philosophy, but because it's a well-defined one it's something the Doctor could work with. He could find a way to use that warrior code to manipulate the Ice Warrior, Grand Marshall Skaldak, into doing what he wants. That would make sense. It would be a sort of intellectual judo; if written well, it would be fascinating to watch.

But that's not what we get. Instead, the Doctor appeals to its better nature – which we've been explicitly told it doesn't have.

Now on one level it's touching to see the Doctor trying to cultivate mercy. But everything about the Ice Warriors' nature says that this is the wrong enemy to try it on. From Skaldak's perspective, mercy is not just weakness, it's dishonour. He would probably conceive it as a deadly insult to the recipients of the mercy. It's great that the Doctor is so humanitarian. But with such an implacable soldier as Skaldak, it's weak plotting that not only is this something the Doctor tries, but it turns out to be the right approach to take.

Come to think of it, there's an awful lot of implacability in the classic Doctor Who menagerie. When it comes down to it, who *can* the Doctor appeal to for mercy? Obviously not the Daleks, as they believe it is right and proper that all non-Dalek life should be eliminated. Not the Cybermen, as they believe that humans are better off when converted into more Cybermen. Not the Weeping Angels, as they scarcely communicate at all and certainly don't negotiate. And of course not the Ice Warriors, because of their rigid code of warrior honour. Four classic enemies, four very different, but equally solid, reasons why you can never expect mercy from any of them.

Against that backdrop, it becomes all the more important that we have the Silurians. Alone among the great Doctor Who monsters, they are capable of empathy, understanding, compromise and mercy. That of course makes it all the more unfortunate that the new series' Silurian stories have so far been bungled, and all the more imperative that they return in a story worthy of them during the Twelfth Doctor's tenure.

The more I think about *Cold War*, the more unsatisfactory I find its resolution. When the Doctor's appeal for mercy seems to have failed, he explicitly threatens Skaldak with mutually assured destruction. Given that he is generally the very embodiment of the peaceful approach, it's very out of character. And then Clara butts in with another appeal for mercy, and an allusion to Skaldak's daughter. And, KAPOW, just that like, it's enough. Skaldak violates his ancient warrior code, shaming (as he would see it) both himself and the humans, and relents. Skaldak's response is even more out of character than the Doctor's MAD threat.

Beyond the sheer inconsistency, there are two things about this that bother me.

One is that we're increasingly seeing the Doctor try to solve problems by emotional appeal rather than by clear thinking. Both of these approaches are perfectly valid of course, and it's right that the Doctor should use both when appropriate. But it's a problem that he seems to be tilting more and more towards the touchy-feely (or humany-woomany, if you must) and away from the scientific. For me, the Doctor is at his best when he is clever. Not the talk-nonsense-so-fast-that-all-the-words-run-together "clever" that we saw so much of in late Tennant, but the carefully-piecing-things-together clever that characterised early Smith.

The second thing that bothers me about the resolution is this. For the second episode running, we have the Doctor attempting some specific solution. (In *The Rings of Akhaten*: overloading the pumpkin with memories and lost potential. This week: appealing for mercy). For the second successive week, he's insufficiently persuasive to make the solution work. And for the second episode running, Clara then steps in and does *exactly* what the Doctor did, but for her it works. What's the message here? That a cute smile counts for more than intelligence, empathy, knowledge, experience, and the years of hard work done to attain those qualities? Is Skaldak overcome by Clara's *sex-appeal*? Is that what it's come to?

Well, all of this seems very negative, and I suppose it does reflect *Cold War*'s failure to grip me. It should have been tense, but I didn't feel it. Some effort was made to draw distinct characters among the submarine crew, but I didn't buy them. Taken together with the lack of a sense of place, and with the incoherent conclusion, I can only say that I didn't consider *Cold War* a success (although I understand a lot of other people did).

Episode 7.9. *Hide*

A couple of days before I wrote this, Terry Pratchett wrote in the Guardian about his response to the revived series when it appeared in 2005: "It reminded me of my childhood, which is always a nice thing at my age. But, at last, we had a Doctor who could act – and I mean could really act." He was talking about Christopher Eccleston, of course, but he's put his finger here on a broader issue – to my mind, the single most important one separating the pre-1989 Doctor Who from New Who. And it's this: standards of acting have increased tremendously during the gap. We see it in the Doctors (and let me throw in once more that Smith is the best yet), and in the companions (Rose was the pioneer, but Amy was the first one I've ever seen look genuinely terrified).

I mention this because the best part of *Hide* was not the plot, the writing or the special effects – or even the Doctor. It was the pitch-perfect performances of the two supporting characters: Dougray Scott as Professor Alec Palmer and Jessica Raine as Emma Grayling.

Almost every Doctor Who episode introduces us to a handful of brand new characters, expects us to care about them, then resolves their story all within 45 minutes. Not surprisingly it's usually too rushed to really work. But this time, it does. It's largely down to the marvellously understated performances by Scott and Raine. But it probably also helps that the cast is small: apart from the Doctor and Clara they are the only characters on screen until very near the end. As a result they have time to grow on us, and for their story to slowly develop.

And it *is* slow. It needs to be – that's in the nature of the rather repressed, or perhaps merely over-cautious, relationship between them. It can only progress step by faltering step – to take a leap would shatter the personalities that these two people have developed. I love that at the end, the Doctor's advice to them about their relationship is so very low key: "hold hands". That's all they need at that point, and probably all they're capable of. Having overcome their coefficient of static friction, they'll figure out the rest when they're ready.

Here as elsewhere, Palmer sells the scene convincingly by doing almost nothing. You can see the wheels turning in his skull, but he conveys this with the subtlest of touches. We see the same approach elsewhere. One of the most affecting scenes is in the darkroom, as the Doctor and he are waiting for photographs to develop. The Doctor asks about the choices that led to his current lifestyle: "How does that man, that war hero, end up here in a lonely old house, looking for ghosts?" Palmer considers, just for a moment, and replies "Because I killed". It's a perfectly undemonstrative statement. It's not an anguished confession, just a statement of fact. "It does tend to haunt you", he explains. The emotions are there, but they're under the surface – exactly as with his relationship with Emma. The scene is beautifully underscored with very subtle music that perfectly complements the acting. It draws out the emotion rather than clubbing you over the head with it. The difference from, say, Christopher Eccleston's histrionic reaction to the lone Dalek in the episode of that name is palpable. (That's not in any way to criticise Eccleston – his reaction in that episode was absolutely right and proper for that character in that situation. But it's excellent that Doctor Who isn't locked into that one approach.)

All of this shows that modern Doctor Who is often at its best when dealing with a small, self-contained situations (*Blink*, *Midnight*, *Vincent and the Doctor*, *The Lodger*). When it reaches for Big, it often just can't fit everything into the available time, hence the plague of rushed resolutions (*End of the World*, *Gridlock*, *The Power of Three*, *Cold War*). The alternative of course is to make two-parters, but there are none of those in Series 7. By now it should be perfectly clear that it's just not possible to show us a whole new civilisation (in many stories), introduce us to characters, make us care about them, bring in a threat, advance the series arc and resolve the threat all in 45 minutes. So standalone episodes need to resign themselves to only doing *some* of those things, but doing them properly; and two-parters need to ensure they fully justify their extended running time.

Elsewhere, there are welcome signs of the Doctor's relationship with Clara sparking – something that's not been much in evidence since *The

Snowmen. This exchange is particularly unforced and rather delightful:

Clara: So where are we going?

Doctor: Nowhere. We're staying right here. Right here on this exact spot, if I can work out how to do it.

Clara: So *when* are we going?

Doctor: [Chuckles] That is good. That is top notch.

Clara: And the answer is?

Doctor: We're going always.

Clara: "We're going always."

Doctor: Totally!

Clara: That's not actually a sentence.

Doctor: Well, it's got a verb in it.

For a while there I was encouraged that perhaps this heralded a return to the much sparkier and sharper Clara of *Asylum* and *Snowmen*. But sadly it seems I was tricked by episode ordering. *Hide* was the *first* of episode of Series 7B to be filmed, so in fact the Clara that I liked was a continuation of, rather than a return to, the *Asylum/Snowmen* model; and the Clara that I've found annoying in episodes 6–8 is the development, or rather regression, of that character.

Oh well, let's not harp on about that. Let's enjoy *Hide* for what it is – a near perfect episode of Doctor Who, marred for me only by the bizarre use of the TARDIS to visit the pocket universe after we'd been explicitly told that it couldn't survive there. That wrinkle aside, the whole episode was rock solid, beautiful to look at, lovely to ride along with, and warm, gentle and frightening all at once.

We often talk about the flexibility of Doctor Who in terms of its ability to do sci-fi one week, body horror the next and a celebrity historical the week after. We talk about its flexibility in being able to set stories anywhere in time or space. It delights me that it also has the flexibility – if rarely – to tell an honest-to-goodness love story.

Episode 7.10. *Journey to the Centre of the TARDIS*

Journey to the Centre of the TARDIS has a lot going for it. The timey-wimey plot can be seen as a condensed version of the whole Series 5 arc, eventually resolved by the Doctor slipping back through a crack in time to un-happen the events we've seen; but it doesn't feel like Reset Switch cheat because we've watched him work to reach the point where he can do that. Visually, this is one of those episodes that is just nice to look at, with the TARDIS library particularly gorgeous. It's certainly a step up from the dingy stairwells of the TARDIS interior in *The Invasion of Time*, and indeed from the maze of twisty corridors, all alike, that engulf Amy and Rory in *The Doctor's Wife*.

It's true that the three salvage brothers are rather throwaway characters, and not particularly convincing ones. But once you look past that, the plot is not just extremely neat, but also truly disturbing. The nature of the zombies on the TARDIS is revealed slowly, left hanging as a mystery for us to think through before the Doctor spells it out. I particularly enjoyed the moment when the zombie pursuing Clara through the console room tilts its head on one side in that characteristic way. And I admired how Clara is shown flashes of her own past as hints of what she's seeing when she looks at a zombie.

The zombie versions of the characters, transformed by exposure to the Eye of Harmony, would be reasonably frightening just as monsters; they're worse as examples of body horror; but truly horrible as visions of what we might become. A recurring theme in Doctor Who, going right back to *The Aztecs* in William Hartnell's first series, is changing the past and its effect on the future. *Journey* gives this a twist by having the past, present and future all existing simultaneously. The zombies represent one possible future – one that will come into existence if the Doctor, Clara and the Van Baalen brothers are trapped in the Eye of Harmony room for too long. In another possible future – the one we end up in – those zombies never came into existence. Which of course is why they don't remain on the TARDIS at the end of the episode. We see, in this episode perhaps more clearly than ever, how the choices we make in the present affect the future.

And that's the point, isn't it? Going back into the past to change the future is a great sci-fi conceit, but the truth is that everything we do in the *present* changes the future. Once we get to the future (and we can't help but travel into it), we will look back on what we did now, in what will then be the past, and see how it changed the then-present. How is that any different? We imagine that if we could travel back a thousand years and make some small but significant change to what happened then, we might return to the present and find that the world is radically different. But if that's true, then it's also true that the choices our ancestors made a thousand years ago had profound effects on us; and if *that's* true, then it's also true that the choices *we* make today have profound effects on our descendants a thousand years into the future.

I find that a very positive message, if a little frightening. It's all very well for a post-apocalyptic survivor to go back in time to the present and warn us to change our future by doing something about global warming. But we're *already* in the present. What's to stop us changing the future *now*?

Although Doctor Who makes an effort sometimes to brush up against predestination, its heart is with free will: the power to make our own choices, and the awesome responsibility that comes with that power. The invention of "fixed points", however incoherent as a concept, is a useful plot convention that allows the writers to both have their cake and eat it. Certain special events (the eruption of Vesuvius, the destruction of the Teselecta at Lake Silencio) are fixed, so we can have predestination-based stories when we want them. But everything else seems to be up for grabs, and that's definitely the right way to go for a drama.

Constructing plots that have to arrive at an already known fixed conclusion is always difficult – as anyone who's watched *Revenge of the Sith* lumber towards its Vader-falls-into-a-volcano climax will know. To build an actual *story* under such constraints requires a great deal of craftsmanship. When we already know *what* the conclusion is going to be, the writer has to introduce tension by leaving us not knowing *how* we're going to arrive there. If such a story is to be anything more than a mechanical process of shifting the colours of the Rubik cube into place ready for the last couple of moves that complete all six faces, then it has to surprise us. That means bringing about an expected event in an unexpected way: ideally despite, or even because of, the protagonist's deliberate attempts to avoid that conclusion. That kind of writing can be done; I believe Mr. Shakespeare is considered to give uniform satisfaction. But to pull it off in 45 minutes while also fitting in all the usual Doctor Who stuff (aliens, monsters, exotic civilisations, character development, arc advancement) is nigh on impossible. (This is one reason why *The Fires of Pompeii* is such an incoherent mess.)

So given that what we did in the past affected what is now the present, and that what we do now affects the future, does it follow that it's our actual choices that determine this? There are scientists who will tell you no, on the basis of the following chain of reasoning: decisions are made by the mind; the mind is a property of the brain; the brain is made of matter; matter behaves deterministically (at the macroscopic level) or purely non-deterministically (at the quantum level). On this view, all our choices are either predetermined or random. If that's so, then we ourselves don't have any actual choice in the matter.

It's obvious to me (though I realise not everyone agrees) that this is nonsense. I know that *I* am making decisions, even if I can't convincingly explain what I mean by "I". For that matter, I think it's obvious that there is an "I" separate from the processes we're discussing from the very fact that we say things like "we ourselves don't have any actual choice in the matter". What does that "we ourselves" mean? Something other than the physical processes of the brain. The mere fact that there's part of us outraged (or, I suppose, delighted) at the possibility of not having free will shows that we're more than mechanism.

So when the Doctor and Clara see their zombie selves from the future, they're not seeing a fixed, unchangeable destiny. (That much is obvious, I suppose, from the fact that the zombies are gone by the end of the episode, never having actualised.) But it's more than that. They're not seeing one of several possible futures chosen randomly by non-deterministic physical processes in their brains. They are making actual *choices*; the outcomes are ones they have earned, rather than been handed by a mechanical universe or allotted by chance.

If this seems like a fine point of metaphysics, I don't think it is at all. To switch fictional universes for a moment, one of my favourite moments in all of the Harry Potter books comes towards the end of the otherwise rather forgettable *Chamber of Secrets*, when Harry is worried that his abilities suit him for Slytherin House rather than Gryffindor. He confides to his headmaster, Dumbledore, that the Sorting Hat had been about to place him in Slytherin until he argued it into changing its mind. Dumbledore's reply is widely recognised as a classic: "It is our choices, Harry, that show what we truly are, far more than our abilities." I like it that Doctor Who evidently agrees with Dumbledore.

So despite some flaws, chiefly regarding the one-shot characters, I found *Journey to the Centre of the TARDIS* satisfying both dramatically and philosophically, and a worthy follow-up to *Hide*.

Episode 7.11. *The Crimson Horror*

The Crimson Horror, like *Cold War*, is a real old-school Doctor Who story. It's very easy to imagine Tom Baker starring in it, in a way that you really couldn't see him in *Vincent and the Doctor*, or *The Angels Take Manhattan*. And of course it's none the worse for that. Once more, we're reminded that Doctor Who really can do all sorts of stories, and this sort of period-drama horror has something of the *Weng-Chiang* quality.

Structurally, the big difficulty this story faced was how to pack a classical four-parter into a single episode. Back in the old days, we might not have seen the Doctor at all in the first episode – it might have been entirely the story of Vastra, Jenny and Strax investigating the crimson corpses. The Doctor would have been discovered early in episode 2, and restored to his usual self in episode 3, ready to resolve the mystery and save the day in episode 4.

In fact, *The Crimson Horror* does a very fine job of compressing all that story into its 45 minutes, and is perhaps a rare example of the New Who episode that really does resolve all its issues cleanly without rushing. This is all the more impressive given the broad range of ideas it introduces: the crimson bodies in the river, the model community, the blinded daughter, Mr. Thursday's preliminary investigation, Jenny and Vastra's more ambitious attempt, the Doctor as monster, his and Clara's own investigation (in flashback), the prehistoric leech, the rocket full of venom and of course Mrs. Gillyflower herself. Just listing all the elements is a little exhausting, but there's a craftsmanlike quality about the writing that keeps it all straight and clear.

I find myself surprised to be writing those words, as I'm not particularly a fan of Mark Gatiss's previous episodes (*The Unquiet Dead, The Idiot's Lantern, Victory of the Daleks, Night Terrors* and *Cold War*). But looking at that list of episodes, they do seem to represent a fairly consistent upward trend – which is promising if, as some have speculated, he is Moffat's anointed successor as showrunner.

So how does it hold together so well? Part of it is probably just that the story is mostly linear, and that the only exception (the flashback to the Doctor and Clara's investigation) is so clearly marked out by the rather fetching device of the vintage-effect film. It's the sort of trickery that you wouldn't want to see every week, but which charms when you see it as a one-off. Then there is the very clean delineation of threads. The Jenny/Vastra/Strax thread has an altogether different feel from the Gillyflower/Ada thread, being light-hearted where the latter is harrowing. We always *feel* where we are in the story. Then there is the deliberately two-dimensional sketching of the minor characters: Mr. Thursday, always fainting; the undertaker; Abigail, who is so obviously there only to help Jenny sneak through the locked door. All of these characters are sketched economically, in a way that lets us know up front that we don't need to worry about them. They're scenery. And that's not an insult to the writing: scenery is what's needed, not yet more human drama on top of that of Mrs. Gillyflower and Ada.

Speaking of which, the Gillyflower/Ada relationship really works, partly because Diana Rigg does such a good job of keeping a pantomime villainess about as believable as she could be. Her treatment of Ada is genuinely repulsive, so that when Ada finally rebels at the end it's a cathartic moment. (I also enjoyed how Ada's crushing Mr. Sweet is initially played for laughs as an accident, but quickly turns into an enraged flogging. That's decades of suppressed rage all coming out at once.) If we're taught early on not to bother expending emotional energy on Mr. Thursday, we're given every chance to invest in Ada; and that investment pays off.

(Sudden thought: Mr. Thursday is an unusual name. He is the man who was Thursday. Was the name chosen in tribute to G. K. Chesterton's brilliant *sui generis* novel? It's nice to think so. Anyone who's not read *The Man Who Was Thursday* should get over the Project Gutenberg right now, and download it for free – it's in the public domain. It's one of my all-time favourite books: ambiguous, thrilling, funny, profound, disturbing and moving. Seriously. Stop reading this; read that instead.)

Meanwhile ... I continue to be delighted by Strax: although his character is almost pure comic relief, it's *funny* comic relief. ("Horse, you have failed in your mission."). Why is it that I enjoy Strax so much when I hated Peter Jackson's comic-relief Gimli? For one thing the execution is so much better. Strax is written well; movie-Gimli is written in a way that somehow contrives to be both stodgy and juvenile. I'm convinced he's the part of the *Lord of the Rings* films that Tolkien would have hated most. But another part of the reason for this is that the humour of Strax comes from his playing against type. We all know how a Sontaran is supposed to behave, and Strax is funny because he is *not* a merciless warrior. In the same way, Marvin the paranoid android is funny because robots are supposed to be unemotional. But, as best as I can understand Jackson's and Boyens' intention, Gimli is supposed to be funny because he *is* a dwarf (and therefore short). But there's nothing funny about merely being a dwarf. That's a foundation that you build humour *on*.

There's nothing funny about being a sat-nav, either. The scene with Thomas Thomas giving Strax directions is a bizarrely tone-deaf inclusion.

Oh well. No need to dwell on that one bum note. *The Crimson Horror* was interesting, funny and clever, and packed an emotional punch, too. A fine episode as we approach the climax of this rather disjointed series.

Episode 7.12. *Nightmare in Silver*

After what I felt was a run of excellent episodes (*Hide, Journey to the Centre of the TARDIS, The Crimson Horror*) I was very ready to love *Nightmare in Silver* – especially as it was the work of Neil Gaiman, whose previous episode *The Doctor's Wife* was arguably the highlight of Series 7. Gaiman's natural writing idiom – rich, dark, complex, lots of connections that become apparent only as the story progresses – is a great match for Doctor Who. So I expected a lot from *Nightmare in Silver*.

And it didn't really deliver.

It got off to a shaky start with one of the most unconvincing alien landscapes New Who has ever given us: a very small, constrained bit of moonscape with very obviously cardboard rocks and a very lame door-in-the-rockface prop that reminded me of nothing more than the Blue Peter Doctor Who Theatre made from breakfast-cereal packets, aluminium foil and sticky-backed plastic. It would be nice to think this was a deliberate (if misjudged) homage to some of the Old Who sets; but I saw nothing in the episode to support that charitable reading, and I think we have to conclude that it was simply bad.

Dodgy sets are easy to forgive, though. After all, every Old Who set looks dodgy by modern standards, but I hope we're sophisticated enough viewers to see them as signifiers, like theatre sets; to look past their technical quality to the story being told. (Anyone who thinks a sophisticated viewer is one who *does* get hung up on mechanical failings has completely missed the point.) What's much more damaging is bad characterisation, and here is an area where *Nightmare in Silver* fails horribly. I'm talking about Angie, one of the two kids that Clara is responsible for. Her very first words in the episode are:

"Your stupid box can't even get us to the right place."

There's just no excuse for it. Even given that the goal was to establish Angie as peevish and frankly obnoxious, there is simply no way that *anyone*, walking into a phone box that's bigger on the inside, then walking out of it into a completely different planet, would respond that way. Not even the most spoiled kid. So there goes whatever suspension of disbelief we'd managed to hold on to in the teeth of the cardboard moon-rocks.

I can hardly believe that Gaiman wrote something so tone-deaf. This opening line must surely be the work of a committee. A script committee whose members have read Making A Great Script Awesome and everything Joseph Campbell ever wrote, and who know everything there is to know about scripts except for everything that's worth knowing. I bet if we could see the draft script that Gaiman submitted, it was nowhere near so stupid, but some genius decided that it was important to "cut to the chase", to establish Angie's character up front. Even at the expense of making us loathe her.

And that's fatal. Because pretty much from the word go, I was rooting for the Cybermen to convert her. She gives us more ammunition later on with a string of additional complaints: "How long do we have to stay here?", because it must be *such* a drag having to find interesting things to see and do for an hour on an alien planet; and "I hate the future. It's stupid. There's not even phone service", which is simply moronic. The Cybermen's conversion process removes the emotions and personality from its subject, leaving an empty shell lacking in any individuality. For Angie, that would be a significant improvement.

Although I suppose it would be a shame for Artie, who seems like a nice kid. I assume he must have some residual affection for his sister, however unappealing she is. Artie's given much better lines than Angie, and delivers them well. I particularly enjoyed the moment when Webley asks whether anyone plays chess, and before the Doctor can reply, Artie chips in – slightly shy, but also endearingly proud – with "Actually, I'm in my school chess club." The Doctor's peeved look in the background is priceless. This is characterisation done right – which makes the horribly misjudged handling of Angie all the more baffling. When she's impressed by the lame conjuring trick of producing a penny from behind her ear, it adds insult to injury. What? This, you're impressed by? Dimensional transcendentalism, time travel and aliens, not so much?

All of this put me in a bad mood, so that I was less forgiving than I usually am of other careless points in the story. Why was the emperor powering a chess-playing mechanical Turk? Granted that he wanted to run away from his responsibilities, could he really not find a better situation anywhere in the universe? Why was he wearing a pilot's helmet? Why did he have the stupid, patronising, "comical" name Porridge? No-one's called Porridge. Why would he adopt such an alias? None of this makes any sense. It all smells of un-revised first draft. But it can't be that, because having won the 2012 Hugo Award for Best Dramatic Presentation, Short Form, for *The Doctor's Wife*, Gaiman said in his acceptance speech that he was already on the third draft of his Series 7 offering.

And maybe worst of all is a gigantic yawning plot hole. For all the Doctor's tour-de-force split-personality acting, the resolution is a big, fat *deus ex machina*: the most blatant in New Who history, which is saying a lot. In the end, the emperor sets off the Destroy-The-World bomb, and all our heroes are rescued by being teleported into his ship. But there is no reason at all that he couldn't have done that right at the beginning. So the whole episode turns out to have been a waste of time, and all the Doctor's plans a waste of intelligence. Porridge should have just pushed the big red Happy Ending button as soon as the first Cyberman turned up, and we could all have gone home early.

So what with the unlikeable supporting characters, the incoherent cover-story of the emperor, and the nonsense surrounding the bomb, this is turning out to be a relentlessly negative review. That may not be completely fair. There were some fine moments, for sure. And yet the Doctor's Hitch-Hiker's Guide-like line "And you lot: no blowing up this planet!" – while funny – was more than a little undermined by the fact that they actually *should* have blown up the planet.

That's not to say there's nothing to like in *Nightmare in Silver*. There's a nicely played little exchange as Clara leads the rag-bag of lazily stereotyped troops from Central Casting to the castle where they're planning to hold out against the Cybermen. "I trust the Doctor", she says. "You think he knows what he's doing", comments Captain Ferring. Clara shoots back, "I'm not sure I'd go that far". It's cleanly done, and captures the nature of the Doctor (and Clara's relationship with him) both efficiently and wittily. The Doctor's line when facing the suspicious guns of the Central Casting soldiers is also fun: "Don't shoot! Don't shoot! I'm nice!" But really, such moments are few and far between. They're not enough to rescue an episode with such fundamental flaws.

I expected so much more of Neil Gaiman and Cybermen.

Finally, there's this speech by the Doctor, as he approaches the climax of his chess game against his cyber-self: "When I win, you get out of my head. You let the children go. And nobody dies. You got that? *Nobody dies!*" I was struck by the phase "nobody dies". In literal terms, it means the same as the famous "Everyone lives" from the end of *The Doctor Dances*; yet it feels so much less. A negative never strikes home like a positive does. That negativity, that lack of convictions, feels sadly emblematic of the episode as a whole. The ingredients are all there, but there's no cake.

Episode 7.13. *The Name of the Doctor*

Is *The Name of the Doctor* good? Yes. Is it a good episode of Doctor Who? Questionable. What *is* it a good one of? I really couldn't say. It's a very hard story for me to wrap my head around, not because the sequence of events is unclear – it's not – but because it's not clear what any of it *means*.

We start with the serial killer Clarence DeMarco, in his prison cell, reciting a poem about the Whispermen. Why? How does he know they exist? Madame Vastra comes to talk to him. Why? How is she connected with him? He tells her he has information about the Doctor. Why? How does he know who the Doctor is? He gives her the co-ordinates of Trenzalore. Why? How does he know them? How does he even understand what space-time co-ordinates *are*? We're not off to a good start, and as far as I can make out from having watched twice, the episode never bothers to go back and explain any of this. DeMarco is only there to deliver plot coupons. Vastra might just as well have read the Trenzalore co-ordinates off the back of a cereal packet, for all the significance the method of delivery had.

It's hard to escape the feeling that Moffat just had the image in his mind of the half-insane mass-murderer babbling a mixture of nonsense and wisdom – not unlike Dalek Caan in *Journey's End* now I come to think of it – and just darned well wanted to use that image.

It's a feeling that pervades much of *The Name of the Doctor*: that Moffat started with a grab-bag of images, and figured out a way to more or less shove them all into the story. And we may as well admit that they are stunning images. The joyous revisionism of Clara telling the First Doctor which TARDIS to steal; all the different Doctors running past Clara in her mind; the Doctor impossibly catching ghost-River's hand; and most of all, the giant decaying TARDIS looming over the Trenzalore battlefield. Even though this last one is not particularly well realised, it's a superbly resonant image.

It took me a while to realise why the giant TARDIS affected me quite so strongly, before I realised that it's an echo of the cover of a computer magazine from my youth. It was the March 1982 issue of *Practical Computing*, a special issue about Adventure games such as Crowther and Woods' *Colossal Cave* and Anderson et al.'s *Zork*. It shows an archaeologist squatting down on a square rock which we realise (though he may not) is one of the keys of a gigantic stone computer keyboard, with the screen looming behind – decayed by age, just like the TARDIS at Trenzalore. If one thing stays with me from the heady days of early-1980s computer programming, it's the sense we had that these machines were bigger on the inside. The *Practical Computing* cover somehow conveyed that internal size by making it external.

The interesting thing is that I only had that magazine for a couple of years before it got thrown out, but the memory of the image stayed with me for more than twenty years. Then I had a lucky break: Diana MacKay, a kind reader of my old web-site, read what I'd written about it there and sent me a hardcopy. I was delighted to get it, of course; but paradoxically I was really disappointed by the artwork when I saw it again for the first time in two decades. The execution was so much weaker than I'd remembered: it looked over-bright, washed out, half-finished. Here's the point: with images like this, it's not the execution that matters, but the idea it embodies.

C. S. Lewis wrote something very similar about what he called "myths" – by which he meant stories whose value is in their ideas rather than the specific words in which they are told. For example, he said that he immediately loved Kafka's story *The Castle* when it was described to him; but that subsequently actually reading the novel added nothing to his enjoyment. So despite its recent origin, *The Castle* is a myth in Lewis's sense. By contrast, the story in any given Jeeves story is trivial; but the specific perfectly-chosen words that Wodehouse uses to tell that story are magical. So the Jeeves stories are the opposite of myth in Lewis's sense of the word, being all about the execution and not at all about the ideas.

The idea of the giant TARDIS is very much myth in the Lewis sense. That means it doesn't actually matter much if it's not very well done on a technical level – just like my *Practical Computing* cover. The power resides in the idea itself. Which is just as well, because in fact it's just rather a shoddy painting. The concept deserved, but didn't need, more.

Of course, there's nothing intrinsically wrong with starting with an image. To go back to C. S. Lewis for a moment, famously the germ of *The Lion, The Witch and the Wardrobe* arrived in his mind as a mental picture of a faun rushing through the snow with a stack of parcels. That book may be my all-time favourite – it's certainly up there as one of the two or three books I've re-read the most times, comfortably into double figures along with *The Hitch-Hiker's Guide to the Galaxy*. But the reason *LW&W* works so well isn't just that Lewis started with an arresting image; or even that (in the manner of Moffat) he piled on more and more arresting images. Quite the opposite, in fact. For Lewis, that image of a faun in the snow was a seed from which a story grew, not one of the set of bricks from which an edifice could be assembled. He used that image as the root of a *story* that touches on the most profound themes – personal choice, the excuses we tell ourselves, grace, forgiveness and redemption, even the character of God. By contrast, Russell T. Davies suffered from a malady that led him to believe crashing together enough ideas would either give rise to a story by magic, or – more likely – conceal that fact that there *is* no story, for 45 minutes at least. There are times when we feel that Moffat has a tendency to succumb (in a less virulent form, thankfully) to that same malady.

Well, now I am getting over-harsh on *The Name of the Doctor*. It's not at all fair to imply that there's no story. There is one, and it's not bad (though it does turn on the classic idiot-plot point of River deciding to sacrifice billions of lives by opening the tomb, in order to save four). As all this is going on, Strax continues to delight: "What is the light?", asks Vastra; "It's beautiful", Jenny comments. "Shall I destroy it?" asks Strax. As with so much comedy, what makes Strax funny is that he doesn't *know* he's funny, any more than Nigel Tufnel does. Dan Starkey delivers those lines as though he really is a Sontaran warrior. He sells the idea.

More importantly, Matt Smith surpasses himself with his reaction on hearing Clara name Trenzalore. You can see his heart shrinking and his soul freezing right there on his face; and the only actual words that come out are a tiny "oh dear". It must have taken courage to write that line – just those two trivial words in reaction to what is supposed to be devastating news. Moffat, in other words, has a lot of trust in Matt Smith to make such moments work. That trust is not misplaced. We're really going to miss Smith when he's done.

But then the sense of seriousness is undercut by strange intrusions of very lazy writing. "I'm linking you into the TARDIS's telepathic circuit", The Doctor tells Clara, "It won't hurt a bit." She shrieks as he does so; and he says ... he says ... I can hardly bear to type it, but he said "I lied". Yes. "I lied." Like Arnold Schwarzenegger in *Commando*. Like Kirk in *Star Trek III*. Like that horrible moment when Gollum says it at the climax of *Return of the King*. "I lied" is now so dreadfully clichéd that *TV Tropes* has a whole page about it. It's not big and it's not funny.

And speaking of lazy: the stars are going out *again*? Seriously? Just like in *Turn Left*. And in *The Pandorica Opens*. And indeed in the venerable Arthur C. Clarke short story *The Nine Billion Names of God*. Aren't we done with this yet? Can't we find a different signifier for "bad things are happening"?

There are other signs of can't-be-bothered, too. At one point, the Doctor discards a flaming torch, dropping it on a straw-covered floor. We even get a close-up of it landing. The principle of Chekhov's Gun tells us that the torch is going to start a fire which will be important later; but no, it just gets forgotten. Is it left over from a plot thread that had to be cut? Then why did that moment survive?

More seriously, there's that line that Clara tells the kids early on, then produces as though it's a profound insight just before walking into the Doctor's time stream: "The soufflé isn't the soufflé, the soufflé is the recipe". I've tried pretty hard to figure out what that means, and I just can't come up with anything. I don't understand what it means with regard to actual soufflés, and I *certainly* don't understand what bearing it has on Clara's decision to go into the Doctor's time stream. (I also don't understand why both the Doctor and River advise her not to do this, when they know that if she succeeds then billions of lives will be saved.)

And while I'm riding the "I don't understand" horse, how about this exchange?

Doctor: There is a time to live and a time to sleep. You are an echo, River. [...] You should've faded by now.

River: It's hard to leave when you haven't said goodbye.

Doctor: Then tell me, because I don't know. How do I say it?

River: There's only one way I'd accept. If you ever loved me, say it like you're going to come back.

Doctor: Well, then. See you around, Professor River Song.

River: Till the next time, Doctor.

Now. The whole issue that the Doctor is addressing here is that River is clinging onto her not-quite-life past the point where she should. She can't let go as she ought. And if the reason she's doing that is because the Doctor has never said a proper goodbye – a real, final, this-is-it goodbye of the kind that he finds so difficult because "he doesn't like endings". Then how can River possibly think that what she needs is for him to *not* say goodbye but *au revoir*? "See you around" is not a goodbye, and can hardly be expected to dismiss her shade to rest in peace. Both the Doctor and River know this. Moffat knows it. So why is it there? The scene is played as though it's supposed to be a tear-jerker. But it's nonsense.

Yes, I am whining a lot. I don't like to do that, because I *did* enjoy *The Name of the Doctor* a lot. And yet these aren't minor failings. The consistently muffed moral calculus, whereby the Doctor and River repeatedly value the lives of one or two people close to them ahead of those of billions of strangers, is not endearing or heroic, it's weak and stupid. The line about the soufflé recipe is (I assume) supposed to be telling us something profound about Clara, but it doesn't. And if ever a character in Doctor Who needed to be permanently put out of her misery, it's River Bleeding Song, but Moffat just can't seem to summon up the courage to give her the lethal injection. It's cowardly writing. I can't help but compare with the ruthless way Joss Whedon kills off major characters, and they stay dead. By refusing to do that, Moffat lowers the stakes: we never really believe any of the characters are in danger – not even the ones who are already dead.

Well, this is turning out to be one of those episodes, like *The Wedding of River Song*, where my review turns out much more relentlessly negative than how I actually feel about it. There was a lot to enjoy, and the epic scope of the multiple rewrites of time – three of them! – did feel appropriate to the end-of-series finale. As an explanation for Clara's "impossible girl" status, it pretty much works: it's not just that there are lots of her all over the universe but that specifically they are where the Doctor needs them to be. And I can just about buy that her last words before stepping into the time stream – "Run, you clever boy, and remember" – somehow remained with all the Clara fragments through space and time.

I had feared, and half expected, that the central point of the episode would be the revelation of the Doctor's actual name, something that could only have been anti-climactic. The actual meaning of the episode title was much stronger and more important. "My real name is not the point", says the Doctor. "The name I *chose* is the Doctor. The name you choose, it's like, it's like a promise you make." Yes. Exactly. We're back to the crucial importance of free will, as discussed in *Journey to the Centre of the TARDIS*. In fact, we're back to Dumbledore's advice to Harry: "It is our choices that show what we truly are, far more than our abilities". The Doctor has abilities to spare, but it's his choices that make him what he is.

Which is what makes the words of John Hurt's Doctor at the end all the more paradoxical: "What I did, I did without choice." But that's not really true, is it? Circumstance can constrain what choices we make, but not determine them. John Hurt's Doctor is lying to himself (quite literally, given that he's talking to Matt Smith). He's trying to justify his choice by saying he didn't have one.

I did it "In the name of peace and sanity", he says. And Matt Smith's Doctor replies: "But not in the name of the Doctor." That's powerful. That's the way to end a series.

A quick thought on *The Name of the Doctor*

"Introducing John Hurt as The Doctor", says the caption.

But our Doctor (Matt Smith) says that what that Doctor (John Hurt) did was in the name of peace, yes, and in the name of sanity, yes, but not in the name of the Doctor.

So what did he do, and when?

First of all, I think it has to be something that he *has* done, rather than something that he *will* do. The grammar alone invites that conclusion – the past-tense references to what the Doctor did.

So the obvious guess is that this refers to the Doctor's bringing the Time War to an end by destroying Gallifrey. It's something that we already know he did, and it seems a bit much to multiply entities by assuming he has *two* atrocities in his past.

We've always assumed that this was the work of the eighth Doctor, and that the ninth was his post-Time War incarnation – hence some of the more erratic aspects of his behaviour, especially in the first series' sixth episode, *Dalek*. My take is that there was another regeneration in between – that Paul McGann regenerated into John Hurt, and it was this Doctor (the eight-and-a-halfth, if you like) that destroyed Gallifrey. When he regenerated in Christopher Eccleston, the new Doctor disowned the previous one, did not allow him the title "Doctor", and took the number nine for himself. So Matt Smith is really the twelfth body that the character has had, but only the 11th to bear the name Doctor.

Is all this terribly obvious?

Series 7 summary and retrospective

It's hard to know what to make of Series 7, because in a real sense there *was* no Series 7 – just a little Series 7a with Amy and Rory, and a little Series 7b with Clara. However much we try to think of them as a single, coherent work, the year that elapsed between the halves just makes it impossible – especially with a Christmas Special in the middle. I can't think of, say, *A Town Called Mercy* and *Hide* as part of the same series. In retrospect, I wonder if Moffat wishes he'd called the two halves what they really are, Series 7 and 8.

And what that leaves us with is two series whose arcs are necessarily rather anaemic, because they just didn't have enough episodes to work up a head of steam. By the time we got to *Boom Town*, we really wanted to know what Bad Wolf meant. By the time of *The Pandorica Opens*, we knew what the crack in time was about, and wanted to understand what had caused it. And needless to say, by the end of *Closing Time*, we *really* wanted to understand the Lake Silencio incident (though arguably we never really did). By contrast, we weren't able to develop that level of curiosity over the mystery of Clara – and the Doctor's going on about her being the Impossible Girl, which was clearly meant to help us grab onto that mystery, really only served to highlight how little engaged we were. It was telling us to care rather than showing us why we should. The one thing that did help lend some weight to the Series 7b arc was having seen Clara in *Asylum of the Daleks* way back at the start of Series 7a – an episode that, as it turned out, was probably her highlight. I like Clara more as a Dalek than as a human.

Still, Clara's half-arsed arc at least achieved one more buttock than poor Amy and Rory were afforded. (That metaphor is shamelessly stolen from Matt Wedel – I only wish I could claim it as my own.) So far as I can make out, there was not even a token attempt at imposing a larger story across the five episodes of Series 7a, and as a result my favourite companions were sent off with five quite unrelated adventures. Even at their best (*Asylum*, *Angels*) these standalone episodes weren't able to generate the weight that a good arc gives. I've seen some suggestion that there's a through-line of the Ponds progressively readying themselves to separate from the Doctor, but I don't see that at all. They are just as attached to him at the end of their mini-series as at the start – as indeed they must be for the parting at the end of *Angels* to have the emotional punch it does.

I'm reminded of the last few episodes of Veronica Mars, which is probably my second favourite TV series ever (after Doctor Who, naturally). Series 1 of Veronica Mars was an absolutely perfect self-contained 22-episode murder mystery. It really couldn't have been improved on, and so Series 2 trod perhaps rather too much of the same ground – in particular, it followed Veronica through another year at high-school, a setting that Series 1 has already mined richly. As superb as Series 2 is, it doesn't quite touch the heights of the first; and ratings, which had never been high, declined. So for the third (and as it turned out final) series, showrunner Rob Thomas tried something different: instead of a single series-long arc, VM3 was to have three separate arcs, each seven or eight episodes long. But when the contract came through, it was for only 20 episodes rather than the US standard of 22. As a result, the third arc was abandoned, and the last few episodes were stand-alone stories. When this approach was announced, quite a few people were pleased by the idea; but in the end, those episodes were an anticlimax. They were fine in isolation, but it turned out that people really missed the sense that they were part of a running story. So Veronica Mars, having started with the single best series of TV I've ever seen, fizzled rather than exploding. Much the same is true of Amy and Rory.

(If you get nothing else from this book, get this: go and watch Veronica Mars – at least the first series. You can pick up a DVD box-set for £15, which is an absolute steal. You'll thank me.)

In the end, although I was pleased to have five more Amy-and-Rory episodes, part of me wishes they'd been written out at the end of Series 6 – left to a life of fruitful domesticity, and revisited briefly in *The Doctor, The Widow and the Wardrobe* just so we can see how well they're doing.

That, really, would have been the natural moment to let them go. Their relationship arc was essentially complete by the end of *The God Complex*, when Amy's idealised image of the Doctor was taken down. A couple more episodes to say goodbye properly, and we could have left it there. But then I wouldn't have wanted not to have *Asylum*. Ah, I don't know what to think. I'm conflicted.

Meanwhile, I'll raise a glass to Brian Williams (or Brian Pond, as the Doctor thinks of him), the companion that got away. He could have been the new Wilfred Mott but better; but he was just introduced too late in the game.

50th Anniversary

The fiftieth anniversary of Doctor Who was a Big Deal, in a way that the original makers back in 1963 could surely never have imagined. It's worth taking a moment to celebrate the fact that one of the most popular programmes on British television is one that celebrates intelligence, insight and wit, and that routinely challenges viewers with complex concepts. It could hardly be a better antidote to X Factor and Strictly Come Dancing.

Although the main event of the 50th celebrations was unquestionably the anniversary special, *The Day of the Doctor*, this was preceded by two shorts to set the scene: *The Night of the Doctor*, and *The Last Day*.

Mini episode: *The Night of the Doctor*

[I am not crazy about the word "minisode", which is what the world seems to be calling these things. I'm going with the relatively staid "mini episode", which is what the BBC is calling them.]

So I was right about the order of Doctors: John Hurt's "not in the name of the Doctor" character from the end of *The Name of the Doctor* was indeed an interstitial incarnation, between Paul McGann's Eighth and Christopher Eccleston's Ninth. And the terrible things that he did "in the name of peace, yes, and in the name of sanity" were his actions in the Time War – presumably the destruction of both Gallifrey and Skaro.

It was a delight to see Paul McGann bookend his Doctor Who career in the six-and-a-bit minutes of *The Night of the Doctor*. We saw his first moments seventeen years ago in the TV movie, and now – after many off-screen exploits in the 73 books of the *Eighth Doctor Adventures* series – we've seen his last moments. His opening words "I'm a doctor ... but probably not the one you're expecting" are a cheeky bit of metatextuality, reminiscent of George Lazenby's sardonic aside "This never happened to the other fellow" in *On Her Majesty's Secret Service*.

Usually when we've seen previous Doctors turn up again, their advanced ages have been a continuity problem. When Patrick Troughton teamed up with Colin Baker in the dreadful *The Two Doctors*[1], how could we be seeing that incarnation at an age so much more advanced than when he regenerated into Jon Pertwee? On the whole we simply ignore such problems. But this time, it's not a problem at all; it's a plot point. McGann's Doctor has been through a lot. It's *right* that he should look a good seventeen years older than he did when we last saw him. And it's even more right that John Hurt's "War Doctor" (that title is in the credits) should look much older, more eroded, still.

It's tough tying together all the threads of something like Doctor Who. Fifty years of continuity are enough to challenge anyone, and Moffat's increasingly non-linear story-lines make things even more complicated. Figuring out what happened to whom and when, and in what order, can be challenging verging on impossible. Given that backdrop, it's rather a relief that *The Night of the Doctor* happens in the right order, with a small, self-contained cast, and has a beginning, a middle and an end. It may be the first episode in a long time to join up the pieces of existing continuity rather than inventing a whole lot more. For once, things seem clearer at the end than they did at the beginning.

I like the Doctor's clear statement: "I'm not part of the war. I swear to you, I never was." I like Cass's terror, nevertheless, of Time Lords: "I'm not a Dalek" he says; "Who can tell the difference any more?", she replies. And I like the idea that, even in light of that fear and disgust, the Doctor deliberately decides to be the warrior that the Time War needs, rather than getting drawn into events unwillingly and progressively. I'm not sure that McGann quite sells the moment of decision, but this is quibbling.

---

[1] I watched *The Two Doctors* with my three sons. It was the first time any of us had seen a Colin Baker episode or Nicola Bryant as Peri. The boys found her so insipid and unlikeable that they spent most of the story cheering on Shockeye in the hope that he'd kill and eat her.

Mini episode: *The Last Day*

The world at large seems to have seen and loved *The Night of the Doctor* (quite rightly), but for some reason *The Last Day* slipped under the radar, and very little has been written about it. That seems a shame. It's very good.

It's a very short passage, less than four minutes, filmed rather audaciously in the point-of-view of a Gallifreyan soldier who's been given an implant to record his vision and memories. Or, reading between the lines, we're watching those memories from a storage device recovered from his dead body. This approach comes off superbly. It allows a very low budget – we mostly look at the face of the officer who is inducting him, with a couple of vague sets in the background – and forces the writing and acting to carry the scene without much help. Which, really, is as it should always be.

The Last Day is a welcome reminder of how tangential special effects are to Doctor Who: so much more is conveyed by traditional means. I think of the very simple effects of *The Empty Child* for example – basically they just shoved gas-masks on everyone. The one notable effects shot is the moment when Doctor Constantine transforms into a gas-mask child. The pinpoint clarity of the moment, and the sheer, simple sadness of his succumbing, scored with perfectly judged, understated music, is what makes the effect fly. The transformation is powerful because of how it's written, acted and scored, not because of how good the effects are.

So now we're set up for the 50th anniversary special itself, *The Day of the Doctor*. I'm actually writing this eighty minutes before transmission, having carefully avoided all potential spoilers including all the trailers. We know that the War Doctor has embraced his role as a warrior, and that many Daleks have penetrated the defences of Arcadia. We're set up for what I hope will be an actual *story* about the Time War, rather than a *Wedding of River Song*-like melange of disconnected scenes, out of order and perhaps not even actually *having* a natural order.

I think by this point we all recognise that Moffat's facility with time paradoxes, first seen in *The Girl in the Fireplace* but hardly left alone since, can be both his greatest strength and his most vulnerable point. He has a tendency to overdo it to the point where even the most dedicated fans can't agree on what it all means. The temptation to go completely overboard with the timey-wimey for a Time War episode must be strong. But unless Moffat has something utterly brilliant prepared, I suspect it would be much better to take the simpler path for once, keeping the story about as linear as a story about a Time War can be. One good approach might be to tell the story strictly linearly from the point of view of a companion character, with the Doctor himself appearing several times out of order. But, you know how it is, for some reason they didn't ask me to write this episode.

Finally: I wonder what we will see of the Time War itself. In a frankly rather brilliant bit of writing in the otherwise extremely uneven *The End of Time*, Russell T. Davies had the Doctor refer to "The Skaro Degradations; the Horde of Travesties; the Nightmare Child; the Could-Have-Been King with his army of Meanwhiles and Never-Weres". These are magnificently evocative names, and I have to hope that Moffat doesn't try to actually show any of them to us, because whatever he comes up with it won't be as powerful as what lurks in the darkness at the back of our own minds when we hear those words. These images are best left undrawn, merely suggested.

I read a couple of reviews last year arguing that Jackson is making the same mistake in the *Hobbit* movies that Lucas did in the *Star Wars* prequels – filling in details that the original only hinted at ("the Senate has been dissolved", "the Clone Wars", etc.) with concretised versions that aren't as interesting as what we independently imagined. Actually, that's not right: in Tolkien the exact opposite is the case, and the "back story" is actually the primary story; the well-known parts were made up to sit on top of it and, if you like, act as an advertisement for it. By foregrounding these, Jackson is arguably being more true to Tolkien's original vision than J. R. R. was himself in writing *The Hobbit*.

But Davies' Time-War creations didn't start out as a fully-realised mythology like Tolkien's. They are ideas. And they should stay that way. If we see the Nightmare Child and it's just (for example) a giant space-squid, that will be a crushing disappointment.

The Day of the Doctor

I'm writing an hour after *The Day of the Doctor* finished. As the boys get older and bigger (15, 13 and 11 now), it's getting harder and harder to squeeze all five of us onto the sofa together, but for special occasions like this, we find a way. I'm still reeling – not quite able to take it all in, but delighted and excited, and with a big, silly grin on my face.

It's not just the fannishness. Yes, I was enchanted to see and hear the original 1963 version of the title sequence, and to spot the references to Totter's Lane and Coal Hill with its chairman of the governors. Yes, I enjoyed the pin-board of past companions in the Black Archive and the parade of all twelve Doctors at the end. But if that had been all that Moffat brought to the party, it would have been just that: a party. This was much more than a celebration or reconstruction of the past. What made it so successful was not just the performances of the three best actors ever to play the Doctor, but the fact that the whole story made perfect sense.

You can argue that that shouldn't be cause for celebration, but business as usual. I'm sympathetic to that. But, really, given the scope and ambition of *The Day of the Doctor*, holding it all together (with only two parenthetical exceptions, which I'll discuss below) is quite an achievement. At every point in the story, I understood where I was, what was happening and why. Whenever we saw an effect before its cause (like the fez dropping through the anomaly to the War Doctor's hut), it was followed up and explained. I wasn't left at the end of it saying "But wait, how did he get Thing X from Person Y to Place Z?"

That's impressive because, as we might have expected, *The Day of the Doctor* came with the regulation set of time paradoxes – as indeed could hardly help but be the case when three doctors were involved. (It's a bit odd to have one of those three also effectively making his debut, but there it is.) Why did it work so effectively when (say) *The Wedding of River Song* didn't? I think a big part of it has to be the running time. At a healthy 75 minutes, the anniversary special was fully two thirds longer than a regulation episode, i.e. only quarter of an hour short of a two-parter. In fact, given the need to recapitulate a certain amount of ground in the second half of a true two-parter, *The Day of the Doctor* probably came in at close to the same amount of usable screen time. And it made full use of that time. Everything I've been saying about the need for more two-parters to avoid Doctor Who being too rushed is vindicated by the clarity of the tricky plot this time around.

I also feel vindicated in what I said about special effects last time around. Let's admit up front that the battle scenes on Gallifrey were very well done; but they really didn't add anything once we'd seen, say, the first five seconds as a signifier that a war is on. One thing Doctor Who has never been is an action adventure: only rarely has the Doctor used any form of physical force to overcome his enemies (mostly in his Jon Pertwee incarnation), instead relying on empathy, wit and intelligence. As a result, movie-like destruction scenes like the ones on Gallifrey always feel rather out of place, as though they've wandered in from a completely different film. In the end, all the sound and fury of the Gallifrey battle scenes signified less than *The Last Day*'s poignant and bewildered sighting of a lone Dalek, followed by the silent emergence of its accompanying squadrons. By showing less, *The Last Day* allowed us to imagine more, and so feel more.

On the positive side, Moffat did resist the temptation to show us the Nightmare Child, the Could-Have-Been King, and all the others. I'm convinced that would have been a terrible let-down; against that dodged bullet, the relatively mundane Time War that looked like a regular war with spaceships and lasers is easy to forgive.

What's ironic here is that outside of those expensive battle visuals, the episode looked fabulous – as so many recent episodes have. The Elizabethan-period fields and woods, the clean spaces of the art gallery, the Black Archive and the War Doctor's desert hut were all beautiful in their very different ways. I think this matter of sheer visual beauty is one of the ways in which the later days of Smith's reign have surpassed his earlier days. In the superlative Series 5, which has to stand as his best, only two episodes (*Vampires in Venice* and *Vincent and the Doctor*) were breathtaking to look at. This years it seems that half the episodes have been. It's a welcome development. We all recognise that the semi-mythical wobbly sets and papier-mâché rocks of the old series were always functional at best. But even looking back just eight years to Christopher Eccleston's one series, nearly every episode looks grimy and half-finished. Now that may have been a deliberate choice: it would have made sense to make the re-launched series look as grounded in reality as possible. But I'm glad we're past that now, and that when Doctor Who takes us to lovely places they *look* lovely.

And so to the key development in the fifty-year arc. Famously the Time Lords were never part of the original conception of Doctor Who. He was introduced as a mysterious loner. ("I am the Doctor. I travel in time and space.") They were introduced at the end of Patrick Troughton's last story, *The War Games*, as a convenient *deus ex machina* to bring about both his regeneration into Jon Pertwee and his budget-saving exile to Earth. But subsequent stories, especially *The Deadly Assassin*, brought the Time Lords front and centre, to the point where their continuity began to be weight that the series had to lug around, not always to its benefit.

Against that backdrop, Russell T. Davies decided very early on in the new series to clear all that baggage away. At the end of the second episode, *The End of the World*, we see one of the most affecting scenes in the whole of New Who. Having spent the previous forty minutes with aliens billions of years in the future, Rose and Doctor Chris arrive back on present-day Earth, into the anonymous bustle of a crowd of people in central London – and Rose sees all those people as though for the first time. And then we have this dialogue as the crowd passes, oblivious, past them:

Doctor: You think it'll last forever: people, and cars and concrete. But it won't. One day, it's all gone. Even the sky. [Long pause.] My planet's gone. It's dead. It burned, like the Earth. It's just rocks and dust. Before its time.

Rose: What happened?

Doctor: There was a war, and we lost.

Rose: A war with who? [No response.] What about your people?

Doctor: I'm a Time Lord. I'm the last of the Time Lords. They're all gone. I'm the only survivor. I'm left travelling on my own, because there's no-one else.

Rose: There's me.

It was a bold move, and executed brilliantly – largely because of the superb acting: Eccleston's flat, affectless delivery, as though the words are costing him something to say; and Piper's puppy-dog eagerness to understand, to help; to do something, anything, that will make things better.

As a result, we've had a radically different backdrop to the revived series: no Time Lords, no Gallifrey, and the Doctor as the last of his species. On the whole, that's worked superbly, lending the series a poignancy quite lacking from Old Who – most notably in *The Hungry Earth* when the Doctor is interviewing the captured Silurian warrior Alaya. "I'm the last of my species", Alaya insists. "No", says the Doctor, kindly but very firmly, "You're really not. Because I'm the last of *my* species, and I know how it sits in a heart. So don't insult me."

And now ... it's not true any more. Gallifrey is not destroyed but hidden. And although the Doctor did this, the knowledge of it is hidden from him. Because of timey-wimey. If that sounds like I'm being dismissive, actually I'm really not. Whenever you have a multiple-Doctors story, you just have to have some form of magical forgetfulness pixie-dust, otherwise you run into completely unavoidable continuity errors arising from later Doctors remembering the experiences from the point of view of their earlier selves. Usually, the problem has been ignored; this time we got a little bit of technobabble about time-streams being out of sync; and the forgetfulness was extended to the Eleventh Doctor as well as his predecessors. That's an important bit of ret-conning, because unless he absolutely believed Gallifrey was gone forever, much of what the Doctor has said and done for the last eight years makes very little sense. (Of course, the abortive return of Gallifrey in *The End of Time* makes very little sense even with the ret-con; but then that was true back when we all thought Gallifrey was gone, too. We can't go worrying about whether *The End of Time* makes sense. It just doesn't. Never did, never will.)

But what's done here is really rather clever. It's the same time-paradox judo that we saw in the resolution to Series 6, when we all thought the Doctor had been killed at the fixed point at Lake Silencio. Both then and now, it looks like the past has been changed, but it hasn't. The past turns out in both cases to have remained exactly as it was, but our understanding of that past is shown to have been incorrect. Just as we all thought the Doctor's death was the Lake Silencio fixed point but it turned out to be the destruction of the Teselecta, so we all thought the destruction of Gallifrey was the resolution of the Time War but it turned out to be the hiding of that planet (and the consequent self-destruction of the Daleks). As Allyn Gibson put it, it was a clever way of rewriting the assumptions of the RTD era without rewriting the text.

And I rather like it that this recalibration was brought about by the combination of New Who's oldest and newest companions, Rose and Clara. I admired the steely yet compassionate resolve of the three Doctors as they decided to proceed with the apparently unavoidable genocide; but in common with pretty much everyone, I imagine, I was relieved that they found a different way. I'm also gratified that the "Rose" character was not actually Rose, wrenched across the unbridgeable gap between universes yet *again*, but a simulation of her produced by the sentient super-weapon, the Moment. Between her words to the War Doctor and Clara's to the Eleventh, the seemingly predestined genocide is averted by the realisation that three Doctors, with their TARDISes, can do what one could not.

And here we come to one of the neatest parts of the story but also one of the two places where I couldn't quite see how it hung together. First, here's the neat part. The idea of three TARDISes being able to instantaneously hide a whole planet is beyond anything we've seen a

TARDIS do before – but it stretched credulity less that it might have because we knew that one of those TARDISes had had four hundred years to figure out the details and calculations of how to do it. It would have been a bit much to spring the "Start your TARDIS thinking now, War Doctor!" idea on us at that point. Instead, the concept of pre-preparing artefacts starting from the War Doctor's time had been neatly established earlier on, with the multiple-sonic-screwdriver escape from the Tower of London. So that only a passing word was needed when the same tactic was used for the TARDISes.

But here's the bit I don't understand: why did the other nine Doctors in their TARDISes also turn up at that point? If it's possible to summon them from the past of the Doctor's own timeline, why didn't the War Doctor do this in the first place? I can only assume that Moffat really, really *wanted* to have all thirteen TARDISes buzzing around the place, and the thirteen faces appearing on screens. Well, I have some sympathy with that. I guess you can cut a 50th anniversary episode some slack.

While I'm mentioning problems, the other part I couldn't straighten out in my mind is what the aged Tom Baker was doing in the museum at the end. Again, I suspect this is the work of simple sentiment: who wouldn't have wanted to find a way to bring back Doctor Tom? I tried to justify this to the boys using the fannish theory that each of the Doctor's incarnations somehow outlives the regeneration process and goes on to its own retirement. But my heart wasn't in it, because it's a bit of a stupid theory. And even if you buy it, it doesn't explain how Doctor Tom knew what the three modern Doctors had done about Gallifrey, and the true title of the painting that encodes that information.

So those are the two imperfections I mentioned earlier. Pretty small beer, I think, and both of them easy to overlook as they gave us such enjoyable moments. The 50th anniversary would have been poorer without them.

And of course there was so much more to love about *The Day of the Doctor*. The misdirection as we're gently invited to believe that it's Weeping Angels lurking under the sheets in the art gallery. The Doctor's completely missing that his horse, not Elizabeth I, is the shape-shifted Zygon. His threatening the rabbit. The fezzes coming through the anomalies. The War Doctor's impatience with the immature behaviour of his successors. The Doctors' clever use of the Black Archive's memory-wiping machine. The very brief first glimpse of Peter Capaldi as the Twelfth Doctor (assuming we're sticking with the old numbering). The War Doctor's last words, "wearing a bit thin" recapitulating those of the First Doctor, and the Tenth anticipating his own last words, "I don't want to go". All of this in an episode that told three complete stories: modern Zygon invasion, Elizabethan-era Zygon pre-invasion, and Time War.

Shortly after the broadcast, I saw a tweet (from someone whose identity I will protect), saying "Thought the special was lame shit". It's hard to know what to do with a person like that. Just ignore them till they go away, I suppose. I'm reminded of the dwarves in C. S. Lewis's *The Last Battle*: sitting, huddling together, in the paradise of Aslan's Country, insisting that they're in a filthy stable, refusing to be "taken in". I can only hope these guys are enjoying their feeling of superiority, because they certainly need something to compensate for the superb TV they're missing.

I love Doctor Who! I just *love* it!

Christmas 2013: *The Time of the Doctor*

And so to Matt Smith's valedictory episode – one which set out to tie up all the loose ends of the Eleventh Doctor era and came closer to succeeding than it had any right to. The purpose of the crack from Series 5? Check. The genesis of the Silence religious order? Check. The origin of the Silence species? Check. The reason that "no living creature can speak falsely" on Trenzalore? Check. The reason why the Question must not be answered there? Check.

Of course, it doesn't *all* quite fit neatly in the box. There remains the confusion over the first mention of the Question – the Teselecta's claim in *Let's Kill Hitler* that the Silence's core belief is that silence will fall when the question is *asked* rather than answered. I think that now has to be written off as Just Plain Wrong. There's also still some confusion over whether and when the Silence consider silence to be desirable: their main concern is to *prevent* silence from falling when the Question is answered; yet they want to achieve that by means of the Doctor's silence, and they adopt the name Silence for themselves. These wrinkles make me sceptical that Moffat had everything planned out before he started. Still, I admire how much it does all tie together in the end.

One foundational plot question does remain for me: why did the TARDIS explode back in Series 5, causing the crack in time and space? Two hypotheses seem to have legs. One is that the Silence caused the explosion in their attempts to kill the Doctor, with the unwitting and ironic result of creating the very crack whose existence imperilled them. The second, which is not really supported by the text but makes more sense to me, is that the Time Lords engineered the explosion, in order to create the crack and so make a way for themselves to get back into our universe. I doubt this will ever be definitively answered now: it feels like a question that belongs to the Matt Smith era. And that, sadly, is over.

As to *The Time of the Doctor* itself: perhaps the heavy plot burden it carried prevented it from touching the heights of the very best standalone Christmas episodes, but there was plenty to love. I enjoyed the sudden shifts of tone throughout the episode: the naked-at-the-dinner-table farce in Clara's flat leaping in one bound to the high drama in the Church of the Papal Mainframe, then to the played-for-laughs honesty field in the town of Christmas, and then the reveal of the crack. From there, through the long, slow ageing of the Doctor (I wonder how old he canonically is now?) to the emotional finale.

Even for Doctor Who, the story structure was ambitious. All those locations, with their different tones, and the Doctor shown at three stages in his life-span. I suppose we should be grateful that the story did at least happen in chronological order. Some of the cameos were perhaps disposable: the brief scene with the Weeping Angels felt very much a throwaway, bunged in at the last minutes as part of a Moffat's Greatest Hits anthology. But the overall shape held together, and Smith's ageing was superbly portrayed. I loved the way the most aged version of the Eleventh Doctor recalled William Hartnell visually, while unmistakably retaining Smith's personality.

I have reservations that in the end the way the Doctor defeats the Daleks is by being more powerful than them. Shades of Bad Wolf. It didn't feel right because the Doctor never overcomes by power, but overcomes more powerful foes by being cleverer. We saw this done beautifully with the wooden Cyberman on Trenzalore: tricked into shooting itself by the Doctor's sneaky circumvention of the truth field. That was a classically Doctorish move, and perhaps my favourite moment in the episode. Still, the final defeat of the Daleks is acceptable because the raw power that the Doctor uses to defeat them is not his own, but bestowed by the Time Lords from the other side of the crack – along with a new batch of regenerations.

Which was jolly nice of them. This Time Lord behaviour of course completely ignores the events of *The End of Time* parts 1 and 2, which I think is the wisest cause of action. In 2013, the Doctor talks and acts as though none of the 2009 Christmas special ever happened. Implicitly, those episodes are relegated to non-canon. And I'm pretty cool with that. *The Time of the Doctor* is a much better send-off for Smith than Tennant got in *The End of the Time*. In retrospect, Tennant was particularly ill-served by the long-drawn out coda after the actual story had ended, outstaying his welcome by hanging around when he had nothing to do but try rather crudely to pull at our heartstrings. It reminded me of the frankly interminable sequence of endings that drag out the last reel of *Return of the King* to a full half-hour after the ring goes into Mount Doom. By contrast, Smith's farewell was more like the ending of the original *Star Wars*, in which less than three minutes elapse from the explosion of the Death Star till the credits roll.

Not that his farewell was skimped — it just wasn't dragged out. I loved the poignant hallucination of young Amelia and then adult Amy. And her final words to him — "Raggedy man: good night" — were a joy to hear. A farewell, yes, but not a sad one; more of a Nunc Dimittis. As we've come to expect from Smith, pretty much every part of this was executed convincingly.

And then, with an abrupt regeneration and a very brief introduction to Twelve, it was over.

Smith was the Doctor. And he always will be. But times change, and so must the Doctor. I will not forget one line of this. Not one day, I swear. I will always remember when the Doctor was Matt Smith.

The Eleventh Doctor's place in the pantheon

It's fair to say that each of the first four Doctors left their mark not only on the series but on the character. William Hartnell created the role, establishing his eccentricity and otherworldliness. Patrick Troughton brought a new whimsicality to the role, along with flashes of powerful intelligence. Jon Pertwee gave us elegance, and an unruffled attitude to danger. And Tom Baker of course added a clownish, impetuous aspect that's now central to how we think of the Doctor.

Against the backdrop provided by their predecessors, it might appear that the next three doctors – the last three of the classic series – left less of a mark. I am honestly hard-pressed to think of much to say about Peter Davison beyond the observation that his Doctor was quite nice. Colin Baker attempted to add a potentially interesting ruthless streak to the Doctor, but whether due to his own limitations or a sequence of dreadful scripts he was never able to make it work convincingly. Sylvester McCoy might have been going somewhere with his cynical, manipulative take on the Doctor, but Michael Grade ensured that we never saw how that would have worked out. And of course Paul McGann never had a chance to show us how he might develop the character past the 85 minutes of the TV movie.

So my reading is that Christopher Eccleston's Doctor was built on the foundation of the first four Doctors, with the next four chipping in with only minor aspects of the role. All of which context makes Eccleston's performances more superb still.

It's easy for us to forget in 2013 just what a risk Doctor Who was in 2005. No-one particularly expected it to become the pop-culture phenomenon and perennial Christmas-day favourite that it now is. Doctor Who was killed off in 1989 because it was already on its last legs, and there was no very compelling reason to think that the 2005 revival would succeed. That it did is largely due to Russell T. Davies' vision, of course, and some superb writing especially by Steven Moffat,

Paul Cornell, Rob Shearman and (some of the time) Davies himself. But the one person who is surely due the bulk of the credit is the Doctor himself, Christopher Eccleston. He completely reinvented the character while simultaneously retaining its core – and by doing that, reset our expectations of what we were watching while keeping it rooted in what we'd loved about the classic series. Eccleston was believable both as a cosmic jester and as a PTSD victim of the Time War. Within a couple of episodes, he'd made the part his own – which was just as well, since we found out before Episode 2 that he'd be leaving at the end of the series.

Losing Eccleston so quickly could have been crippling for the new series, and it's greatly to David Tennant's credit that he took over the role so effortlessly that Eccleston quickly started to feel as though he'd been only a caretaker. Tennant's best work was done when it counted most: at the start of his run, and especially in his debut, *The Christmas Invasion*. Whatever my own feelings on the subject may be, there's no doubting that most people, and especially most casual fans, prefer his take over Eccleston's, and he is in many people's minds the defining modern Doctor, just as Tom Baker is the defining classic Doctor.

And then, Matt Smith.

Here's the thing. Doctor Who is good because it has the Doctor in it. When the Doctor is fun, the programme is fun. And Smith's Doctor is fun.

In *Nightmare in Silver*, as the kids prepare to go to sleep in the Emporium, the Doctor warns them:

"Don't wander off! Now I'm not just *saying* 'Don't wander off'. I mean it. Otherwise you'll wander off. And the next thing you know, somebody's going to have to start rescuing somebody."

"From what?", asks Angie.

"Nothing. Nobody needs rescuing from anything." A beat. "Don't wander off." Another beat. "Sweet dreams."

Smith is consistently, effortlessly brilliant in such exchanges. (Although like most things that appear effortless, doubtless it only got that way because of all the effort he put into it.)

Andrew Rilstone once wrote in a blog post that Doctor Who mustn't be about the Doctor. I initially disagreed in the comments, but eventually I realised that we were at cross purposes. He meant that the programme can't be about how special and magical and wonderful the Doctor is. The idea of the Oncoming Storm was powerful when it was first introduced by Doctor Chris in *The Parting of the Ways*, but when it becomes the Doctor's identity rather than a surprising aspect of his history, all is lost. That far, I agree with Andrew.

But in another sense, Doctor Who absolutely does need to be about the Doctor, because he's by far the most interesting character in the series. Attempts to do Doctor Who without the Doctor can range from the competent (The Sarah Jane Adventures) to the contemptible (Torchwood series 1 and 2), but never come close to touching the heights of the parent programme. Russell T. Davies probably came to recognise this, perhaps because of the failure of Torchwood, and that is no doubt the reason Rose Tyler: Earth Defence never came to fruition.

The programme works when the Doctor works, and it's the glory of the revived series that – so far at least – all of the leading actors have been superb. I criticise David Tennant at times, but that is by the standards set by Eccleston and Smith. Realistically, his work is streets ahead of what any of the Classic Series Doctors ever achieved. Even Tom Baker's episodes, seen now, appear mannered and pantomimesque by comparison. Baker rarely attempted any emotion beyond dry amusement (which admittedly he was superb at), and on the occasions when he was called upon to enter unfamiliar emotional territory the result was usually pretty awful scenery-chewing. For example, the much-lauded "do I have the right?" scene in *Genesis of the Daleks* does not stand up at all well when you actually watch it. None of this is to criticise Tom Baker, who by general consent was the pick of the first seven Doctors, but to make the point that the ante has been raised dramatically since the 1970s. It seems clear to me that even the least good of the New Who Doctors is better than even the best of the Old Who incumbents.

This of course leaves a lot of work for Peter Capaldi to do. He has not one, not two, but three quality acts to follow. And it seems pretty clear from his age alone that he will have to play the role very differently from his immediate predecessors. I applaud that: when Matt Smith began, I was worried that his take would be too similar to David Tennant's – a fear that proved unfounded once he'd found his feet, but nevertheless a trap that would have been terribly easy to fall into. Moffat could easily have played it safe by choosing another Bright Young Thing as Smith's successor; but by picking an actor 24 years older than Smith, he's burned those bridges. The new Doctor can't possibly play the role in the same way as Smith – he *has* to be his own man from day one. That's exciting.

And it will be a bit of a relief to have a Doctor who (we presume) is liberated from the now rather ubiquitous romantic entanglements. There was something refreshingly other-worldly about the apparently asexual quality of William Hartnell's, Patrick Troughton's and (most of the time) Jon Pertwee's Doctors. I'd be happy to see that return – and with it, a stronger focus on the Doctor's intellect rather than emotions (without discarding the latter).

I'm sad that Matt Smith is leaving: just in case it's not completely obvious, let me say again I think he has been superb, and made himself by some distance the best of the eleven Doctors so far (or twelve if you count John Hurt). But I'm delighted for him that he leaves behind such a superb body of work. And I'm excited about Capaldi.

Looking forward

The new Doctor

Despite how very highly I rate Matt Smith, part of me is pleased that he jumped before he was pushed – that he's avoided the trap that David Tennant fell into of reiterating the same character for so long that he's reduced to self-parody. He walks away from Doctor Who with his head held high, having been consistently the best thing about the programme throughout his four years. At the same time, he leaves the stage clear for his successor.

I hope that Capaldi will play the role very differently. The great thing about Smith was that, despite his tender years, he was believable as a much older man. The very serious core of that man kept showing through the (sometime self-consciously) zany exterior in a way that Tennant never really managed to pull off. (Where Tennant ranted and raved, Smith just quietly bled.) As Capaldi is visibly much older than Smith (at 55 years old, more than twice Smith's age when he made his debut) he can hardly produce a similar kind of performance. Instead, I hope to see him played as fiercely intelligent, and impatient with those who can't keep up. Way back in *Father's Day*, Christopher Eccleston says of Rose, "I did it again, I picked another stupid ape". I liked that sense of assumed superiority – a sense that only appears in flashes, as the Doctor mostly tries to stay polite, but which is always there beneath the surface. I'd like to see more of that.

While I'd like to see the new Doctor's raw intelligence as the most obvious and visible part of his character, I also want to see (relatively rare) impish moments showing the other side to his character. In other words, Smith's performance turned inside out. Without that other aspect, the character will not be likeable, and that would be catastrophic. It's not enough that we should respect the Doctor – we have to like him, too.

Clara

What now for Clara? With her mystery solved, she will presumably be downgraded to being a normal human. I am very OK with that. Rose became Bad Wolf, the most powerful being in the universe; Donna became part Time Lord; Amy was told by the Doctor that "quite possibly the single most important thing in the history of the universe is that I get you sorted out right now". Clara was the impossible girl. I'm about ready for a companion who is just a companion – the regular person through whose eyes we see the Doctor.

With Capaldi playing an older Doctor, we should presumably be safe from the threat of more Doctor/Companion romance. If the idea of a 1200-year-old man with a 27-year-old woman doesn't creep out the audience, then putting her with an actor twice her age ought to do it.

Because that romantic subplot really isn't necessary at all in Doctor Who, in fact it's a distraction. Every week, we're shown brand new things – the wonders of numerous new civilisations, of races with morals incomprehensibly alien to us, of the universe. It's anticlimactic to come down from those high planes to mere soap-opera, and terribly insulting to the audience to think that none of that other stuff is of value to anyone without some snogging. If we're going to see The Doctor In Love again, the something like the River Song story-line is the way to do it: matching him with something like an equal, not an ordinary person plucked from present-day Earth. I say something *like* River Song because of course *actual* River Song is unbearable. I suppose when we look at the pig's ear Alex Kingston has made of that role, we should be all the more grateful that the role of the Doctor himself has been so well cast all through the revived series (notwithstanding my criticism of Tennant's later years).

Story structure

I think that if Series 7 proved anything, it was that splitting a single series into two halves in different years just doesn't work. If for some reason we really can't have more than half a dozen episodes in a year, the Moffat should just be honest with us and himself, and call them what they are: a short series. That way, expectations can be set properly, and Moff needn't make narrative promises he can't keep. Really, I'd like to see a single solid block of thirteen episodes, as we had for the first five series.

The other lesson of Series 7b is that we do need a series-long arc to tie all the stories together. You could make a case that the average quality of the five episodes of Series 7a was higher than those of the eight episodes of Series 7b, but there's no question that the second half as a unit was stronger than the first half. It had a sense of narrative propulsion which, though flawed, did at least give us a sense that we were headed somewhere.

Series 7 didn't really give us the promised return to the Doctor as anonymous wanderer. It certainly seemed we were headed that way at the end of *Asylum*, when Clara wiped the Daleks' memories of him; and some of the individual episodes – *A Town Called Mercy*, *Hide* – had that intimate quality where the universe wasn't under threat, just one or two human lives. But the lure of the large was too strong for the Moff and his buddies, so that the last three episodes crescendoed through the end of all human life on Earth (*The Crimson Horror*), the end of the pan-galactic human empire (*Nightmare in Silver*) and finally the complete rewriting of time and the destruction of many (most? all?) stars.

I'd be happy to see bit more cosmic hobo from Peter Capaldi, and a bit less Saviour Of The Universe. Don't misunderstand me – I'm in favour of saving the universe. But not every week. Once every year or two seems about right.

Unfinished business

I still want to know why the TARDIS exploded back in Series 5. We've waited three years for the explanation, and that doesn't seem reasonable to me. Should I just accept that we're never going to know, and that Moffat has dropped that whole thread on the floor?

And the end of *The Day of the Doctor* strongly suggested that we've not seen the last of Gallifrey, and that the Doctor is likely to go looking for it. I have mixed feelings about this. But let me just call it now: Gallifrey will turn out to be inside the painting *Gallifrey Falls No More*. How they ret-con that with *The End of Time* I couldn't possibly speculate.

Appendix A: most memorable episodes

At first, I titled this appendix "best episodes", but I quickly realised that wasn't going to work. Under Russell T. Davies, it would have: not many people would dispute the selection of *Dalek*, *Father's Day* and *The Empty Child/The Doctor Dances* as the stand-out episodes of Series 1, nor of *Human Nature/The Family of Blood* and *Blink* as the best of Series 3. But under Moffat, things have become more complicated, and most episodes seem to split opinion. *The Lodger*, for example, is some people's very favourite Series 5 episode, but other people's most hated. Similarly, I loved *The God Complex*, but lots of other critics found it pointless.

Why this difference between the two New Who eras? I think there was more consistency of approach in the Davies era, while Moffat encourages his writers to try more different things – to lunge out in different directions, and let the ashes fall where they may. It's notable that the most distinctive of all the Davies-era episodes, *Midnight*, came about by accident: it was written in a hurry by Davies himself when another writer's script fell through at short notice. Yet the Moffat era has included all sorts of other kinds of stories besides the Doctor Who staples of base-under-siege and alien-invasion. Stories like *Amy's Choice*, *Vincent and the Doctor* and *The Girl Who Waited* simply wouldn't fit in a Davies series. Moffat attempts more. That means that he fails more, but also succeeds more. I'm in favour of that. Doctor Who is all about adventure: that has to apply to how the programme is made as well as to its content.

With that said, then, here is my highly personal list of the Eleventh Doctor episodes that stuck in my memory the most strongly – in chronological order.

The Beast Below

The episode where I *got* Smith's Doctor, after having been

disappointed at how Tennantish he seemed in *The Eleventh Hour*. Not only intelligent, not just eccentric in a bundle-of-mannerisms way; but empathetic, quick of insight, and kind to children in a decidedly non-patronising way. You can quibble with how much sense the plot makes, but as a showcase for the new Doctor it was just about perfect.

The Time of Angels/Flesh and Stone

This highest density of wonderfully Doctorish moments, with every knob turned up to eleven. The flamboyance of the "12,000 years later" caption near the beginning perfectly heralded how the episodes would be.

Vincent and the Doctor

Although flawed by the unnecessary and clumsily grafted monster mystery, this story was a joy to watch, and at its strongest in the scenes of just the Doctor, Amy and Vincent. The carefully handled relationship between Vincent and Amy was a delight – half thoughtless flirtation, half hero-worship and half unspoken sympathy. Yes, that makes more than one whole: that's completely appropriate for this episode, which also scores highly for its stone-cold refusal to take the obvious happy ending.

The Big Bang

Packed with surprises from start to end, and taking a refreshingly unexpected slapstick approach to the time-travel paradoxes. One of very few examples whether the second half of a two-parter has unequivocally surpassed the first half, and perhaps the most *fun* Doctor Who has ever been.

A Christmas Carol

Doctor Who in the small, with the Amy-and-Rory-on-a-crashing-spaceship subplot really being only a placeholder and a distraction. *A*

Christmas Carol succeeded brilliantly by being basically all about one person, and a most unpromising character at that. A rare episode where we wanted good outcomes for everyone, and more or less got them. Part of me feels that I ought to sneer at the climactic scene of a sleigh-ride drawn by a flying shark, but I can't make myself do it.

The Impossible Astronaut/Day of the Moon

The most ambitious Doctor Who has ever been, and the beginning (or at least so we thought) of a series-long arc of unprecedented complexity and richness. Also, the first appearance of a truly uncanny enemy in the Silence. We can look back at Series 6 as a whole and feel that it didn't keep the promise that this opening salvo made, but at the time it was absolutely sensational.

The Girl Who Waited

Perhaps Karen Gillan's finest moment came as the aged Amy who has survived thirty years by rigid self-discipline. She never ostensibly lets on that her heart is breaking, but it's apparent in every scene. A fantastic example of Doctor Who going off into completely alien territory, and exploring in depth emotions that no other TV programme can even approach.

The Doctor, the Widow and the Wardrobe

The super-happy ending is a delight, but it's the opening twenty minutes or so, with the Doctor as Caretaker, that really lingers in the memory. All that zaniness, but providing such a shallow layer over the empathy and vulnerability beneath.

The Angels Take Manhattan

Amy and Rory's farewell was always likely to be emotional, but it was all the more so in an episode that was built around that farewell. Martha's departure was rather low-key; Donna's was very emotional, but over quickly. This episode gave us the first extended goodbye since Rose's in *Doomsday*, and it hurt to watch.

The Day of the Doctor

It would be churlish not to choose the 50th Anniversary special, an episode with three superb Doctors all at the top of their game, contriving to rewrite a key piece of mythology without cheating. The interplay between the three of them was the highlight, and there was just enough nostalgia to leaven the episode without overpowering it.

And the winner is ...

It's tough to pick one, but if I had to choose a single Doctor Who episode to show to an unbeliever, I think it would have to be *A Christmas Carol*. Easily comprehensible even to those not immersed in the backstory, it nevertheless hits all the key aspects of what makes the programme great.

Appendix B: Magic moments

I was surprised, in assembling my list of magic moments, that on the whole they weren't from what I considered the best episodes. Some of them are little moments of genius in the writing; some are simple magic on the part of Matt Smith, sometimes when working with the most unpromising material. Here they are, once more in chronological order.

Victory of the Daleks

Interior, Dr. Bracewell's laboratory. A Dalek glides in. "Would you care for some tea?" it asks him. "That would be very nice, thank you", he replies. A shocking juxtaposition of the evil and the mundane – funny and disturbing at the same time.

Flesh and Stone

Amy is left alone with the church soldiers, feeling lost and abandoned as the Doctor and River leave her to find the flight deck. The Doctor tries to reassure her:

Doctor: Amy, you need to start trusting me. It's never been more important.

Amy: But you don't always tell me the truth.

Doctor: If I always told you the truth, I wouldn't need you to trust me.

The Vampires of Venice

We switch from Rory's stag night, with the Doctor as the stripper, to the interior of the TARDIS. I loved Rory's quick acclimatisation. Right from the off, we can see he's no fool.

Doctor: It's a lot to take in, isn't it? Tiny box, huge room inside. What's that about? Let me explain.

Rory: It's another dimension.

Doctor: It's basically another dimension. What?

The Hungry Earth

My favourite part of any Doctor Who episode ever: the Doctor's conversation with Alaya, the captured Silurian warrior. It's full of wonderful moments, but the best may be these:

Alaya: I'm the last of my species.

Doctor: No. You're really not. Because I'm the last of my species and I know how it sits in a heart. So don't insult me.

And:

Alaya: Our sensors detected a threat to our life support systems. The warrior class was activated to prevent the assault. We will wipe the Vermin from the surface and reclaim our planet.

Doctor: Do we have to say vermin? They're really very nice.

The Big Bang

I've never, ever been so totally taken by surprise as in that moment just before the title sequence when young Amelia opens the Pandorica in the museum to find not the Doctor but her own grown-up self inside. "OK, Kid", says Amy, "This is where it gets complicated." So gloriously true!

A Christmas Carol

Oh, yes, this! Remember I said the Doctor's interview with Alaya was my favourite part of any episode? Sorry, my mistake, it's my *second* favourite. The very best is the part of *A Christmas Carol* where the Doctor shows grizzled, cynical Sardick an old film home-movie of himself, then appears in that film as he's watching it:

Sardick: Get out! Get out of my house!

Doctor: Okay. Okay, but I'll be back. Way back. Way, way back.

He steps into the TARDIS; we hear its distinctive sound, and the boy on the screen reacts to it. The Doctor appears inside the film.

Doctor [on the screen]: See? Back.

Every part of that scene is superb – and what leads up to it, and what follows. Just perfect.

The Impossible Astronaut

However flawed the eventual resolution of the Death Of The Doctor thread turned out to be, the actual moment when the impossible astronaut shot him once, then again as he was regenerating, was completely unexpected and absolutely shocking.

The Doctor's Wife

The Doctor has been fooled by old Time Lord distress signals into thinking there are live Time Lords in the bubble universe. He is desperate to find them:

Doctor: There are Time Lords here. I heard them and they need me.

Amy: You told me about your people, and you told me what you did. [...]

Doctor: I can explain. Tell them why I had to.

Amy: You want to be forgiven.

Doctor: Don't we all?

Let's Kill Hitler

Another glorious Rory moment. In the confusion of the Teselecta's assassination attempt, Rory punches Hitler, grabs his gun, and points it at him.

Rory: Sit still, shut up. [...]

Hitler: He was going to kill me.

Rory: Shut up, Hitler.

Doctor: Rory, take Hitler and put him in that cupboard over there. Now do it.

Rory: Right. Putting Hitler in the cupboard. Cupboard, Hitler. Hitler, cupboard. Come on.

Hitler: But I am the Führer!

Rory: Right, in you go!

Flustered but unshaken, absolutely competent. It's pure Rory.

The Doctor, the Widow and the Wardrobe

I've already quoted this exchange earlier in the book, but it's so very, very perfect that I'm going to do it again. The Doctor has been showing Lily and Cyril the wonderful house where they're going to spending Christmas, and their mother, in a burst of not-quite-rational rage, has sent them downstairs. She turns to the Doctor:

Madge: Lily and Cyril's father, my husband, is dead and they don't know yet, because if I tell them now, then Christmas will always be what took their father away from them, and no one should have to live like that. Of course, when the Christmas period is over, I shall. I don't know why I keep shouting at them.

Doctor: Because every time you see them happy, you remember how sad they're going to be, and it breaks your heart. Because what's the point in them being happy now if they're going to be sad later. The answer is, of course, because they are going to be sad later.

Has there ever been a finer moment of empathy, understanding and wisdom in the Christmas TV special?

Asylum of the Daleks

The clues were all there, but I was caught completely unawares by the reveal of Oswin when we finally saw her, and realised she was a Dalek. What made it work was that this shocking moment wasn't played for shock value. Instead it was given to us simply as what it is: a desperately sad moment, when we realised along with Oswin that whatever outcome she might have hoped for was never going to happen. Truly horrifying.

Dinosaurs on a Spaceship

An episode that should have been full of visual wonders somehow wasn't – until the very end. The highlight was the wordless shot of the Earth seen from space, then the pan back to see Brian sitting above it, in the doorway of the TARDIS, with his cup of tea and his sandwich. Someone simply enjoying the wonder of travelling with the Doctor. Ah, Brian. I miss him.

The Name of the Doctor

This piece of script reads as mundane, even vacuous, on the page:

Clara: The Doctor has a secret he will take to the grave. It is discovered. Doctor?

Doctor: Sorry. And it was Trenzalore? Definitely Trenzalore?

Clara: Yeah.

Doctor: Oh dear. Sorry.

But Smith absolutely sells it with the most astonishingly intense performance. Who would ever have believed the two simple words "oh dear" could mean so much?

Acknowledgements

For this project, I owe the most to the readers who have stuck with my blog, and contributed fascinating comments, as that blog has wandered progressively further away from its original conception as being mostly about computer programming. For a writer, nothing is more encouraging than responses – not congratulations or compliments, but actual engagement. Commenters at *The Reinvigorated Programmer* have forced me to think more deeply about Doctor Who, and the later reviews in this book would not have been anywhere near as interesting without the cross-pollination of their ideas.

I also owe my gratitude to other bloggers who have written fascinating, insightful pieces on Doctor Who, and whose own work in this area inspired mine. Top of the list is Andrew Rilstone, whose blog *The Life and Opinions of Andrew Rilstone* is fascinating, infuriating and thought-provoking by turns. Other provocative reviews include those of Andrew Hickey (*Science! Justice Leak!*), Gavin Burrows (*Lucid Frenzy Junior*), Richard Flowers (*The Very Fluffy Diary of Millennium Dome, Elephant*) and Allyn Gibson (*Made of Awesome & Guinness and Bright Shiny Pennies*). It's maybe not coincidence that all these blogs discuss a wide range of subjects, not just Doctor Who: their authors have interesting things to say about Who because they're interested in a lot of other things.

Anna Nordling (anna@annaway.fi, http://annaway.fi/) very generously designed the front cover image, based on my amateurish mock-up, and even paid to licence the image of Matt Smith. Nothing made this book feel more real for me than seeing the final version of the cover.

The book has benefitted greatly from two phases of proof-reading: first, before Christmas, on the near-complete manuscript by Alex Chan and Martin Keegan; then, after I'd written the final sections, by Gabriella Marino and Jon Wensley. I am greatly in their debt. It's traditional in acknowledgements to say "any mistakes that remain are my fault", but instead I'm going to blame them on Jon. (He can take it.)

Finally, it takes a very special family to put up with the amount of time I put into all my extra-curricular activities, including writing this. My deepest thanks go to Fiona, Daniel, Matthew and Jonno.

Image and font credits

Images

The cover is composed from modified versions of three photographs — one commercially licensed, and the other two from Wikimedia commons:

— **Matt Smith arriving for the Evening Standard Film Awards, County Hall, London. 06/02/2012** by Steve Vas / Featureflash, copyright © Featureflash | Dreamstime.com. Clearance kindly negotiated by Anna Nordling.

— **2009 07 31 David Tennant smile 04** by Rach from Tadcaster, York, England. CC By. https://commons.wikimedia.org/wiki/File:2009_07_31_David_Tennant_smile_04.jpg

— **Christopher Eccleston London** by Emma Marie's Photos. CC By. https://commons.wikimedia.org/wiki/File:Christopher_Eccleston_London.jpg

The "crack in time" art for Series 5 uses **Wall texture 6** by Chrisseee. CC By. http://www.flickr.com/photos/chrisseee/5142832945/sizes/o/. I drew the actual crack from a *Victory of the Daleks* screenshot.

The "impossible astronaut" art for Series 6 uses parts of two photographs:

— **Mono Lake Reflections** by Henry Lydecker. CC By. https://commons.wikimedia.org/wiki/File:Mono_Lake_Reflections.jpg. It turns out there is no Lake Silencio in Utah, but Mono Lake in California is a great stand-in. It's the lake where the back cover photo of Pink Floyd's *Wish You Were Here* was taken.

— **Buzz Aldrin Apollo Space-suit** by NASA /Neil Armstrong.

Public domain. https://commons.wikimedia.org/wiki/File:Buzz_Aldrin_Apollo_Space suit.jpg. This is a classic photo, and I didn't want to edit it more than absolutely necessary – which is why you can see the lunar lander and Neil Armstrong reflected in the helmet.

The "Clara's leaf" art for Series 7 is based on **Red maple leaf with veining** by Benny Mazur. CC By. https://commons.wikimedia.org/wiki/File:Red_maple_leaf_with_veining.jpg

The "about the author" photo of Mike Taylor with a Dalek was taken by a member of BBC staff who was my handler as I did the *Xenoposeidon* interview – someone whose name now sadly escapes me (if I ever knew it). I assume that person, in taking the photo, was giving it to me, and I now dedicate it to the public domain.

Fonts

The fonts used on the cover are as follows:

"THE" – Univers Extended (modified)

"ELEVENTH" – Revue

"DOCTOR" – Univers Bold Extended

"A critical ramble …" – Eurostile Extended #2

"by Mike Taylor" – Eurostile Bold Extended #2

A reminder: Copyright and licence

The text of this book is copyright © Mike Taylor, 2010–2014.

The text is made available under the Creative Commons Attribution 4.0 International licence (CC By 4.0), which means you are free to read, share, copy, modify, remix and redistribute it provided only that you credit me as the original author and do not misrepresent me as endorsing any changes you may make.

If you downloaded this book for free, and enjoyed reading it, I ask but do not demand that you buy either an official copy of the e-book or a hardcopy. Actual sales reward me for the work that went into this, and encourage me to write more. But if you can't or won't pay, I'd still rather you read the book than not.

Artwork is provided under a variety of licences and involves a variety of copyright holders, as detailed in the Image and Font Credits section. All but the cover can at least be freely redistributed in unmodified form for non-commercial purposes.

About the author

Mike Taylor is a man of many parts.

By day, he earns his living as a computer programmer (though his actual job title is Software Guy) with Index Data – the world's tiniest multinational, with fifteen staff of eight different nationalities scattered across five countries. His work is a pleasantly varied diet of analysis, design, programming, testing, debugging, documentation and presenting, mostly in the areas of information engineering for libraries.

At night, he works (unpaid) as a palaeontologist specialising in sauropods, the biggest and best of all the dinosaurs. His academic publications in this field include the papers describing and naming two new dinosaurs *Xenoposeidon* ("alien earthquake god") and *Brontomerus* ("thunder-thighs").

As a spin-off from his academic work, Mike is a passionate advocate of open-access publishing – the idea that all academic research should be freely available to the public whose taxes paid for it, and open to any form of re-use. It seems ridiculous that such an obvious idea should even need advocating, but apparently it does.

On his evenings off, he's an occasional folk-singer and guitarist, with a tendency to slip Beatles covers into settings more used to protest songs and traditional harvest dances. His claim to fame is his acoustic-guitar-only version of *Shine On You Crazy Diamond*, and his lasting shame is that he's never written a song of his own.

In between all this, he is the father of three delicious sons and the husband of one delicious wife – all four of them amazingly tolerant of the time he spends on all this other stuff.

Mike has two main blogs: *Sauropod Vertebra Picture of the Week* at http://svpow.com/; and The Reinvigorated Programmer at http://reprog.wordpress.com/, whose tag-line is "Everything except sauropod vertebrae". Despite all that writing, *The Eleventh Doctor* is his first book.

The author. I met this Dalek at the BBC Television Centre at Shepherds Bush in 2007, when I was there to do interviews about the new dinosaur *Xenoposeidon*. In a disappointingly predicable act of cultural vandalism, the BBC sold the iconic building earlier this year.

Where next?

Discuss this book on my blog: http://reprog.wordpress.com/book/

Read Andrew Rilstone's Doctor Who books, *The Viewer's Tale* and *Fish Custard (The Viewer's Tale volume 2)* or his forthcoming *The Complete Viewer's Tale*, covering the whole of the revived series.

Read Andrew Hickey's very different Doctor Who book, *Fifty Stories For Fifty Years*, surveying the broad sweep of Doctor Who's narrative history.